MURDER AT
Heartbreak Hospital

Published in 1998 by
Academy Chicago Publishers
363 West Erie Street
Chicago, Illinois 60610

ISBN 0-89733-463-9

MURDER AT
Heartbreak Hospital

Henry Slesar

Academy
Chicago Publishers

All the characters in this book are fictitious, and any resemblance to actual persons, living or dead, is purely coincidental.

Contents

Contents

Cast of Characters

Gene Badger: Producer of "Heartbreak Hospital."

Captain Bagley: Head of the Movie/TV police unit.

Lou Blankenship: Director of "Heartbreak Hospital."

Kiki Carney: Associate producer of "Heartbreak Hospital." Formerly, Gene Badger's secretary.

Luis Compos: Vice squad detective. Once Troy's partner. Friend of Norman Levi after Robin Dillard leaves him.

Milo Derringer: Actor who plays Dr Jonathan Masters on "Heartbreak Hospital."

Robin Dillard: Minor actor on "Heartbreak Hospital." Norman Levi's boyfriend.

Ramsey Duke: Black actor who plays Lieutenant Rick Savage on "Heartbreak Hospital."

Daisy and Noel Earnshaw: William Troy's sister and brother-in-law.

Keith Ellenberger: "Outside" writer who contributes story ideas for soap operas.

Fiona Farrar: William Troy's ex–live-in girlfriend.

Norman Levi: Scriptwriter who works for Bob Neffer.

Dan Lipschultz: Detective, friend of William Troy.

Abel McFee: Executive producer.

Mitzo: Secretarial assistant to Captain Bagley of the Movie/ TV police unit.

Bob Neffer: Head writer of "Heartbreak Hospital."

Gary Naughton: William Troy's friend on the Movie/TV police unit.

Julia Porterfield: Actress who played Andrea Harmon before Sunday Tyler took over the role.

Carl Rivera: Homicide detective.

William Troy: Detective with the Movie/TV unit of the NYPD.

Sunday Tyler: Actress who plays Andrea Harmon on "Heartbreak Hospital."

Ophelia Utley: Associate head writer.

Phyllis Wykopf: Supervising producer.

1 Our Gal Sunday

"We can't just have her killed," the man in the checked shirt said, with an earnest expression only slightly marred by the fragment of shrimp tail he was picking out of his teeth. "I mean, that's a given. It can't be anything blatant, like a knife or a gun. We've got to do this right."

"Cleverly," one of his eating companions said. He was a thin man with shoe-polish-black hair and a hawklike profile. "Not an obvious murder. A believable accident." He looked into his linguine. "Food poisoning, maybe."

"We get her to eat here," the third man said gloomily, staring at a grey wedge of meat on his fork.

William Troy, sitting alone at the next table, sneaked another sidelong glance at the third speaker and realized it was a woman. The tweed jacket and short haircut had fooled him for a moment, but the voice, for all its throatiness, was definitely feminine. Two men and a woman, casually plotting murder in their lunch hour, choosing a public place for their sinister conference and ignoring the possibility of eavesdroppers, including a member of the New York City police force.

The risk may have finally occurred to them, because now both men were suddenly canvassing the crowded restaurant with darting, apprehensive eyes.

"Don't worry," the woman said, in a tone of dry derision. "She wouldn't eat here if she was starving. She's probably at

Aureole right this minute. André Soltner is lighting her cigarette."

"I'm not just worried about *her*," the hawklike man said.
"We've got to make sure that nobody knows. It's got to happen
so fast that they just don't see it coming."

"You're forgetting something," the woman said. "She's on
a fifty-two-week cycle with twenty left to go."

"We'll just have to eat the guarantee," the first man said.

"It'll probably taste better than this veal." She stabbed at it
viciously. "Why do we eat in this place, for God's sake? Do we
have a death wish or something?"

"I have a death wish, all right," the hawklike man said darkly.
"And I can hardly wait."

William Troy wasn't sure he should wait either. He had,
after all, a sworn duty to apprehend felons before, during, and
after the commission of a crime, preferably the first. It had been
some time since the NYPD had allowed him to uphold it, not
since he had been a patrolman in a Village district, piling up a
hefty number of vice arrests in that fertile area. He was making
all the right moves towards detective status when, on his twenty-
sixth birthday, a hooker with a face like a Botticelli angel and
the mental attitude of a Borgia plunged a six-inch kitchen knife
into his chest, narrowly missing his heart. The emotion which
surfaced first was surprise. Troy hadn't planned on injury in his
police career. He wasn't a notably physical type, barely making
the required weight for his six-two frame, and it had been an
effort of will to meet the seventy percent passing grade of the
Academy's Physical Education unit. Troy's image of his future
had been a cerebral one. He saw himself solving Baffling Crimes
through Brilliant Analysis and Deduction. In other words, he
was a child of the television age.

He hadn't been sure if he was making a step in the right
direction when he put in his request to join the Movie/TV unit

of the NYPD. His friend Gary Naughton had suggested it on the first day Troy was allowed visitors at the hospital. Troy still hadn't had the breath to answer him, but he had managed to shake his head "no." His picture of the work had been that of a bunch of Blues standing idly around the perimeters of a city street closed off by a movie crew shooting an inane TV commercial. Gary had done everything he could to rebut his argument, and he had had plenty of time in which to do it. Troy's convalescence had been a long one, and Gary was his most frequent visitor, apart from Fiona, the blonde with whom Troy shared his Village apartment. Gary had made the work seem like cop heaven: he received his assignments at home and used his own vehicle to get to the location sites. Every job was different, he had said with enthusiasm, and there was plenty of clout from the mayor's office—they were doing backflips to encourage the Hollywood types to use city locations; it was good for business. The truth was, Gary was starstruck, and he had just come from a downtown area where he had stood two feet away from Cher. Besides, he had said, didn't Troy once tell him he took a film course someplace? (It was at the New School, and lasted three weeks.) Captain Bagley would love him, Gary promised; Troy would be able to talk to these movie guys in their own arcane language. There was a long list of applicants, but Gary was sure he could get his name on the list. All he had to do was nod his head again, this time up and down. What do you say?

By the end of his hospital stay, Troy had said a qualified yes. He had taken a ride out to the Special Operations Division located in the old press building at Flushing Meadows. The offices of the Movie/TV unit were minimal, with no hint of the glamorous function they supported. There was also no hint of a showbiz influence in the commanding officer: Bagley was the type who got cops the appellation of "bulls" in the first place, a big man with fists like Smithfield hams, although Troy had suspected there was something slightly defensive in his muscular swagger.

"I'll tell you what I need on this job," he had told Troy, fixing him with a blue-eyed stare. "I need common sense. Now I'll tell you what I *don't* need. I don't need guys who drop their batons every time they see a movie star. You got a problem with that, Troy, you don't belong in this command."

It turned out there was something else Bagley needed. One of his most trusted deputies, a sergeant named Horner, had just opted for early retirement. Horner had been the man Bagley had relied on most to assist him in the liaison work that was crucial to the operation. When Bagley learned that Troy was a college graduate, that he could talk film jargon, he had put on some selling pressure. Within a week, Troy's name had travelled to the top of the list.

The job wasn't entirely without perks. This lunch was one of them, although the conspiracy at the next table raised some doubts about the quality of the meal still ahead of him. Two days before, Bagley had shown him a request from a daytime serial produced in New York for the extended use of city locations ranging from the Battery to Central Park. The TV people had already posted the required million-dollar bond, and were now asking for Department help to scout the areas. Troy was less than delighted. There were six feature movies in town at the same time, and he had hoped to be assigned to the one called *Heat Wave.* For one reason, it featured two rugged male stars he had admired from childhood. For another, it was a cop picture, the kind that created the most problems for the unit since phony uniforms, vehicles, and firearms would be employed. Troy liked problems. He had never watched a soap opera in his life but was nevertheless convinced of their cultural worthlessness.

He had been feeling better about the whole thing later that afternoon, when he had had a preliminary meeting with the producer. She was about twenty-five, a state-of-the-art blonde.

"Associate producer," she had corrected him. "That really means I'm Gene Badger's glorified secretary. He's the producer. There's also a supervising producer named Phyllis Wykopf and an *executive* producer who works at the network, named Abel McFee, but you'll never see him so it doesn't matter."

"It's your name that matters to me," Troy had said, with a smile that compensated for his broken nose and too-narrow face. He had been gratified to see the answering light in her large violet eyes.

"It's Kiki," she had said apologetically. "Kiki Carney. My mother thought it was cute. Anyway, all you really have to remember is the name of the program."

"I don't think I ever heard it," Troy said.

"It's 'Heartbreak Hospital,'" Kiki said.

Now, waiting for his first briefing session at the restaurant Kiki had chosen, Troy had already forgotten the name. He was far too distracted by the unholy three he had under surveillance. Like all cops, he was trained to be suspicious, warned to be wary of men sitting in cars near schools or playgrounds, of people walking late at night, or carrying large packages, or—a new one for the list—plotting homicide in a public restaurant. But there was no way Troy could put a move on them simply on the basis of what he had overheard. Conspiracy to commit murder was a crime, but conversation wasn't hard evidence.

Then there was a new complication. Kiki Carney, looking even better than he remembered, threaded her way between the tables and waved her hand in greeting. Only the acknowledgment wasn't for him. It was for the Murderers' Lunch Club. With a start, Troy realized that *she knew these people.*

A few moments later, Troy knew them, too.

"Phyl Wykopf," Kiki said, and the woman held out a surprisingly soft hand. "Phyl is our supervising producer."

"How nice of you to help us out, Lieutenant." She locked her blue eyes into his as if trying to send him a telepathic message. He corrected the title, but she shrugged her tweeded shoulders. "Sorry," she said. "On soaps, every cop is a lieutenant."

"I'm Gene Badger," the man in the checked shirt said. He had an engaging, open face under sandy hair with random streaks of grey. "You look like an actor yourself, Mr Troy. Ever do anything in that line?"

"I did a little in college before a linebacker stepped on my nose."

"Badge of honor," the hawkfaced man said. "The American Heidelberg scar." Kiki introduced him as Bob Neffer, head writer of "Heartbreak Hospital." "This week's head writer," Neffer added glumly. "Don't get too attached to me, Lieutenant. I probably won't be around that long."

Troy didn't bother to make the correction a second time. Instead, he muttered a few polite words to the assembled trio and allowed Kiki to guide him back to the table where he had been waiting for her. He was relieved to see the group pay their bill and leave, so he could make a full confession.

"Get ready to laugh," he said. "I thought those three were cold-blooded killers. I should have realized your studio was right across the street, that they were just . . . plotting a soap opera."

Kiki didn't laugh. In fact, she looked downright solemn.

"They weren't plotting," she said. "They were just daydreaming. There's no way they're going to kill off Sunday Tyler. They probably talk about it every time they have lunch together, but it just isn't going to happen."

"I suppose I should know who Sunday Tyler is, but I don't. Is it the actress or the character?"

"The actress," Kiki said. "But you can bet your badge the name is just as phony as she is."

Troy grinned. "Sounds like you're a member of the same fan club."

"Oh, everybody hates Sunday," she said lightly. "Just as they're supposed to hate Andrea Harmon."

"Who's Andrea Harmon?"

"Not an actress. The character. The one Sunday plays. Only of course, people *love* Andrea because she's so hateful. And Sunday makes her so hateful because Sunday is very good at making you hate her. That's why they're never going to be able to get rid of Sunday, because they can't get rid of Andrea. . . . What's the matter?"

"I'm thinking of giving you a speeding ticket."

"Sorry. What I mean is, Sunday Tyler is a miserable bitch, but she's very good at *playing* a miserable bitch, so we can't fire her or kill her off without hurting the show. Are you with me now?"

"Clinging to the running board."

"Cars don't have running boards any more."

"Mine does, practically. It's a twenty-year-old Volvo. If you're not busy this weekend, I'll show it to you."

"I think we'd better talk about 'Heartbreak Hospital.'"

They ordered drinks, Kiki asking for the predictable glass of white wine and Troy, in minor deference to duty, a bottle of beer.

"We've been on the air for eight years. That's not really a very long time in this business. Serials like 'As the World Turns' and 'The Guiding Light' went on television before I was even born. They're like turtles. They move slowly, day after day, and live for a hundred years."

"You mean soaps *never* get canceled?"

"Of course they get canceled. Sometimes in their infancy. Sometimes after thirty-five years, like 'Search for Tomorrow.' They wear themselves out, or the Nielsen pendulum swings to another network, or they get stuck in a bad time period. And when that happens, it isn't like one of those prime time ax jobs—everybody expects night-time shows to be canceled. When a daytime serial falls, it's like a dinosaur dropping. *Whoomp!* The earth trembles."

"I see," Troy said slyly. "They're like turtles *and* dinosaurs."

"So I mix metaphors," Kiki said, nettled. "Do me something."

"What did you have in mind?"

She gave him a quizzical glance. "You don't think much of soap operas, do you? Or am I just being sensitive?"

Troy shrugged. "I don't know anything about them. But something tells me that the fate of Western Civilization wouldn't be affected one bit if they *all* fell like dinosaurs. Whoomp!"

Her small red lips parted, showing very white teeth that were slightly, charmingly, protruding. Troy felt guilty at once and murmured an apology.

"It's all right," Kiki said, still with a hint of grumpiness. "Most people feel the way you do about soaps—if they never watch them."

"One thing I never knew is that they shoot soaps outside the studio."

"They do it all the time, to hype the ratings. Usually, they're running off to the Caribbean and places like that for their location sequences. We thought 'Heartbreak Hospital' should use the city itself. I mean, there's everything here."

"That's the problem," Troy said. "There's everything, including eight million people and four million vehicles. I just hope you're aware of all the problems you're going to have."

They ordered lunch, Troy choosing what he hoped was a chef-proof item, a pasta that arrived tasting like library paste. Kiki nibbled at a large salad, and answered his questions.

"I got hooked on soaps in college," she said. "There was a funny kind of counterrevolution going on at the time—it was almost groovy to be square, if you know what I mean. I don't know when it started, but suddenly all the dormitory kids were congregating in the lounges with their eyes glued to the tube, waiting to see if Laura would ever forgive Luke for raping her, and if they would ever escape from the gangsters on their trail and find true love and. . . . Oh, I know it sounds ridiculous, and I guess it was, but it became a kind of shared experience. Even if we didn't know each *other,* we knew the same imaginary people and rooted for them. . . . That's still the basic reason why soaps are so popular, I guess. But my first job wasn't in soaps, it was with a game show company, Goodson-Todman."

"Goodson-Todman? Sounds like something Jews say to each other on High Holy Days."

"It was just a temporary job, but I met people in the business, including a guy who worked for the producer of 'The Edge of Night,' Nick Nicholson. Nick needed a secretary, and I had sworn to myself that I would never, never, never take a job where I brought the boss his coffee in the morning. But the minute I walked into that studio on 44th Street, and saw Sky Whitney in the flesh *and* Geraldine Whitney and Raven and that terrifying Gunther . . ." She paused, seeing his reaction. "They were characters in the show. These people had become so *real* to me from the television screen that it was disorienting to see them in person. And exciting, too. PS, I took the job."

"And brought Nick his coffee?"

"Some mornings he brought me *mine.* And he also talked to me. And let me learn the business. At least, as much as it's possible to learn about a business so quirky and complicated. . . . I hated leaving that show: there was so much camaraderie around that studio. But when I got the offer from 'Heartbreak Hospital' . . . Well, it was just too good to turn down."

"Any regrets now?"

"Only one."

"Let me guess," Troy said. "Sunday Tyler."

"It's not that she leans on me very hard. I'm small potatoes—not worth the energy. She just acts as if I'm not there. But I am there, and I see her flog everyone around me, and it's not easy to take."

"Who gets it the most?"

"Right now, I'd say Bob Neffer."

"The head writer."

"Sunday absolutely refuses to admit the existence of writers, not even as a necessary evil. When she gets a script, she considers it a personal affront that someone is daring to put words into her mouth. Not that Bob actually writes scripts."

"Then what does he do?"

"The head writer does the long-term story. Then there are three breakdown writers who do the daily outlines. Then there are three more writers who actually write scripts from those outlines. Of course, every now and then the producers get someone else to contribute a long-term story, and sometimes other people write the outlines, and the breakdown writers occasionally write scripts. . . ." She saw his befuddled expression and laughed. "I'm confusing you again. The truth is, most soaps these days are hardly models of efficient operation. The lines of responsibility have got pretty muddled, especially in the last five or ten years. Probably because the stakes have got bigger."

"What stakes?"

"Money, of course. Soaps are big business. Did you hear the capital letters? BIG BUSINESS. Most of the network profit comes from day parts, because the production is relatively cheap compared to prime time. It's all those weepy women and unwanted babies who are paying for those helicopters and car chases on prime time."

"So that makes them inefficient?"

"It makes them *nervous*. Everybody is a bundle of nerves in soap opera. They're so worried about the ratings and the network and their jobs that they spend half their time covering their ass." Troy's pasta-filled mouth drooped slightly. He should have been accustomed to every degree of bad language by now, but coming from Kiki Carney's delicate lips . . . "Look," she said, "I didn't mean to tell you what was wrong with this business. It's still a lot of fun if you relax and enjoy it. Unfortunately, Bob Neffer, the head writer, can't. His job is definitely on the line."

"Then it wasn't a joke? About his not being around very long?"

"Let's say there are . . . rumors."

"Doesn't he have a contract?"

"He does—for the next two years. But most actors and writers have a cute little clause in their contract which gives the show the option to fire you every thirteen weeks."

"And you think they're about to exercise it?"

"It wouldn't surprise anybody. 'Heartbreak's' already chewed up and spat out five head writers in the past year and a half. The last two were pure and simple hatchet jobs, and guess who was wielding it."

"Our gal Sunday?"

"Smart cop. And now Bob Neffer is on her list. He made the mistake of ignoring her latest story suggestion."

"So she's a writer, too?"

"Actors are always coming up with story ideas, starring themselves, naturally. Usually, they get a friendly pat on the hand and that's the end of it. But not in Sunday's case. These days, you can hear the sound of a blade being sharpened all the way to the studio control room."

"Does she really have the power to get people fired?"

"Sunday has the network convinced that she's the only reason the show is in the top five of the ratings. Unfortunately," Kiki said ruefully, "she might even be right."

"Is she that good?"

"She's *The Bitch*. I can't tell you how important that job is on a soap. It's unthinkable for a daytime serial—or night time, for that matter—not to have at least one world class Bitch making trouble for everyone, seducing every man in sight, including the married ones, lying, cheating, scheming . . ."

"You'd think women would find someone like that threatening."

"They *identify* with her. They want to *be* her. You go to these focus sessions—"

"What are those?"

"It's a type of research. They put a dozen or so women viewers into a room and ask them about the soap they watch. Meanwhile, another group of show people and agency executives are watching *them*—through a one-way mirror. Or is it two-way? I never could get that straight."

"And they like the Bitch, is that it?"

"They may 'like' the 'good' women. But they admire and envy the wicked ones. Many of them wouldn't watch the show without her. And of all the Bitches in daytime, there isn't one they love to hate more than Andrea Harmon. Now you can see why Sunday Tyler is such a menace to oncoming traffic."

"Not quite," Troy said judiciously. "I know Success Spoils, but—there must be exceptions."

"You're right," Kiki nodded. "There are plenty of successful show people who don't turn into Yetis. But that's just the problem. Sunday doesn't believe she's successful. Deep down,

Sunday actually *hates* 'Heartbreak Hospital.' She thinks she ought to be in Hollywood, being a *star*. Like Kathleen Turner, for instance—she was on a soap once. Sunday keeps waiting for that lightning to strike, and it just won't."

"So she's dropping her own thunderbolts."

"Anywhere she can. That's why I'm really afraid for Norm—I mean for Bob Neffer." Troy didn't comment on the slip, but Kiki decided to explain it. "Norman is a scripter who works for Bob. A friend of mine. He'll be out of work, too, if Bob gets the ax. That would be a shame. He's very good."

"And what about the producer? Your boss Badger? And Phyllis What's-her-name? And yourself, for that matter?"

"Nobody's safe from *her*," Kiki said. "Whatever Sunday wants, Sunday gets. And we've already wasted too much time talking about her."

"Yeah—what about this 'police' story? If you're not going to kill off Sunday, what *are* you going to do?"

"We're going to kill someone else." She looked at her watch and bit her pretty underlip. "It's almost one-twenty. The dry run of today's show is at one-thirty. Do you have time to go back to the studio with me?"

"I'm all yours," Troy said.

Studio 22 was housed in a West Side building he had passed a hundred times without speculating about its tenants. The wait for the elevator was interminable, so Kiki led him through a dimly-lit hallway to the largest freight elevator he had ever seen, big enough to hoist elephants playing grand pianos. It stopped only once before they reached their third floor destination, and the most stunning woman Troy had ever seen stepped inside. He wasn't too surprised when Kiki greeted her as "Sunday." What did surprise him was the fact that she was carrying a blood-stained ax.

2 The Secret Storm

(SCENE: MRS ARMSTRONGS LIMO. MRS ARMSTRONG IN BACK, HERBERT AT WHEEL. HE BRAKES SUDDENLY)

MRS ARMSTRONG

What's the trouble, Herbert?

HERBERT

A young man on a bicycle, Madam. Driving rather recklessly.

MRS ARMSTRONG

He called me something as he went by. What is a "douche bag," Herbert?

HERBERT

I believe it's a hygienic device, Madam.

MRS ARMSTRONG

Oh. For a moment, I thought he was being insulting.

Norman Levi stared at the glowing amber screen and cackled softly to himself. For a full minute, he considered keeping the scene intact in the document he had designated as HH-3994, the number of the episode he was writing from Ophelia Utley's outline. Two years ago, before Sunday Tyler stepped into the role of Andrea and transformed a minor league Bitch into the centerpiece of the serial, he would have allowed the parodical scene to slip through, trusting to Kiki Carney's sharp eye to excise it, *after* she had chuckled with appreciative amusement.

That appreciation had been Norman's entire motivation, a game he delighted in playing with Gene Badger's pert new secretary. He had discontinued it not merely because Kiki had been elevated to "associate producer." It was the humorless wrath of Sunday Tyler he feared. Somehow, Sunday had managed to bypass all the customary production taboos. She had access to every script, every outline, every projection, every story decision made in chambers at both the studio and agency level. In Norman's opinion, her privileges weren't only the result of her preeminent role in "Heartbreak Hospital"; it was also the role she played in executive producer Abel McFee's bedroom.

With the sigh of the thwarted artist, Norman pressed the DELETE key on his Compaq and watched his dialogue wink out of existence. Then, settling down to the job, he reread Ophelia's turgid paragraph describing SCENE 2B and wrote:

> MRS ARMSTRONG
> Do hurry, Herbert. The hospital board meeting is
> at three, and Dr Grayson is so disgustingly punc-
> tual.
> HERBERT
> Yes, Madam.
> MRS ARMSTRONG
> Oh, dear! Isn't that Miss Harmon waving at us?
> HERBERT
> Yes, Madam. I believe she wishes to speak to you.
> (ANDREA APPROACHES THE LIMO)
> ANDREA
> (dryly)
> What a lovely coincidence! I've been trying to
> reach you all morning, Mrs Armstrong. I was *so*
> disappointed that you couldn't make my dinner
> party last night.
> MRS ARMSTRONG
> (flustered)
> Yes, I was, too—

ANDREA

And I'm *so* happy to see that you're all recovered from the flu! Obviously you have a marvellous doctor. You must give me his name!

MRS ARMSTRONG

Some other time, my dear. I'm rather late for an appointment . . . Go ahead, Herbert . . .

(LIMO DRIVES OFF. ANDREA LOOKS AFTER IT WITH HOODED AND DANGEROUS EYES)

ANDREA

(to herself)

Yes, Mrs Armstrong. . . . I hope you have a *very* good doctor!

Norman Levi sighed again, this time in relief. The scene was briefer than the one Ophelia had outlined, with less of a confrontation between Andrea and the dowager (her rich weakling of a son was madly in love with The Bitch, at least according to the latest story line). But since there was another scene between them in Act Six, Norman opted to wait until then for the full fireworks display. Writer's privilege, he told himself—if a soap writer *had* any privileges left in this era of big bucks and network domination and autocratic superstars.

He got up from his Door Store desk, patted the head of his drowsy Dobermann, and padded into the kitchen, his bunny slippers flapping pleasantly on the tiles. Norman always wore his bunny slippers when he worked. Before he had met Robin, he used to wear Mouseketeer ears with concealed stereo headphones. He never admitted that he wore them to conceal a bald spot.

Like a number of writers in the field, Norman had once been an actor. He had played smarmy young men too handsome for their own good. He had married an heiress in "Love of Life," undergone a liver transplant in "The Doctors," fallen off a horse in "Texas," and been stabbed to death in "The Edge of Night."

When he remained out of work for the next two years, he had decided that his association with canceled shows had given him a reputation as a Jonah. Then his roommate brought home a script from "Heartbreak Hospital," groaning at the lines he was supposed to commit to memory. Norman had rewritten them for him, and the supervising producer had agreed it was an improvement. More important, Phyl Wykopf, the supervising producer, had asked Norman to try his hand at a complete script, and it had turned out good enough to air.

Norman considered himself fortunate to have the steady work, and in his eagerness to please never complained about the inconsistency of the story quality and occasional downright idiocies of the plot. The first group of scripts he wrote concerned a hidden castle whose residents still believed they were living in the Middle Ages. In urgent need of medical assistance, a knight errant had left the kingdom in quest of a physician and had wound up abducting Dr Jonathan Masters, one of "Heartbreak's" bachelor heartthrobs. The patient, of course, had turned out to be a beautiful young girl, and Dr Masters had cured her with modern alchemy and promptly fallen in love with her. True to form, it was Andrea Harmon, the castle-wrecker, who broke up the romance.

In truth, Norman enjoyed writing for Sunday Tyler. The role was juicy, the actress skilled at delivering his lines. The problem was, Sunday never recognized that they *were* his lines. Her contempt for writers was in direct proportion to her ego. She complained bitterly at every read-through, her sharp red pencil darting through every speech labelled ANDREA, changing "can't" to "cannot" and "won't" to "shan't"; reversing the order of sentences until reeled the mind. But by the time of final taping, with a great show of reluctance, she abandoned most of her changes, "saving" the scripter from artistic embarrassment by the quality of her performance. Sunday was convinced she could read football results and make audiences weep.

But she *was* talented. Norman was the first to admit it. Her talent was her power base. As the head writer Bob Neffer put it, it was no longer possible to tell where Sunday Tyler stopped and Andrea Harmon began. Thinking of Bob, Norman returned to the living room, carrying a tall iced tea glass with an engraved bumblebee. He wondered if he should call the head writer to ask if there had been any word regarding his renewal. He was painfully aware that Bob and his script writers were joined at the hip, their contract periods coinciding. If Sunday succeeded in her vendetta, Norman's head would roll at the second sweep of the ax.

Ax. Why did that remind him of something?

Before he could make the connection, the door opened. Robin was home. For a moment, Norman forgot their morning quarrel and almost greeted him cheerily. Remembering in time, he swivelled his chair round and booted the computer.

Robin came up behind him and kissed the bald spot.

"For your information," Norman growled, "that is not an erogenous zone."

"It is for me, Babybuns."

"I thought you were in rehearsal," Norman said, trying to keep an edge of displeasure in his voice.

"They flip-flopped today's show," Robin Dillard said. "The Spider Woman has a guest shot on Dave Letterman tomorrow, so she's on today and I have the afternoon off. Maybe we could do a movie."

"Maybe I could do a script, if you'd get off my back."

"Still mad about last night? I told you, I was just *talking* to this guy Carlos. He's got a pair of Quicksilver amps he may be selling."

"I'll bet that's not all he's selling. . . . He called this morning, you know."

"Who?"

"Your Latin lover. At least I think it was him. He's got an accent you can cut with a machete. When he heard a man answer, he hung up."

Robin laughed, and went into the kitchen, returning a moment later swigging a bottle of Perrier. He was tall, with wide square shoulders and snake hips. He could have been cast in cowboy movies, but he couldn't overcome his slightly nasal Boston accent. He was a dayplayer on "Heartbreak Hospital," portraying an intern whose lines usually consisted of, "We're doing everything we can."

With his free hand, Robin snapped the lock on his T. Anthony attaché case and removed a manila envelope.

"I have a present for you," he said.

"I don't need any peace offerings, thanks."

"Don't you want to know what it is?" When Norman didn't reply, he said, "Does the phrase 'ax murder' do anything for you?"

Norman spun round, his eyes blazing with eagerness. "Did you get it? The Ellenberger story?"

"Right from the horse's ass's mouth, if that's the phrase. Of course, I had to imply a promise of sexual favours, but it'll be a cold day in hell, naturally." With a slight bow, he handed the xeroxed copy to Norman, who quickly studied the title page.

HEARTBREAK HOSPITAL
Story Projection
by
Keith Ellenberger

Norman had fully expected to see a red TOP SECRET stamp on the manuscript. It was, of course, illicit. Even though the show's producers were within their rights to have a projection written by an outside writer, the Writer's Guild agreement, to which "Heartbreak" was a signatory, required them to inform the head writer of the fact. Norman was certain that Bob Neffer knew nothing of Ellenberger's involvement. Nor would he have been greatly shocked, having been victimized by this form of deceitfulness in the past—in fact, Neffer himself had written illicit story projections without the knowledge or consent of the contract writers. It was all part of the game, where rules were made to be broken and hurt feelings were dealt with by a mocking-serious comment: "That's why you get the big bucks, fella."

"So they really went to Ellenberger," Norman said. "He must be eighty by now, and they still run to that guy."

"He's sixty-five," Robin said. "And there's nothing wrong with his libido, the dirty old queen."

"They say he's written for every soap that was ever on the air except 'Ma Perkins.'" He flipped to the first page. "Did he mention Sunday Tyler at all?"

"Of course not. He'd never admit he wrote the projection for *her*. He claims he did it on pure speculation."

"My ass," Norman said. "Sunday gave Ellenberger this job. But I'll bet she got the money out of Abel McFee. I'd love to know what they paid for this piece of crap."

"How do you know it's crap? You haven't read it yet."

"I've got a nose, haven't I?"

He leaned back in his swivel chair and started to read.

ANDREA, infuriated by JONATHAN'S engagement to MARIBETH ARMSTRONG, doesn't try to hide her feelings. When MRS ARMSTRONG

gives her daughter an engagement party, she naturally omits Andrea's name from the guest list. But
Andrea, like the Uninvited Witch, shows up anyway on the arm of her "intended," Maribeth's
younger brother, MONTY. Andrea looks sensational, making Maribeth feel plain in contrast, but
Jonathan assures her that the past is dead, that he
loves her far more than he ever loved his ex-wife.
The apparent failure of her tactic makes Andrea
all the angrier. She gets drunk and vows publicly
that the wedding will never take place, that she'll
see Jonathan in his grave before she'll see him
married to anyone else. She storms out. But in the
mansion's front hallway, seeing the suit of armor
with the ax, she mischievously seizes it and buries
the blade deep into the portrait of Montgomery
Armstrong, Sr., as a gesture of her contempt.

"There it is," Norman chortled. "Sunday's famous ax! Bob
says she's been talking about doing that ax scene ever since
they put that dumb suit of armor in the Armstrong set."

"I saw her in the prop department just this morning, watching them put bloodstains on it."

"*Bloodstains*?" Norman said. "What for?"

"Read on, Macduff."

Norman hurriedly flipped pages.

It is past midnight at Hartford Hospital. A weary
Dr Jonathan Masters is just coming off duty, after
sixteen long hours. He bids goodnight to a young
intern and walks down a lonely dark corridor. He
leaves the building and enters the parking lot. Just
as he goes to open his car door, a figure steps out
of the shadows. It is a tall woman shrouded in a
long black coat, her face almost indiscernible in

the shadows. Something gleams metallically in the light and we see that she holds an ax in her hand. There is also a mad gleam in her eyes as she steps into the light, and we see that it is Andrea Harmon. She raises the ax to strike, and Jonathan turns and sees death descending.

"My God!" Norman said. "Am I supposed to believe this? Sunday Tyler planning to make *herself* a killer?"

"Read on," Robin said mysteriously.

Norman did, aloud.

"'Moving swiftly, Jonathan avoids the fall of the ax by a fraction of an inch. But before he can grapple with the crazed woman, Andrea scurries away across the parking lot to the hospital entrance. The young intern, just leaving, sees the incredible sight and screams. Andrea lifts the ax and strikes again. This time, she hits her target and the intern falls to the ground. Jonathan races to his aid, but it's immediately apparent that he is beyond medical help. The intern is dead, and the killer has escaped. All Dr Masters can do is call the police and report the shocking, improbable news, that his own ex-wife has become a deranged killer. . . .'"

Norman lowered the manuscript and his eyes rounded.

"Now I understand," he said, in a hushed voice. "She's finally found a way to get her damned *twin* story into the show! "

Robin applauded lightly. "That's right, Babybuns. It's on page six. Andrea Harmon has a twin sister that nobody knew about. Mad as a hatter, and stashed away in some foreign loony bin for years. Only now she's escaped, and thinks *she's* Andrea—get it? She's been following Andrea's escapades for years, thanks to dear old Aunt Sally, who writes to her every week. . . . Now she's come to solve Andrea's problems the only way she knows how—with a bloody ax. Cute, huh?"

Norman had the dazed eyes of an earthquake victim.

"I can't believe they're serious about this," he said. "Even Abel McFee said he'd be damned if they'd put still another *twin* story on the air! Every stinking serial has had one. There must have been *four* twin stories last year, and there are still two of them going on right this minute! Even 'Heartbreak Hospital' did a twin story, back in 1993, remember?"

"Want to hear a prediction? There's going to be another one on the air."

"No," Norman said, shaking his head vigorously. "I'm not going to believe that. Bob would allow them to do this over his—" He stopped. "What am I saying? Bob's probably dead right now."

"You can count on it. There'll be a new head writer on 'Heartbreak' in a couple of weeks. Maybe even Keith Ellenberger, although I doubt it. He's an asshole, but he's not dumb enough to jump into *this* barrel of sharks."

"You realize what you're telling me, don't you? That I'm out of work again?"

Robin looked pensive at this. He went to the dry bar and poured himself a large tumbler of port. Norman, knowing that Robin didn't like drinking, experienced a small chill on the back of his neck. It proved to be justified.

"There's something else I have to tell you," Robin said carefully. "It occurred to me that you and Bob Neffer might not be the only ones who get separated in the next few weeks. I mean, what if they decide that the 'young intern' who gets the ax in that parking lot is lovable, dispensable Robin Dillard?"

"Why would they do that?" Norman said nervously.

"Why not? How many 'young interns' *are* there at 'Heartbreak Hospital'? And you know I haven't been doing much in the story, have I?"

Norman was staring at him, and must have made him uncomfortable enough for Robin to turn away. His broad back to his roommate, the actor said:

"If Bob Neffer gets canned, which looks like a foregone conclusion, you get canned because you're Bob Neffer's boy. By the same token, if they're looking for a murder victim, they might choose someone like me because . . . well, let's face it. Everybody on the show knows that you're my . . . Significant Other."

"Oh, for corn's sake!" Norman said. "What kind of dumb logic is that?"

"Sunday Tyler logic. . . . Look, don't get upset. I'm just trying to be practical. This is a tough business, and you've got to watch your rear at all times."

"You ought to know—*Babybuns.*"

"Be reasonable," Robin said, turning and holding out his hands. "The Spider Woman has you on her shit list, Norm. And when it hits the fan, I don't want to be around to get splattered. I got *debts,* man. You know that. I can't afford to be out of a job right now. So I figure, why don't we split for a while, until the dust settles?"

"What else have you got in that attaché case, Robin? A Spanish grammar?"

"There's nobody else, I swear it. You know how I feel about you. But I'm scared. That's one mean bitch after your ass and she's out for blood. . . ."

The phone rang. Norman was grateful; it allowed him to swallow the bitter tears that threatened to choke him. He grabbed the receiver and barked:

"This is Norman Levi. I'm not home right now, but if you'll leave your—" He stopped. "Oh—hi, Bob."

"Hey, Norm, how's it going?" Bob Neffer's voice rang out over the phone line like a musical instrument. Jarred by the sound, Norman looked at Robin and said:

"I'm just working on 3994. The one where Andrea has her fight with Mrs Armstrong."

"Yeah, good show, good show," Bob said brightly. "Make sure they really zing it to each other. The audience loves those scenes. . . ."

"Boy, you sound peppy," Norman said. "You're not back on the nose candy, are you?"

"Who, me? I don't abuse this beautiful body, kid. I'm just feeling good, that's all."

"Wait a minute," Norman said. "Have you heard something? About the renewal?"

"No, nothing yet. But it's going to be okay, I can tell you right now. We won't have to worry about the Wicked Bitch of the South any more. She's all through!"

"You're kidding! You mean she's off the show?"

"Who?" Robin said curiously. "Not *Sunday?*"

"She's practically out the door now," Bob Neffer said gleefully, a glee bordering on the hysterical. "If you want to know why, come down to the screening tonight."

"What screening?"

"Meet me in my office at six-thirty, okay? Don't tell any one. All seats are reserved."

He hung up, and Norman looked at Robin.

"*Madre Dios,*" he said wonderingly.

3 Against the Storm

Troy Wayland's guided tour through Studio 22 left him with a confused impression of snakepit underfoot and patchwork quilt overhead. The tangle of cables running everywhere made an obstacle course of the floorboards; beams, catwalks, wires and lighting fixtures made dizzying patterns on the high ceiling. There were a dozen sets partitioned off from each other, including a grand salon whose furnishings looked like Louis Quatorze's best on the screen but Grand Rapid's tackiest to the naked eye. There was a doctor's surgery, complete with adjoining examining room; a bearded man in sweatshirt and sneakers was sprawled across the white table, snoozing. There was a nurse's station, a private hospital room, a small ward which looked enormous in the distorting lens of the camera. Clumps of actors stood among the sets, rehearsing quietly, and Kiki, steering Troy like a blind man, led him to a set that gave him a shock of recognition. It was a police duty room, complete with "Wanted" posters and scarred oak furniture; here, the dilapidated look had verisimilitude. Adding to the authenticity was a cop in shirtsleeves wearing a shoulder harness, and, being young and black, he resembled half the plainclothes cops Troy had worked with in the Village precinct. But he was an actor, of course, and so—more obviously—was the man rehearsing lines with him. He was handsome in an outdated way: a profile too sharp, a nose and jawline forming two promontories that reminded Troy more of the heroes of silent screens than of television tubes.

Kiki introduced him first. "Milo Derringer," she said. "He plays Dr Jonathan Masters in the show. This is William Troy—he's a cop, so don't offer him any illegal substances."

She smiled an "only kidding" smile, but Milo Derringer mirrored it only faintly.

"Nice to meet you, Officer." Troy noticed that he didn't make the assumption everyone else had, that Troy was "Lieutenant." He found that he was slightly miffed; or maybe he just resented the actor's exaggerated good looks. "I hope you can give my friend here some good tips," Derringer said, grinning at the black man. "At least teach him how not to shoot himself in the foot."

"Ramsey Duke." The pseudo-cop stuck out his hand. "Maybe you could talk to the writer, too. He has me putting out all-points bulletins every five minutes. Something tells me cops just don't do that."

"Not that often," Troy said. "But I won't be much help to either of you. I'm not a consultant. I'm with the Movie/TV unit."

"That's too bad. We could use a technical adviser around here. Especially the scriptwriters."

Kiki patted his blue sleeve. "Don't blame poor Norman. We've all got a lot to learn." She looked at Troy. "It's the first time 'Heartbreak Hospital' ever had a major cop character."

"I'd be happy to answer any questions I can handle," Troy said. "But it would be unofficial, of course."

Ramsey said: "Maybe we could have lunch one day."

"Sure. As long as it isn't that restaurant across the street."

Kiki tittered. "I just introduced him to the Green Grotto."

"One of our occupational hazards," Derringer said. "Take him to the Four Seasons bar, Ram." He turned to Troy. "Help yourself to something edible. From the local bakery, and damned good."

Troy looked at the table he indicated, laden with coffee machines and pastry containers, many of them already attacked by cast and crew. "I never could resist lemon meringue," he said, cutting himself a slab.

Ramsey Duke grinned. "I thought cops only like doughnuts."

"I'm a lemon meringue kind of cop."

"Tell him what kind of cop you are," Milo Derringer said slyly. "Ever hear of a dancing detective, officer?"

Ramsey's answering scowl was only half-serious. Later, Troy learned that the actors had worked on another soap together, that Derringer had suggested Duke for the role of Rick Savage. *Lieutenant* Rick Savage, naturally.

"It's true," Duke said. "I was with the New York City Ballet for about four years. But you live fast and die young in that business. That's why I switched to acting."

"And when that gets too rough," Derringer said, "you can try politics." His eyes slid away to another part of the studio, and his voice became citric. "Who knows? I may be running for office myself pretty soon."

Troy tracked the direction of his gaze. Its vanishing point was Sunday Tyler in the salon set, rehearsing her own day's role with a tall, gangling man with a permanent stoop. Troy's natural curiosity was stirred again. Was there some connection between the remark and Sunday's notorious reputation?

"I'd better see if Gene is ready for us," Kiki said. "Be right back." She scurried off, and Troy muttered something about letting the actors go back to work. He drifted away slowly, stepping carefully over the booby-trap cables, and realized he was moving unconsciously towards the magnetic glow of Sunday Tyler. When he was close enough to overhear, he also realized that she wasn't rehearsing lines with the tall, stooped man. She was arguing with him.

"It's not your direction I won't take, Lou," the actress was saying with icy calm. "It's what's in the fucking script. Do I make myself clear?"

The man called Lou had a prominent Adam's apple that now bobbed up and down nervously. "If you had problems with the script, Sunday, why didn't you bring them up at the read-through?"

"I wasn't at the read-through, as you very well know. I couldn't make it. My alarm didn't go off. But we don't have to make a Federal case out of it, Lou, let's just cut the goddam kiss, is that so much to ask?"

"Uh, honey baby sweetie, don't you think the audience is getting a little upset because you never kiss the man you're supposed to be crazy about?"

"Do we cut the kiss or don't we?"

"You better take it up with Gene, Sunday, I'm just directing this show, I don't write the stuff. . . . Excuse me." In his anxiety to escape, he backed into Troy, treading on the foot that had ached ever since a furious prostitute had stomped him on Jane Street. The director apologized without even glancing at his victim. Troy, suppressing a moan, saw Sunday Tyler looking at him with amusement.

"Who are you?" she said. "You're not dressed like an actor, so you must be from the network."

"No," Troy said. "Not the network. Station NYPD."

"What?"

"I'm a police officer," Troy said, uncomfortable under her inspection. She was giving him the same frank appraisal women give men in singles bars—not that Troy had visited one since he broke up with Fiona. It was almost two months, right after his transfer to the Movie/TV unit, since Fiona had walked out of their shared apartment, taking her clothes, her Bruce Springsteen albums, and everything else she could carry. His friend Gary had suggested picking her up on a petty larceny, but Troy had refused, secretly relieved that she had left. Fiona was the cheerleader type, and there was something in Troy which drew him to less wholesome, more dangerous females. Like the one in front of him.

"I know who you are," Sunday was saying, snapping him out of his reverie. "You're going to help us with the location shooting."

"I'll do my best," Troy said. "But I still don't know what you're planning to shoot."

"Why, a murder, of course," Sunday smiled. "Didn't anybody tell you? We're going to kill someone."

From across the room, Kiki was waving at him and heading in their direction.

"I'm sure Little Miss Muffet will tell you what she knows about it," Sunday said sweetly. "Unfortunately, she doesn't know as much as she thinks. If you'd like to learn what's *really* going to happen—why don't you buy me a drink some time?"

Troy blinked, and she recognized the sign of incredulity.

"No, I'm serious. I'm busy tonight, and I'm taping the Letterman show tomorrow evening, but I'll be free the rest of the night. . . . Are you good at remembering numbers?"

"I can only try."

She rattled off a phone number and walked away just as Kiki arrived, apologizing for the delay. As she led him towards Gene Badger's office, Kiki smiled and said:

"Did she make a pass at you?"

"What makes you say that?"

"You looked like you were trying to memorize a phone number."

Troy gave her five points for perception.

The producer's office was reached through what seemed like half a mile of dingy, cluttered corridors. There were only two points of interest along the way. One was a small screening room, occupied by Bob Neffer, the hawk-profiled head writer Troy had met at lunch, who appeared to be waiting nervously for something to happen or someone to arrive. The other was a bulletin board on the stucco wall adjoining Gene Badger's place of business. It was a jumble of notices, clippings, cards and letters, and, since the producer had someone with him when they arrived, Troy spent the waiting time looking them over. The letters fascinated him the most; they were obviously from "Heartbreak Hospital's" most rabid fans. One read:

> How can you let that horrible slut Andrea get away with it? Jumping into bed with two different men THE SAME NIGHT!!! And pretending that she loves both of them when everybody knows she doesn't love anybody but her own slutty self!!! When are you people going to WISE UP to that bitch on wheels?!!! When is somebody going to kick the S—T out of that filthy tramp or stick a knife in her gut? I can't wait to see her get HERS!!! But PLEASE PLEASE don't let it happen on a Monday because I work and don't get home until late.

It was signed: "ANDREA'S BIGGEST FAN".

Most of the other letters mentioned Andrea, although some were addressed to other cast members. Or rather, Troy observed, to the characters they played. Obviously, there was a confusion of identities in the minds of the audience. One letter in particular, addressed to the actor Troy had just met, contained a haunting phrase:

Dear Milo Derringer:
    Dr Jonathan Masters is very lucky to have you
play him.

Someone had also invested in a lengthy Mailgram, but the
occasion seemed worthy.

> DEAR TAMMY AND STEVE. CONGRATULATIONS ON
> YOUR WEDDING AND I HOPE YOU WILL BE VERY
> HAPPY. YOU BOTH LOOKED ADORABLE AND I
> LOVED THE WAY YOU KISSED FOR SUCH A LONG
> TIME THAT EVERYONE WENT OOOOOOO. I THINK
> YOU DID THE RIGHT THING NOT TELLING ANYONE
> WHERE YOU WERE GOING ON YOUR HONEYMOON
> BUT I HOPE ITS SOMEPLACE NICE. MY ONLY WORRY
> IS WHEN YOU COME BACK PLEASE WATCH OUT FOR
> ANDREA. YOU KNOW THE WAY SHE MAKES
> TROUBLE FOR EVERYBODY LIKE THAT WONDER-
> FUL DOCTOR MASTERS. I DONT KNOW WHY HE
> EVER MARRIED HER AND HE HAD BETTER BE CARE-
> FUL BECAUSE SHE IS AFTER HIM AGAIN. I HOPE YOU
> LIKED THE WEDDING GIFT I SENT YOU BUT DONT
> WORRY ABOUT SENDING A THANK YOU NOTE.
> EMILY POST SAYS YOU HAVE UP TO SIX MONTHS.
> WITH LOVE AND BEST WISHES FROM YOUR FRIEND
> LOTTIE.

Troy became aware that Kiki was reading over his shoulder.
Her closeness made the back of his neck tingle.

"The Mailgram's from Loony Lottie," she said. "She sent a
silver tea service when Tammy and Steve got married."

"Tammy and Steve being—characters?"

"Of course. I doubt if Lottie even knows the names of the
actors. I don't think she wants to admit there *are* actors behind
the masks. Incredible, isn't it?" she said. "The *power* of these
shows! It still amazes me—the fact that so many millions of
people believe these characters they see on the screen are *real*."

Troy shrugged. "They think wrestling is real, too."

"No," Kiki said. "It's different. The people in the soaps come into their homes almost every day. They reveal everything about themselves. Every intimate secret! They cry, they laugh, they make love, they betray each other, they *kill* each other! But they also make small talk, and they cook meals, or they just sit around and have coffee, and it all adds up to some crazy kind of reality that's realer than real. . . . Sometimes it's scary!"

"You might be getting a distorted picture. Maybe the only people you get letters and Mailgrams from are the whackos and psychos. Like Loony Lottie."

Kiki stiffened and Troy was instantly sorry he had spoken.

"You'd be surprised at who watches soaps, *Officer* Troy. I assure you, they're not all cooks and maids and invalids and weirdos. . . . I could show you studies—"

"Please—anything but that."

"Soap characters become as real to people as members of their own families. No, there's a difference. They usually know the soap characters *better* than they know their families!"

"And you think all this is healthy?"

"For a lot of people, yes. I remember this one old lady. She was in her nineties, and she got so upset about the *bad* things happening to the characters that a worried neighbour wrote us a letter about it. Gene thought we should be charitable and write to the old woman, assuring her that everything she saw on the screen was make-believe, that there was really nothing to worry about. . . . That's what we did. . . . She died the week after she got the letter."

"Moral? "

Kiki shrugged. "Maybe the show was keeping her alive. Maybe being involved even with imaginary people is better than not being involved at all."

Badger's door opened and the visitor emerged. It was the tall, stooped director, and Troy could guess the substance of their talk. When he emerged, Lou Blankenship looked like a man with a migraine. Gene Badger, however, seemed unperturbed behind his desk, sipping coffee from a plastic container and smiling genially. Later, Troy learned about the support the producer received from the little pill he called his Nice Uncle Val.

"It's true," he admitted, when Troy quoted Sunday Tyler's remark. "We're going to do a homicide story. Nothing unusual about that, of course. Soaps have been murdering people in broad daylight for the past fifty years."

"I thought they were supposed to be family shows."

Badger chuckled. "I can see you don't know daytime. These shows couldn't exist without crime. There are just so many stories you can tell about love triangles and custody cases and marriages on the rocks. . . . Sooner or later, somebody commits a robbery, or plans to murder a rival, or gets involved with espionage. And at least once a year, the syndicate moves into town and starts slaughtering the non-contract players."

"Contract players, too, sometimes." Kiki volunteered.

"Well, murder's one way to get rid of characters who outlive their usefulness. Or who just aren't popular enough."

"Or actors who won't behave. Who make too many demands, or ask for too much money, or . . ."

"Let's not get carried away," Badger said, clearing his throat. "We all know there's such a thing as temperament, and you can't blame these people when you think about the job they do, going up in front of those cameras day after day—"

"I think it's the toughest acting job in the world," Kiki said. "I'm always amazed at how well they do it."

"What baffles me," Troy said, "is how they manage to learn new lines for every show."

"And unlearn the old ones," Badger said. "It's quite a skill, and if you don't have it, you just don't do daytime."

"They can get help from the teleprompter, can't they?"

"We don't use it anymore," Kiki said. "For one thing," she added dryly, "it was costing us sixty grand a year."

"The best ones never used it anyway," Badger said. "It made the difference between a good *reading* and a good performance."

"Would one of the best ones be . . . Sunday Tyler?"

Badger's hesitation lasted only a fraction of a second.

"Definitely one of the best. Probably be the Emmy nominee this year. Maybe even the winner. Why do you ask?"

"I was just wondering if she was also your nominee for Murder Victim."

Kiki sighed. "You might as well know that Mr Troy heard you guys at lunch today. You were talking very loud."

"But that's all it was," the producer said, producing a wide smile with no apparent effort. "It was just talk. We were kidding, of course. Nobody really wants to kill off Sunday."

"You could have fooled me."

"Not that Andrea Harmon wouldn't be a great Victim," Badger said quickly. "I mean, the character is begging for it. She's the Bitch, and the Bitch has lots of enemies, which makes her the obvious murder victim. Except for one thing: we don't want to be killed in the ratings at the same time."

"I've already explained that to Mr Troy," Kiki said, looking slyly amused.

"Sure," Troy said. "I'm hip."

"So . . . we're planning to do something different. Instead of making Andrea the victim . . . we're going to make her the killer."

Troy sat back. "Doesn't that amount to the same thing? You can't allow a killer to get away with murder. I assume there's some sort of rule about that."

"There is," Kiki said. "The NAB code—the National Association of Broadcasters. We can't cause serious harm to a child, we can't offer suicide as a viable alternative, and we can't let killers off the hook. Even if we got around the code some way, there are the network censors. . . ."

"Then what are you planning to do? Not that it's any of my business."

"A lot of what we're planning has to do with the location shooting," Badger said. "We thought it would be interesting to have the whole murder sequence take place outdoors." He looked at Kiki. "Maybe Sergeant Troy should have a copy of the story projection. It'll give him the general idea."

"The general idea being," Kiki said, "that we make it *look* as if Andrea is the killer, even though she's innocent. It's not the newest idea in daytime. False accusation of murder is pretty standard stuff. But we haven't let that stop us yet." She pretended not to see Badger's disapproval. "Actually, we're hoping Bob Neffer can put some kind of spin on it, something the audience won't figure out from day one . . . a blue herring."

"A what?"

Badger said: "Kiki's been talking about it for weeks. She read an interview with some mystery writer who says that audiences have become too smart to fall for the old red herrings. You have to fool them with *another* color herring. Blue, for instance."

"Meaning a false clue that they'll *know is* a false clue?"

Kiki clapped her hands. "Exactly! We make the audience *think* they've outguessed us by dragging a *blue* herring across the trail! Do you see?" she said, directing her appeal to Troy. "Gene *doesn't* see it. I'm not sure Bob Neffer does, either. This story could be so *boring* if the audience is ahead of us, and they'll have weeks to guess the truth. If they guess it right away, we'll have a ratings disaster on our hands."

Badger began showing his irritation.

"What do you want us to do, Kiki? Go with Sunday Tyler's crazy twin idea?"

"What's the twin idea?" Troy asked.

"Sunday came up with her own plot," the producer said, his genial aura tested. "She wants the writer to invent a twin sister nobody ever knew about until now, who escapes from a nuthouse in Outer Mongolia or someplace and comes here and commits the murder, God knows why. Naturally, everybody blames Andrea, including the audience. . . ."

"A little far-fetched, isn't it?"

"You know why she suggested it, of course. By playing twins, Sunday gets twice the air time and twice the salary. But anyway," Kiki said, "there are two soaps using twin stories right this minute, and 'Heartbreak' itself did a twin story not very long ago. The audience just won't stand for it."

"I won't stand for it," Gene Badger said. "We'll do that damn twin story over my dead body."

No director could have timed it better. The door opened right on cue. Sunday Tyler was in the doorway, holding the same bloodstained ax Troy had seen her brandishing in the elevator.

"I thought you might like to see this, darling," she said. She came forward to give the producer a better view. "I asked Freddy to bloody it up for me. Doesn't it give you goosebumps?"

"Take that thing away," Badger growled.

Sunday laughed as if it was a witty remark. "He's squeamish," she said, addressing no one in particular. "But actually, I had another reason for coming to see you. I just spoke to Lou. He says he told you about my objection to the last scene today. The kiss?"

Troy started to rise from his chair, but Kiki gave him a quick nod that meant "stay."

"The kiss is the punctuation of the scene," Gene said, in a tone that would have sounded reasonable except for a slight tremor. "The audience is *waiting* for Andrea to kiss Jonathan. They're *begging* for them to kiss. They're threatening to march on the studio with torches if they *don't* kiss."

"Good," Sunday said sweetly. "Fine. But let's remember the old soap opera rule. *Never give the audience what it wants.*"

"I always thought that was the dumbest rule I ever heard."

"And the dumbest thing I ever heard is in that script on your desk. ANDREA SIGHS AND FALLS INTO JONATHAN S ARMS. THEY KISS. FOR A MOMENT, SHE HAS COMPLETELY SURRENDERED AND BECOME A WOMAN. We'll sell a million sick bags with that one."

"One kiss isn't going to hurt you, Sunday."

"*This* one absolutely destroys Andrea's character. It makes her a weakling. It gives him *power over her.*"

"This isn't a power struggle, sweetheart. This is pure and simple romance. It's what earns us our paycheck every week."

"I don't agree. *Andrea* doesn't agree. And that's why she is *not* going to kiss Dr Jonathan Masters today!"

If she was trying to provoke an explosion, she succeeded. Badger stood up so suddenly that his chair skidded back and slammed against the wall. He jabbed his finger at the Xeroxed document lying on his desk and shouted:

"That kiss is in the script, honey sweetie baby! And if you don't perform, I'm taking it up with Equity. They've got rules about that sort of thing—you know, about following directions? They wouldn't blame us if we fired your ass right off this show!"

There was a moment of hushed silence, making them all aware of their held breaths. Then Sunday took one step forward, lifted the ax with both hands, and brought it down in a short but effective arc that drove its blade deep into the script sitting on Gene Badger's desk, impaling it on the blotter. "All I asked for was one little cut," she said nicely.

Then she turned on her heel and made a perfect exit. The moment the door closed, Troy remembered the phone number. He also knew that he would be calling it.

■ ■ ■

Sunday's acting-school posture lost none of its perfection as she strode down the cluttered corridor towards the studio. But as she passed the screening room, the sound of a high-pitched giggle stopped her in her tracks. There was something familiar about it; there weren't many people who laughed in that precise, fluting way, but she couldn't visualize the mouth from which it was emerging yet again. Then she realized why. She had met Norman Levi, Bob Neffer's pet scriptwriter, only at "Heartbreak" Christmas parties and other celebrations. They had been congruous settings for Levi's peculiar laugh. What was going on in the screening room? There was only one way to find out.

Sunday pushed open the door. The U-matic videotape player was operating, its small green light shining brightly in the darkness. And on the television screen, shining even more brightly for the two-man audience, was a younger, thinner, and nude Sunday Tyler. No, naked was the proper word. The naked Sunday Tyler, reaching out languidly to stroke the equally naked buttocks of another equally lovely woman.

4 Bright Promise

Every man has white nights of the soul. From the day he turned fifty, Abel McFee shifted his contemplative moods to the morning. It was a shaving mirror ritual, enabling the executive producer to conduct a silent dialogue between the image in the glass and the one he carried inside his head. He preferred the latter, because the unseen Abel was ageless, potent, and above all, THIN. The portly imposter spreading Foamy across his puffy cheeks was only there to handle the shaving process.

This morning, his mind was so clouded by dark thoughts he barely noticed the steamy vapor on his mirror. The fact that it was Thursday accounted for some of his depression. Thursday was Nielsen day, and for the last five weeks "Heartbreak Hospital" had been declining steadily in the ratings, losing half a point each week since the wedding of Tammy and Steve. Actually, the decline had started earlier, with the location shoot in the Virgin Islands, a favorite site for soap exteriors and, Abel secretly believed, primarily a perk for cast and crew. The show garnered an inflated 24 share and an 8.2 rating during the week the St Thomas story aired; in the old familiar sets, it reverted to normal just as Abel had feared. Now the share was down to a 17, the rating 6.5. Not a bad slice of a pie that was shrinking every year with the inroads of cable; but it was still a loss of two million homes, and that meant more frowns in the network corridors, more threatening rumbles behind the closed doors.

Abel, watching his impersonator guide the razor past his second chin, decided to believe that the Nielsen families would be kind this time. But the moment of optimism only permitted his other worries to rise to the surface. He was three months in arrears on alimony payments to *both* of his ex-wives. He was afraid to drive his Ferrari for fear of repossession; he kept it in the garage of his country house in Pound Ridge. His present wife, Vera, would be returning from the monkey gland clinic in Switzerland any day now, and there would be more talk about the divorce settlement. His two children, Ryan and Diane, privately renamed Ruin and Disaster, were clamoring for expensive gifts. Somehow, the world had made the assumption that a network vice-presidency was the key to unlimited wealth, when his actual gross was less than ninety thousand a year, far less after the ravages of the national and state taxmen, the social security levy, and all the rest.

There was one other concern which should have been part of Abel McFee's white morning, but some time ago he had learned to bar it from his thoughts as securely as the studio's controlroom door barred visitors during taping. Now, however, watching his portly twin splash on shaving lotion, the door inside his head opened a crack, and the name *Talent Assets* was whispered in his ear, and Abel's two images merged momentarily into one frightened whole. He was grateful for the interrupting sound of the bedroom telephone.

"Ah—you're still there. Good."

"Sunday? What are you doing up so early? I thought you told me you weren't on today."

"I'm not. And you're not going to work until you see me. It's very important."

Abel groaned. "I've got a lousy day ahead of me. Thursday!"

"I don't care if it's Doomsday! I've got to see you. You never get in until ten o'clock anyway."

"If it's about that ax business, I've already heard it. I'm surprised it wasn't on the CBS News last night. Cute stunt, honey, very cute. You're going to get a reputation as a fruitcake."

"It's my reputation I have to see you about," Sunday said. "Are you still in bed?"

"Do you want me to be?" Abel said hopefully. He had been making an unsuccessful attempt at seduction for the past two months, and had become all the more intrigued, even obsessed, with the actress because of her curious resistance. Well, maybe not so curious, he thought ruefully, spotting his paunchy reflection in the full-length mirror on the wardrobe door.

The sight of his soft white body was all the incentive he needed. He opened the wardrobe and removed his jogging suit. Abel hadn't been faithful to his New Year resolution to run in nearby Central Park three days each week. Of course, it would have to be a quickie this morning, since Sunday was on her way. Fifteen minutes would do it, giving him time to shower before she got there. He would still be damp and glowing pink in his terry robe when she arrived. His second wife had once told him he was very sexy when wet. He began to feel better about the day's prospects.

As he left the apartment house, there were three other joggers doing their stretching exercises against the building façade, arms braced against the stone, heads bowed, genuflecting to the great god Exercise. He gave them a brisk wave of camaraderie and trotted towards the park. It was a bright, clear morning. He felt wonderful. Just the same, he was so winded when he reached the corner that he had to stop, missing the light. His heart was pounding, but he didn't think that was so bad. Wasn't that the whole idea of aerobic exercise, to make the heart beat faster, make that tired old blood zip through the veins? He decided he had done his duty, turned the corner and made a slow circuit of the block back to the building entrance. Fortunately, the three joggers had left, and the doorman was busy hailing a cab. He didn't feel the slightest trace of guilt when he got off the elevator. He went back into his apartment, poured himself an enormous glass of orange juice, and then headed for the shower. He sang lustily as the water splashed on his pink, portly body. Sexy when wet! He laughed to himself.

Abel was just tying on his robe when the doorbell rang. Sunday had made good time. As usual, she had flashed through the streets of the city on a silver Peugeot bicycle, wearing dark Porsche glasses, an Hermes scarf streaming behind her. When she sailed into the room, the scarf was around her head, concealing an unkempt hairdo. She didn't remove the scarf, but she whipped off the glasses, uncovering eyes red and puffy from lack of sleep.

"You look terrible," Abel said. "Beautiful but terrible."

"I've been up half the night."

"Worrying? About what?"

"Not worrying—working. Never mind that. I came to talk to you about Bob Neffer and his little poofter."

Abel sighed wearily. "Is that what you wanted? Haven't I heard it all before, Sunday? About Neffer and about Desowitz and Moody and every other writer on this show?"

"You haven't heard *this* before." She flopped on the sofa, picked up a cushion and hugged it like a teddy bear, burying her face in the velvety nap. "Those bastards are out to get me, Abel," she said in a muffled voice. "And somehow or other . . . they found out about . . . Peaches Paree."

It was a good reading. Abel could almost hear the ellipses in the sentence. The only trouble was, it made no sense to him.

"Who or what is Peaches Paree?"

Pause. Wait for curiosity to build.

"She's *me.*"

"What?"

Look up. Meet his eyes. Look pained, frightened, helpless. "It's a stage name I once used."

"You're kidding. Sunday Tyler is peculiar enough, honey, but—*Peaches Paree?* It sounds like the name of a stripper. Or one of those porno queens . . ."

His own performance wasn't bad either. Abel's speech slowed imperceptibly as he came to the end of his sentence; his eyes rounded and his mouth opened, creating a textbook picture of (1) surprise, (2) disbelief and (3) fearful apprehension.

"Sunday, you're not telling me that . . . you . . ."

"Oh, wipe that sickening face off your expression!"

"You said that wrong."

"Fuck you! Did I say that right?"

"For God's sake, tell me what this is all about! When the hell were you 'Peaches Paree'? When did you get the time to be anyone but—what was the name again? You told me but I forgot."

"Eileen Ovitz, and I'm trying to forget it, too." Sunday flung the cushion halfway across the room and got to her feet. "I was seventeen years old. It was the first acting job I had in New York. It was better than becoming a hooker, even if some people think it amounts to the same thing."

"Doesn't it?"

"I made *two* goddam movies!" Sunday shouted. "The first one ended up as mandolin picks. It was shot with a flashlight and a Brownie camera, no pun intended. The second one was called *Ladies in Wading* and it was shot on Rockaway Beach in

October. I almost froze my ass off. They paid me five hundred dollars. No points. I wasn't even the star, just the second lead."

"And," Abel said, not wanting to hear the answer, "I gather this second movie *wasn't* cut up for mandolin picks?"

"I didn't think there was a print left in the world! I still don't know how they got their hands on it, Neffer and that little shit. They were both at the studio last night—*in our own studio!* They were in the screening room, watching a videotape of that damned movie and giggling like a couple of sorority sisters!"

"A videotape! That must explain it. This company you worked for had it transferred to an X-rated tape. They've done that with practically every porno film made. Jesus," he said, in awe. "That means you're in the video rental stores. . . . If Standards and Practices found out about this, Sunday . . . "

"They wouldn't know a goddam *thing* about it! Not unless they were very carefully *shown.* I'm only in two scenes. In the first one, I'm romping in the surf along with three other girls—you can't tell one pair of tits from the other without a score card. In the next scene . . . well, there's a big close-up of me. I was . . . younger, of course. Very young. If somebody didn't *tell* you it was me, you might not guess."

"But if you were pointed out—?"

"Yes. You'd know."

Abel, who had been sitting on an ottoman, rose and went to the bar. Forgetting that he hadn't even had breakfast yet, he poured himself half a glass of bourbon and sipped it. He didn't offer anything to Sunday.

"All right," he said. "Let's think about this. Maybe it isn't as bad as it sounds."

"Why? Because the odds are against anyone finding out?"

"Partly."

"Do you really think Neffer and the Fairy Princess are going to keep *quiet* about it? They hate my guts, Abel, in case that fact escaped you. They're probably going to try to blackmail me with the damned movie. Maybe blackmail you, too, the show, the network, everybody."

"They wouldn't do that. It wouldn't work, and their names would stink in this business. They're too *smart* for that, Sunday, and you've got to be smart, too. Even if they spill the beans, we can probably convince the network that it was only a foolish mistake you made when you were very young. This isn't the McCarthy era, kid, people are more broadminded, it makes them feel good to forgive your peccadilloes. "

"There's only one problem," Sunday said dryly. "Nobody's ever seen my peccadilloes in quite this way before."

"Meaning what?"

"I mean it's not just a porno film. It's a certain type of porno film."

"I don't get you."

"It's an all-talking, all-color, all-girl extravaganza."

"Sunday, will you please—"

"It's a lesbian movie, Abel."

He needed something to eat or he would definitely be sick. From somewhere in her being, Sunday Tyler dredged up a mote of domesticity and went into his kitchen. She had no idea what to do with eggs or bacon or anything else requiring culinary skill, so she found a bowl and a packet of cereal called Captain Crunch. She was too nervous to be amused. She brought a bowl-ful of the stuff into the living room and Abel pointed out that milk might make it more palatable. She brought him the milk and watched him eat slowly, trying to digest her announcement along with his breakfast.

"I don't believe all this," he said. "I think I'm still asleep and dreaming. A lesbian movie. Does that explain why you—"

"No," she said flatly. "I don't swing that way and never have. I'm an *actress,* damn it, and when the director told me to *act* like a dyke, I acted like a dyke. That's all there was to it. Which probably won't help me one bit with the network."

"All right," Abel said, crunching. "I'll talk to Bob. I'll find out if he plans to make trouble. Maybe he doesn't mean any harm. Maybe we're hollering before we're hurt."

"No," Sunday said, her voice as crisp as the cereal. "That won't do any good. Because if Neffer isn't in a vengeful mood *now,* think what he'll be like when he hears about . . . Andrea's twin."

"Oh, God," Abel groaned. "I'd almost forgotten about that, Sunday. Maybe we should—"

She jump-cued him with lightning speed. "Don't say it! Don't you dare talk about scrapping my story! You promised me we would do it! And don't forget the money you just paid Keith Ellenberger for his projection. What was it, twenty thousand?"

"I don't care about the money! We'll eat it!"

"All you're going to eat is your cereal, Captain. We're doing the twin sister story or you'll be very, very sorry!"

"You know what Bob threatened to do if we rammed that story down his throat! He was going to quit!"

"Which is exactly what we want him to do, don't we, lovey? Didn't we discuss all that? Keith Ellenberger is chomping at the bit waiting to take over. Or is it champing?"

"But that was *before* this . . . Peaches Paris business!"

"Peaches Paree. I made the name up myself. I'm very good at names. I'm thinking of calling my twin sister Prudence. Don't you think that would be deliciously ironic, considering that she's a homicidal maniac?"

Abel lost his appetite. He put the cereal bowl down and said, "Sunday, please be reasonable. If you're right about this, Neffer has a loaded gun and he could hold it to our heads."

"Well, I don't intend to spend the rest of my career in 'Heart-break Hospital' with a gun pointed at me. My suggestion is— we bite the bullet. Right now."

"This analogy is getting out of hand."

"I'm suggesting that you fire Neffer immediately. Him and his gay *caballero*. Fire them both and there won't be any incentive for them to blackmail us. His cycle ends in another six weeks, so you'll have to eat that money, too. It will be worth it."

Abel hesitated. "I don't think I can do that, Sunday."

"You're the executive producer, aren't you?"

"Even the boss has a boss."

"Why should you be afraid of Neffer if I'm not? I'm the one whose ass is on the line. Or the beach, in this case."

"Don't ask me to do this, Sunday."

"What makes you think I'm *asking* you?" Abel looked at her. He was sitting, she was standing. She looked taller than usual, more imposing, more dangerous. He didn't know why the last word occurred to him.

"Do you mean you're ordering me? Now is that nice? To bully a friend?"

"My darling, I learned a long time ago that it's one's *friends* who require the most bullying."

He tried out a chuckle, rose to his feet, and slipped an arm round her waist. She didn't resist the gesture. She just looked into his eyes, located a fraction below her own, and said:

"Talent Assets, Abel."

She might as well have said: "Saddam just dropped the Bomb, Abel."

"Now what's that supposed to mean?" he said, admiring his own calm.

"God, how I hate that line," Sunday said flatly. "Script writers use it all the time, have you noticed? I suppose it fills up the page. I think this is the first time I've heard anyone say it in real life."

"I'm saying it. What is 'talent assistance' supposed to mean?"

"Good," she smiled. "Very good. Pretend to get the name wrong. Nice little touch, Abel, but not effective. You know very well that the name of the company is 'Talent Assets.' I'm sure you dreamed it up yourself. I don't like it much. It has an awkward sound. You're not as good at names as I am."

He moved away from her, even though he knew she would interpret the move as eye avoidance. The truth was, he *couldn't* keep on meeting her eyes.

"All right, say what you have to say," he told her, his voice sounding distant in his own ears.

"You're smarter in the office than you are at home, darling. I'm sure you don't leave incriminating papers right on top of your desk for everyone to see. But at home—well, you tend to be careless. That's how I first realized that Talent Assets was more than it appeared to be. More than the network thinks it is. Do I have to go on?"

"Yes. You do."

"Remember the night you got me drunk and brought me here? To wreak your will on me, as they used to say?"

"I didn't get you drunk on purpose. I didn't realize you had no tolerance for alcohol."

She smiled sweetly. "Oh, you knew, lovey. That's why I got a Bloody Mary instead of the Virgin Mary I wanted. But no matter. I didn't mind being lightheaded, even if I didn't much care for the vomiting afterwards. Vomiting is so unfeminine, isn't it?" Her smile broadened. "It also discourages romance, as you found out. And so . . . I ended up sleeping quietly in your bed. Alone. And when I woke up the next morning . . . I was still alone."

His eyes went to the bedroom door.

"My God," he said. "The stationery."

"I wasn't snooping. I was merely looking for a painkiller. You know what a hangover is like. This was my very first. "

"Why didn't you look in the medicine cabinet?" he said harshly.

"I didn't want *aspirin,* darling. I assumed you might have something more 'interesting' around. You usually do—or would you like to deny that, too? Anyway, I thought a logical place to look would be in your bureau drawers, and that's what I did. And lo and behold, what did I find? Boxes full of stationery. Talent Assets. And a nice checkbook in a ring binder. And a pretty little stamping thingamajig with a corporate seal. Why, even a dummy like me could figure out that my little sweetie Abel was running a little business on the side."

"There's—nothing wrong about that, is there? For God's sake, what's wrong with a little private enterprise?"

Sunday laughed, and it had a genuine relaxed sound.

"Oh, you're wonderful, Abel, you're a sort of comic genius. A little private enterprise. Emphasis on private, of course. But as I said, the name was pretty awful. Especially considering that you didn't deal in Talent, and that there were no Assets. So what could I possibly conclude from all that?"

"You tell me." Abel noticed that his tie was choking him. He went to loosen it, and then realized he was still in his robe.

"Why, I had to think that Talent Assets was a fake, and that all the network checks you wrote to the company went right into your own pocket. Do I get an A, Professor?"

Quietly, Abel said: "Ten minutes ago we were talking about blackmail. What are we talking about now?"

"Mutual assistance," Sunday said promptly.

"A deal, you mean."

"A handshake deal, lovey, made in friendship. I *am* your friend, you know. Think how long I've known about this little scam of yours and said absolutely nothing. Did I say little? The balance in that checkbook was over a hundred thousand dollars."

"You were just waiting for the right moment, is that it?"

Sunday went to her handbag. It was large and flat, but it collapsed when she removed the manila envelope inside.

"Let me leave this with you," she said.

"What is it?"

"It's what kept me up last night. I was rewriting Keith Ellenberger's projection."

"So you're a writer now," Abel said. "Do you want that job, too?"

"No, my sweet. Playing *two* roles in 'Heartbreak Hospital' will keep me busy enough. And I wasn't trying for the Pulitzer Prize. I merely made some small changes in the Ellenberger story line. We can talk about it after you've read it. I've got to get myself together for the Letterman interview now. I'll be at NBC for most of the afternoon, but you can reach me at home this evening after eight." She patted his freshly shaved cheek. "Don't look so unhappy, darling. Everything is going to be fine. The story is going to be wonderful. The ratings are going up, up, and away. Hi-yo, Silvercup!"

"It's 'Hi-yo, Silver,'" Abel corrected sadly. "Silvercup was the Lone Ranger's sponsor. It was white bread."

"And so are you, angel," Sunday Tyler said.

Abel didn't know what to do with himself after she had gone. He took the cereal bowl back into the kitchen and put it in the sink. He thought about getting dressed, but realized that would entail sartorial decisions, and he wasn't prepared to make decisions of any kind. Then he realized that the most practical thing to do right now was open the manila envelope and see what Sunday Tyler, the Great Communicator, had left behind.

There were only two double-spaced pages in the envelope, kept neat by a cardboard stiffener. Had it really taken her half the night to rewrite two pages? He read it slowly.

It is past midnight at Hartford Hospital. A weary Dr Jonathan Masters is just coming off duty after sixteen long hours. He bids goodnight to a young intern who asks him about his forthcoming wedding. Jonathan says he's the luckiest man on earth, and the intern agrees with him. Then Jonathan leaves the building and enters the parking lot. Just as he goes to open his car door, a figure steps out of the shadows. It is a tall woman shrouded in a long black sequined cape, her face almost indiscernible in the shadows. Something gleams metallically in the light. It attracts Jonathan's eye, and he turns to look at the source of the distraction. He sees the woman and asks who it is. She doesn't reply. But when she takes one more step, her features are revealed. It is Andrea, looking beautiful but strange. He calls out her name in surprise. What is she doing there?

Suddenly, he realizes what created the metallic gleam. It is a broad ax, the same terrible weapon that was missing from the front hallway of the Armstrong mansion. He is startled to see it in her dainty hands, and asks what in the world is she doing with that? Again, she doesn't reply. But as he comes closer, the woman suddenly lifts the ax and lets it fall! And while we don't see the actual blow, we hear his cry of terror and the sound of his body crumpling to the ground. . . . A moment later, the young intern, alerted by the cry, dashes out into the parking lot. He stoops over the body and says: "My God—it's Dr Masters! And—he's been murdered!"

It had been a morning of shockwaves. If Abel had to list them in Richter scale order, this one was a close second. Sunday Tyler was actually planning to kill off the single most popular male character in "Heartbreak Hospital."

5 Road of Life

Troy didn't meet Ramsey Duke at the Four Seasons bar.
Duke chose a Chinese restaurant instead, and nibbled happily at a large order of honey spareribs. He grinned when he
picked up his third piece and said: "Those people sho do know
how to make ribs, don't they? Now if only they had rhythm."

Troy smiled at Duke's black black humour, but it was only a
mechanical movement of mouth muscle. It had been a bad morning at the Movie/TV unit of the NYPD. Captain Bagley was in a
filthy temper after a run-in with the mayor's office, and bawled
Troy out for not providing the paperwork on the "Heartbreak
Hospital" assignment. There had been a call from Troy's sister
Daisy, demanding to know if he planned to attend their parents'
anniversary dinner the following week. Her belligerent tone
made it clear that she anticipated a refusal, and she was right.
Troy argued that a 29th anniversary wasn't significant enough
to warrant a home visit; he didn't see how he could get the time
off for the trip to Dutchess County. In a voice that could have
dried up the Croton Reservoir, she asked him if crime would get
completely out of control if he missed a day on the movie set.
With that low blow, Daisy hung up, leaving him feeling depressed
and guilty. To complete the morning, he had left the building at
noon and found Fiona waiting outside in the sunshine of Flushing Meadows in her little red Mercedes. Her hair was blonder

than he remembered it, but the way she pulled it back from her forehead made her look less like a high school cheerleader and more like an assistant principal. She said she needed to see him, that there was something she had to talk to him about; could they have lunch? When Troy said lunch was impossible, adding quickly that dinner was even more so, Fiona only looked more determined. She would see him later that night, she said and, choosing not to hear his objection, stepped on the accelerator and roared off at illegal speed, right past the long row of parked police vehicles. It was only when she was out of sight that Troy remembered that she had never returned his apartment key.

"What did you think of the story line?"

Troy brought himself back to the present and tried to construct a reasonable answer. He had read Bob Neffer's projection the night before, but had awakened that morning with only a hazy recollection of the intricate plot. He forestalled his reply by asking a question of his own.

"How did you know I read it?"

"The Badger doesn't keep secrets," Duke said. "Some producers play their cards close to the vest, never let actors see breakdowns or story projections, but not Gene. He believes in sharing. He says actors aren't cattle, even if Hitchcock thought so. But if you want my opinion . . . but hell, you probably don't."

"Sure I do," Troy said politely.

"Badger is scared. The pressure on the guy must be ten thousand pounds per inch. He wants as many people on his side as possible, so he's always Mr Nice Guy to the cast."

"Anything wrong with that?"

Ramsey Duke shrugged. "There are times when actors *need* a little toughness, a little prodding. Take Milo Derringer, for instance. Now he's a pal of mine, but I have to tell you, the guy goes to pieces unless he's kept in check. He mugs all the time, chews the scenery too much. He needs somebody to sit on him."

"Isn't that the director's job?"

"There are four directors on this show, so none of them has any overwhelming authority. It's up to the producer to keep people like Milo from going off the deep end. And lately. . ." He stopped and stared at his half-eaten rib. "Anyway, what did you think? About the murder story?"

"You want literary criticism or a police opinion?"

Duke grinned. "Either one."

"I couldn't understand it. There were too many names that were unfamiliar to me, too many motives I didn't understand. And—it wasn't finished. The killer wasn't named."

"That was deliberate. They don't want the actor to know."

"Because he'll be out of work?"

"And for other reasons. There's a famous story about an actor who went on a talk show and was asked about his soap. He said, 'Oh, I won't be on too long, Merv, I'm the murderer.'"

Troy grinned. "I see what you mean."

"They're also afraid the actor might foreshadow his guilt by rolling his eyes or skulking around in the shadows. Personally, I think that's a lot of crap. A pro would never do that. Although if it were Milo, I suppose it's possible."

"It couldn't be him, could it? Doesn't he play one of the Good Guys?"

"No, it won't be Milo. He's number one in the Q ratings. "

"What's that?"

"It's another measuring gimmick. Only instead of counting audiences, the way Nielsen does, they study which actors are best liked. Or maybe I should say which *characters*. It's hard to tell the difference between the two."

"Has Milo been on the show very long?"

"From Day One. He *is* Dr Jonathan Masters. I doubt they'd ever recast the role if he decided to leave."

"Could that ever happen?"

Duke shook his head. "Milo would never leave voluntarily. He's threatened to, every time he gets into a hassle with the Wicked Bitch of the South—I suppose you know who that is by now."

Troy didn't reply, reluctant to join the chorus. Especially since he had a date with the WB of the S that night.

"Anyway, he'd never do anything drastic. Milo's so identified with the role that he's afraid nobody would hire him to play anyone else. He might be right. Look at George Reeves."

"Who?"

"The actor who played Superman in the original movie serial and TV show. When it was over, the poor guy couldn't get arrested. He ended up a suicide. And if I know Milo . . ." He stopped.

"What do you think he would do?"

"Fall out of his tree," Duke said worriedly. "He's hanging from the branches right now. . . ." He shook off the mood and turned on a toothy smile. "But, hey, why worry? He's not the Villain of the piece, he's the Hero. You read the projection. Even though I run the investigation, Jonathan Masters is the one who finally comes up with the answer. That's what is known as honky justice."

Troy looked up, his eyebrow shaped like a question mark.

"Don't get me wrong," Duke said, delving into his pork lo mein. "I'm glad I got this part. If there weren't cops on daytime serials, there might not be jobs for black guys at all."

"You mean all cops are black on soaps?"

"Not all. Just a lot. It's a good way to take care of what they call the 'minority' problem, you dig? Cops don't have to have love interest and stuff like that. They just help the white folks get out of trouble. There are exceptions, of course. But 'Heartbreak Hospital' isn't one of them."

"Okay—so you conduct the investigation. But from what I read last night, you won't have an easy time of it. I couldn't find a single thing that sounded like a clue."

"I'll give you one. Hell, I'll give you the name of the murderer. I think it's Allan Laker. He plays Steve on the show."

"Why do you think that?"

Duke tapped his temple and looked wise. "Elementary. It's contract time. I heard that Allan won't renew without a nice fat raise. Can you think of a better motive?"

"It's not the usual kind, that's for sure."

"Of course, Steve is a popular character, so I can't swear I'm right. For all I know, the killer will turn out to be me."

"You? The investigating officer?"

"Nobody's safe. That's one of the peculiar facts about soaps. You can't kill off George Clooney or Frasier in prime time, but you *can* knock off a soap hero. It's been done."

"I can't see making the investigator the killer. It was done successfully only once as far as I know, by Agatha Christie."

"You mean you actually read detective stories?"

"It's about as close as I can get to crime these days."

Duke met his eyes. "Does that bother you? Not solving crimes, arresting people, stuff like that?"

"Sometimes," Troy admitted.

Duke didn't pursue the subject. "Anyway, I'm not really worried about being the killer. There's a code that protects me."

"Code? Like the NAB?"

"Something like that. Only in this case it stands for—No Abuse to Blacks." He laughed, but with uninvolved eyes. "I mean, let's face it, man, they're not going to have a *black* man going around killing people. Not in a daytime serial. Blacks almost *never* commit crimes in the soaps, don't you know that? We's all decent, upstanding folks. Same goes for Hispanics, Asians, every other identifiable minority. It's the *law*."

"You don't sound too happy about it."

"Why should I be?" Duke pushed away his plate, no trace of a smile on his dark, sculptured face. "It's just Jim Crow turned on its head. The day the soaps really grow up will be the day a guy like Lieutenant Savage *can* be a murderer."

"How's the chop suey?"

It was another voice in the mix. Troy looked up and saw Phyl Wykopf approaching the table, a big-boned woman who made the most of her size in the way she put herself together. Troy started to rise, a move inculcated in him by his mother, but when he saw that Ramsey Duke stayed where he was, he changed his mind.

"What are you doing here, Phyl?" Duke looked at her curiously. "I thought you didn't like Chinese food."

"I'd rather have borscht at the Four Seasons bar," she said lightly. "But you weren't there."

"You mean you were looking for me?"

"Isn't he clever?" she said to Troy. "Maybe you can use him on the Force."

"We've got too many actors right now," Troy said pleasantly. "Uh, won't you sit down?"

"I don't have time, thanks. I just came to ask Ramsey if he wouldn't mind coming by the studio after lunch. We're having a . . . little problem he might be able to help us with."

Troy could sense the actor going rigid beside him.

"Is it Milo?"

"See? He never misses." Despite her first refusal, the woman sat down. "Milo took an early lunch at the Green Grotto. He hates the food, but he likes the drink? He liked it a little too much today."

"Jesus," Duke groaned. "Is he real bad?"

"He's conscious. I'll say that much."

"Thank God for that, anyway."

"It might have been better if he had passed out at the restaurant. He's in what you might call a truculent mood?" Troy heard the question marks at the end of her lilting sentences, and realized that Phyl Wykopf must have been a large Southern belle at one point in her life. Stress seemed to bring it out in her.

"Thank God Sunday Tyler isn't on today," Duke said grimly. "That's all she's waiting for, just one more piece of ammunition. . . ." He threw down his napkin and stood up. "Sorry about this. I really wanted to talk to you."

"It's okay. Tell you the truth, I was going to suggest that you get together with one of our homicide detectives, guy I know named Dan Lipschutz. He knows a lot more about conducting a murder case than I do. Would you like his number?"

"That would be great," Ramsey Duke said. Troy wrote it on a paper napkin and Duke folded it into his wallet, reaching for some bills at the same time. Phyl waved him off.

"The show will pay for lunch. It's the least we can do."

Duke hurried off to the cloak room while the producer tried to catch a Chinese eye.

"Has, uh, this sort of thing happened before?" Troy asked.

"It never happened at all, until we recast the part of Andrea Harmon. I think you can figure out the significance."

"You mean somebody else played the character—before Sunday Tyler?"

"Oh, yes. She didn't create the role. Julia Porterfield was the first Andrea. Then all the goppy articles in the fan magazines went to her head. . . ."

"Fan magazines?"

"Didn't you know? There must be half a dozen of them. Some of them have been around for years, some of them are just quickies. All about the Darlings of Daytime. When I was growing up in Charlotte, I used to read them constantly, until Constant Reader frowed up."

Troy smiled. "Didn't turn you off daytime, though, did it?"

"I *love* daytime," Phyl said soberly. "That's why I object to most of the magazines. They're always writing about the actors, and what they think and what they cook and who they're sleeping with. . . . They don't realize that the audience doesn't want to know what *Sunday Tyler* cooks or who she sleeps with. They want to know what *Andrea Harmon* cooks and . . . well, you get the idea."

"Yeah, I get it. But what happened to this Julia Porterfield? If the role was so good, why did she leave it?"

Phyl shrugged. "The Hollywood bug bit. Her publicity convinced her that she was star material, that being a leading lady in a soap wasn't enough. She went out to the Coast expecting the heads of all the major studios to meet her at the airport."

"And did they?"

"Like they sometimes say in bad pictures . . . we live in two different worlds. I mean nighttime and daytime TV. You'd be surprised at how little attention Hollywood pays to what's on in daylight. Oh, it got better for a little while. Soaps started getting a lot of attention in the media, and that helped some of the actors get prime time and movie jobs. Personally, I don't see what's wrong with a good *daytime* job, but—I'm prejudiced?"

"So I gather Miss Porterfield didn't make it?"

"Vanished without a trace," Phyl Wykopf said. "She managed to get one or two minor roles in a couple of series, then nothing. I don't think she's worked for the past two years. Unless she's behind the cosmetic counter at Neiman Marcus."

"You think she's sorry she left?"

"She must be. Especially when she sees what Sunday did with the part. Sunday's a hell of an actress, even if she is . . ."

". . . the Wicked Bitch of the South," Troy finished. "Yeah, I know. I'm beginning to think that the lady doesn't have a friend in the world."

Phyl had finally caught the attention of a waiter. As she reached into her purse for a credit card, she told Troy:

"You don't have to wait around while I pay this. I'm sure you have more important things to do."

"Maybe I can think of one," Troy said lightly.

He said his goodbyes and headed for the front entrance. Then he remembered that he had put his light raincoat on an adjoining seat, and doubled back to the table. Phyl Wykopf didn't see him approach. She was staring at something she had removed from her purse along with the credit card. It was a photograph, the overhead light bouncing off its glossy surface. He caught a glimpse of a sad-looking young man standing against a brick wall with a coat draped over his arm. What triggered Troy's curiosity was the red grease-pencilled question mark that covered the surface of the photo like some cryptic graffiti.

■ ■ ■

Gary Naughton had gotten the assignment Troy had coveted, coordinating police supervision on the movie *Heat Wave*. On the pretext of conferring with him, but actually in the hope of getting a glimpse of his two favorite movie heroes, Troy drove to the scene of the shooting, a warehouse area on the West Side. There had been problems about the location, engendered by the naivete or arrogance (choice of one, please) of the movie's director, a bearded wonder who could part the Red Seas of Hollywood and expected to do the same in New York. The script called for an elaborate shoot-out involving two stretch limousines, a garbage truck, a BMX, a Porsche, and three patrol cars, winding up in a foot chase ten city blocks long. Most of the action would be filmed from a helicopter, and it was clear that the director intended this to be the Super Bowl of chase sequences. His first choice of location had been Times Square, but Captain

Bagley had quickly disabused him of the notion. They had scouted alternatives the next day with no agreement. That evening, prowling the city on his own, the director had found the perfect spot, a dismal section of abandoned warehouses near the waterfront. Convinced of its viability, he had made immediate arrangements to have cast and crew at the site the following morning. There had been a lot of dropped jaws and expletives when they found the "abandoned" area totally transformed, with thirty trucks filled with fruit and vegetables. To his credit, the captain didn't even laugh. The mayor's office would have been proud of him.

When Troy arrived at the location which had finally proved acceptable, there wasn't a movie star in sight; only a bored gang of crewmen and police officers waiting for the next step in the tedious process. Even the crowd on the perimeter of the set had thinned down to a few stragglers. He found Gary napping in the back of one of the patrol cars, breaking no regulations since the vehicle was leased from a prop house. Gary had a shambling, country-boy look that belied his Brooklyn upbringing, but he had adopted a drawl to go with the image.

"How's the soap opera coming along?" he asked, one eye still closed. "If you feel like switching, we can talk about it."

Troy expressed his surprise. "I thought you wanted this assignment. You know—you and Mel and DeNiro and all that."

"No women," Gary grunted. "Not a female in the whole darned fil-um. At least not the part they're shooting here. They left 'em all back in LA."

"Which reminds me," Troy said. "Would you mind if I stayed at your place tonight? Unless you're expecting company." He didn't wait for the question. "It's Fiona. She showed up again and said she was coming up to the apartment. To *talk*. She may want to move back in, and I've heard all the Springsteen I can take."

"Well, that depends," Gary said, pulling up his cap and yanking at his forelock. "Tell me about this soap opera deal of yours. Must be some good-looking chicks in that studio, right?"

"More than one," Troy said. He looked at his watch. Still six hours to go before he saw Sunday Tyler again. It seemed like a very long time.

■ ■ ■

Gary, of course, had consented to make room for his buddy, and Troy tried not to feel guilty when he visualized Fiona letting herself into the empty apartment on Bleeker Street. He had never liked confrontations, which made his choice of a police career all the more remarkable. Most people thought his decision had been reached because of the violent death of his elder brother Morgan. They believed that Troy had made some kind of vow of vengeance against all lawbreakers after a mugger had ended the young history teacher's life in a dark street not far from the Columbia campus. In fact, there had been no vow, and the only emotional satisfaction Troy sought when he entered the Police Academy was to live a life dedicated to action rather than learning. He had been reconciled to following in his brother's footsteps, to joining the slow-paced parade down the Halls of Ivy which had begun with his great grandparents. But when Morgan died, Troy felt as if the chain had been broken, that his free will had been restored, that he could choose his own career even if his family considered it another plane of existence.

With hours to kill before his date, he decided to use the time by completing the Movie/TV unit's production meeting form. He called Kiki at the studio, but she had a problem.

"I don't *have* an office," she said dryly. "Just a desk in what they call the utility room. Where we store the scripts and the

Xerox machine, two typists, and me. Low man on the totem pole, remember?" She had another suggestion. She and Gene Badger planned to be at Bob Neffer's apartment that afternoon to discuss the location shots; they should have the complete list when he arrived. Troy agreed.

Neffer lived in a residential hotel on the West Side. His suite had a chilling, temporary feel; the furnishings seemed resentful of human presence. When Troy sat in one of the stuffed armchairs, it creaked in protest.

"You, uh, live here all the time?" he asked.

"Only since my divorce," Neffer said. Troy glanced at one of the room's few ornaments, a framed photo on a coffee table. It wasn't a family portrait. It was the picture of a grinning basenji.

Kiki's mood was businesslike.

"We're having some differences about the location sites," she said. "Phyl Wykopf wants to shoot most of the action in Central Park, but I think it won't convey enough city atmosphere. I mean, trees and bushes could be anywhere, couldn't they?"

"What do you think, Mr Troy?" Badger asked. "You read the story projection, didn't you?"

"I skimmed it," Troy said. "I didn't think it was important for me to know the story—only the part that concerns the Movie/TV unit."

Kiki smiled slyly. "I don't think we've made a soap opera convert out of the sergeant."

"I'm not interested in any kind of opera. Even grand."

"Ever hear the plots of some operas?" Badger said. "They make 'Heartbreak Hospital' look like *cinema verité*."

"Really?" Troy said genially. "I asked one of our secretaries about your show. She says there's one female character who's been married six times, kidnapped twice, raped, blinded, paralyzed, and charged with murder."

Badger took it amiably. "She also had amnesia, split per-
sonality, and three kids. One of them became a spy, one became
a killer, and the other went upstairs to do his homework and was
never heard from again."

"It always sounds silly when you summarize these plots,"
Kiki said defensively. "But we're talking about stories that go
on for *months,* even years. You have to make things happen!"

"And to the same characters," Neffer said. "We can't intro-
duce a whole new cast for every new story, although it's a temptation."

"One that hurts us in the ratings," Kiki said. "The audience
wants its longtime favorites involved, no matter how improbable it seems. The longer they're on the show, the more real
they become to the viewer. . . . Anyway, it's getting late. We
ought to get started. . . . What's that?" She watched Troy remove a Xeroxed sheet from his pocket.

"Paperwork," he said. "I've got to turn in a data sheet. I'll
need the names of all the people who'll be involved in the location shooting and what their function is. I'll also need the names
of the actors and get some idea of their popularity. "

"Why would you have to know that?"

"We have to estimate the size of the crowd you might at-
tract. A few months ago we had Michael Jackson on a location,
and practically had to call out the riot squad. Although I don't
suppose soap actors get that much attention."

"Wrong, copper," Kiki said caustically. "You'd be amazed
the way they get recognized. Sometimes *more* than movie stars!
People follow them in the street calling them by their first
names."

"Their *show* names, of course," Bob Neffer said. "That's the
big difference. They think they're the characters they play. . . .
Hey, did you ever tell him the toilet paper story?"

Kiki said: "There's a wonderful actress named Lois Kibbee who played a *grande dame* in 'Edge of Night.' A woman spotted her in a supermarket buying toilet paper, and she gasped: "Mrs Whitney! I never thought you went to the *toilet!*"

Badger, skimming the police form, asked Troy why they had to know if the exterior scenes were period or contemporary.

"Makes a big difference," Troy said. "Not long ago, we worked with a movie that was supposed to be taking place in the Forties. The trouble is, New York traffic lights and parking meters were all different back then."

"What did they do?"

"Changed them. At their expense of course. We took Polaroids of everything to make sure they put everything back the way it was. Except they didn't, actually."

"Why not?"

"The residents of the block liked the old lights so much they petitioned the city to keep them."

"Nostalgia," Neffer said dreamily. "I know just how they feel. If you ask me, *everything* was better in the old days."

"Including soaps?" Kiki said.

"Especially soaps. They used to be about love, sex, jealousy, passion. All those good things. Now they're all about crooks, spies, murderers, blackmailers—cops." He looked at Troy almost accusingly as the phone rang. Kiki reached for it automatically, still a victim of her secretarial conditioning. She looked worried as she covered the mouthpiece and told the writer:

"It's Abel McFee—for you."

Bob Neffer's eyes were even more troubled, but he didn't completely lose the smile. He greeted the executive pleasantly enough, and then nodded in response to a request on the other end.

"Yeah, sure, Abel. I'll come by as soon as we finish up here. We're having a production meeting about the location shoot, but . . ." He stopped, clearly interrupted. "Yes, okay. I'll be there in half an hour." He replaced the receiver as carefully as if it was the final piece of a mechanical puzzle. "McFee wants me," he said unnecessarily.

"Did he say about what?" Kiki asked.

"I wouldn't want to guess," Neffer said.

The meeting was over. Troy didn't mind. Sunday was next on the agenda.

■ ■ ■

Sunday Tyler's apartment was an improvement on Bob Neffer's bleak quarters, but not by much. Troy had expected a seductive ambience: low, velvety furniture and pink-tinged indirect lighting. He wouldn't have been surprised to see a white bearskin rug in front of a glowing fireplace, although that might have lacked subtlety. At the very least, he had expected thick carpeting and a well-stocked bar. What he saw instead, in Sunday's third-floor apartment in a high-rise on East 66th Street, was a well-polished oakwood floor strewn with hooked rugs that might have come from some artsy-craftsy shop in Vermont. The light sources were brass lamps mimicking the kerosene era, and the furniture was vaguely American Colonial. The couch, with its embroidered overstuffed upholstery was hardly the type to support amorous dalliance—not that Troy was optimistic about the possibility. It was the kind of room which should have had a sampler on the wall, praising some simple virtue, and sure enough, there was one. Troy didn't get close enough to read it until after Sunday Tyler had greeted him at the door, wearing an oversized sweater and jeans; she identified it as her David Letterman wardrobe. She had just returned from the taping, which had lasted longer than she thought it would, and she was in desperate need of a shower.

"I sweat like a horse when I'm on one of these talk shows, isn't that funny? I'm never nervous when I'm in the studio, but I think that's because *she's* always in control."

"She who?" Troy said.

"Andrea, of course." She kicked suddenly and a slipper flew into the air; she caught it neatly and then repeated the performance with the other one. Holding both shoes, she sailed off towards the bedroom, urging him to help himself to a drink. Troy, however, failed to find the makings, even after exploring every cupboard in sight. Seeking other diversion, he moved within reading distance of the sampler. It was an antique, all faded greens and browns, the threads so worn that it was hard to distinguish the carefully-stitched message:

Tomorrow shall be my dancing day,
I would my true love did so chance
To see the legend of my play
To call my true love to my dance.

"I never could figure that out," Sunday's voice said behind him. He turned to see her wearing what looked like a peppermint-flavored nightgown. Her legs were bare, and they twinkled disconcertingly when she dropped onto the overstuffed sofa and arranged them underneath her. "One of my golden anuses sent it to me, and said it might help change me. Don't ask me how."

"One of your what?"

"My fans, darling. I call them golden anuses because that's what they are. Assholes, every one of them, but precious—so very precious. I don't suppose you know what it means? The poem?"

"Who, me?"

"I thought being a detective and all." She smiled and lowered her head, causing her blue-shadowed eyes to flash at Troy and make his head spin. No doubt about it. This woman was the bitch-angel of his dreams. The hurried repairs to her makeup made it all the more evident that she was a few years older than he, but it didn't matter in the least. A dazzled Troy tried to remember what she had just said, but it proved unnecessary. "Only kidding," Sunday continued. "I know detectives aren't supposed to be literary. On the other hand, you don't look too much like a detective. You've been badly cast, darling. I think you'd better call your agent."

"I'm not a detective," Troy said. "I doubt if I'd make a very good one, since I couldn't even find your liquor."

"Oh, no!" She bounced off the sofa in a move that swirled her peppermint dress around her, giving Troy a momentary glimpse of a perfect S curve. "That was stupid of me," she said. "The bar is sort of concealed; it was my dumb decorator's idea." She did something to a lowboy of burled maple and a hidden drawer rose from its interior, holding gleaming bottles. Troy accepted the Glenlivet he spotted and was gratified to see her join him.

"No white wine? I thought that's what all the women in New York drank these days."

"I'm not *all* women," she said aloofly. "I am *Andrea!*" She laughed when his eyes enlarged. "It's a line from a script, darling, don't be alarmed. I'm *not* a case study. I never bring Andrea out of that studio with me. I lock her up, the way a ventriloquist locks up his dummy. This is me —Sunday Tyler." She lifted her glass. Troy did the same, asking:

"How did you get *that* name?"

"It seems my grandmother was also a golden anus. She was hooked on the radio soap 'Our Gal Sunday.' She talked my mother into naming me after the heroine. It could have been worse. If I'd been born a boy, she might have named me after Sunday's husband."

"Who was he?"

"Lord Henry Brinthrope." She giggled into her scotch. "I still remember the opening line of that show. My mother used to tell it to me when I was still in my cradle."

"What was it?"

"'Our Gal Sunday . . . The story that asks the question: Can this girl from a little mining town in the West find happiness as the wife of a wealthy and titled Englishman?'" Sunday threw back her head and laughed, a musical, unrestrained laugh that did something to Troy's libido. It was the first time he could remember being turned on by little more than a flashing glance and a free and easy laugh, but Sunday Tyler affected him that way. He downed the rest of his drink and said:

"Uh, what was it you wanted to tell me? About the new 'Heartbreak Hospital' story?"

The remark seemed to alter her mood, and Troy was sorry he had made it. She rose from the sofa and went to put another splash of scotch in her drink, ignoring his own half-empty glass.

"Whatever you've been told is wrong," she said flatly. "Andrea is going to be wrongfully accused of murder. But the victim won't be that stupid fag intern. It's going to be a far more important character, which automatically makes the *story* more important, don't you agree?"

Troy cleared his throat. "I don't think you understand my job, Miss Tyler—"

"Call me Sunday." She turned and gave him a siren smile. "Call me any day, for that matter."

"I'll bet you've used that line before."

"You're not making a morals charge, are you, officer?"

"I was just trying to explain that I have nothing at all to do with the story content of your show. It really doesn't matter to me who gets killed or who does the killing."

"You don't even *think* like a cop."

"My job is to make sure your use of public areas doesn't create problems for other people in this city. That's about all."

She was almost pouting. "And I thought you were some kind of technical adviser. 1 thought you were supposed to be helpful."

"We are. That's the other part of this job, to make it easier to shoot movies and TV shows here. It's good for business."

"Then if you really don't give a shit about the new story, why were you so anxious to hear my version of it? I mean, that *is* why you're drinking my whisky, isn't it, Lieutenant?"

"I *am* interested in your story," Troy smiled. "But not Andrea Harmon's. Sunday Tyler's."

She regarded him coolly for a long moment. Troy wasn't sure she liked his answer, or him.

"I see," she said finally. "You thought I was just making an excuse to get you into my parlor. Sort of an updated version of 'Come up and see my etchings.' Is that it?"

"Am I about to get thrown out?"

"No," said Sunday flatly. "You're about to get what you asked for. Even though you may regret it."

She rose from the couch once more. Troy hadn't noticed that her glass was empty again. She was drinking her Glenlivet as if it was Diet Pepsi. This time she remembered her manners and offered him a refill, too. Then she resettled herself in the center of the cushion, more primly, her back straight, her knees touching, a good little girl about to make a recitation for a visiting relative.

"I was born in North Carolina. My family had a farm there for just years and *years*?" She had activated a Southern drawl. Troy was reminded of someone, but forgot who. "I was the youngest of six children, and I was the actress of the family from the day I could walk. In fact, Mama told me that right after I took my first step I took a bow." She giggled a bit mechanically, and Troy's eyes narrowed. "When I was sixteen, this repertory company came to town and put on a real live stage show and I knew for sure that I had to be in show business or die. So off I ran to the Big City and I met lots of *bad* people and one or two *good* people and I went to acting school? And then got jobs Off-Off Broadway? And then I got to be an understudy to this famous, famous actress and wouldn't you know that she got sick one night and I went on instead and the audience just *loved* me? And then—"

"Hold it one second," Troy said.

"Something the matter?"

"Yes," he frowned. "I think I've seen this movie."

"Why, honeychile," Sunday said, her lashes fluttering, her accent now as thick as Southern molasses. "You're not saying that I'm making it all up, are you?"

"You're pulling my leg so hard it hurts. If you're sore about my not wanting to hear your murder story, okay, I'll listen. Just don't expect any technical advice. That's not my job."

There was a noticeable difference in her answering smile. She finished her drink and said:

"You know something, officer? You're seriously cute."

Troy's face reddened slightly, but it wasn't a blush. "Stop doing that," he said sharply.

"Doing what?"

"Drinking that stuff down like soda pop! You've knocked off two of those babies in the last ten minutes!"

"Did I?" She laughed. "It goes down so smooth I hadn't even noticed."

"You'll notice when your face hits the floor. Do you drink like this every night?"

"Why, how sweet! You sound just like my little old daddy. Most of the men who come here don't mind my having a drinkeepoo or two. In fact, they're the ones who keep my glass filled."

"I'll bet," Troy said sourly.

"It must be because you're a cop," she said, her eyes fixed on him over the rim of her glass. "That's why you're so . . . judgmental. Maybe that's just what I've needed all my life. A man to tell me what to do."

"I knew a girl who used to say that," Troy said, with even more acidity. "She *loved* cops because they represented authority. Father figures with guns, yet. Discipline and sex were all mixed up in her head. There was only one problem. "

"What was that?"

"Like most naughty little girls who get off on punishment, she got naughtier and naughtier. I guess to see how good the punishment could get. One day she found out. Her cop boyfriend shot her in the head."

Sunday winced. "What a horrible story."

"I'm sure it's not as good as yours. For 'Heartbreak Hospital,' I mean. Go ahead and tell it to me."

"Sit over here," Sunday said, patting the seat. "Where you can hear me better."

Troy hesitated only for a second, and then went to the couch. The weight of both of them on the overstuffed cushion flattened it down nicely. She turned her face towards him and he realized what had made her eyes flash so dramatically. She wore contact lenses. She was also wearing a forthright perfume that sent a clear message to his senses, and so did her parted lips. He put his arm round her waist, finding the graceful indentation with no trouble through the thin peppermint fabric since she wore nothing beneath it. She seemed to flow towards him and their lips touched lightly, as if they had both agreed that their first contact would be a tentative one. Then, the rehearsal over, the kiss became hungry, heated, and full of urgency. Troy drew her as close to him as the laws of physical properties would allow. His left hand slid up behind her back until it touched the scoop neck of her gown. His thumb hooked its edge and pulled it down over her shoulder, exposing the whitest clavicle he had ever seen. That was as far as he got before a European wildcat leaped into the living room, shrieking its terrible feline cry, its unsheathed claws raking at him in an attack so swift, sudden, and ferocious that no defense was possible. At least, that was Troy's first impression of what happened, until he realized that the wildcat was Sunday Tyler, and that the claws raking at him back and front were her own well-manicured, well-sharpened nails.

Even as he warded off the lethal onslaught, Troy came to a rueful realization that he knew more about personal combat with women than with men. During his time on the Vice Squad he had scuffled with a dozen kicking, scratching, foot-stomping, groin-kneeing prostitutes, enraged by his interference with their daily, or nightly, occupation, his last encounter resulting in the stab wound that had led to a career move. None of these experiences had prepared him for this assault. He had always been combat-ready on the streets of Greenwich Village; warfare was the last thing he expected in Sunday Tyler's third-floor apartment on East 66th Street. The only defensive tactic that came to mind was to take evasive action, meaning getting the hell out of there. He pushed Sunday away as firmly as he had drawn her to him seconds before. Then he retreated to another part of the room and waited to see if she would come after him, leaping and snarling.

Instead, the actress sagged inside her nightgown, becoming small and harmless within its folds. She looked up at him meekly and said:

"You're bleeding."

Troy touched his face and it felt sticky.

"There's a bathroom in the hall." She nodded at an open doorway. He found his way to a small powder room tiled in black marble. In the mirror, he saw his narrow cheek marked with two parallel red lines, like ski tracks. They weren't deep enough to scar, but they'd still guarantee him some knowing grins from his fellow officers. He splashed cold water on his face, dried it with a towel marked "ITS," and returned to the living room. Sunday was helping herself to another drink.

Troy said: "I knew a woman like you once. Every time she drank too much she became a virgin all over again."

"You've known an awful lot of women, haven't you, Officer?" She saw the handkerchief pressed against his cheek and her tone became more sympathetic. "Is it very bad?"

"I've been wounded in action before."

"I'm sorry—I shouldn't have reacted so strongly. It's just something that comes over me now and then."

"When the moon is full? Or the glass?" She put down the untouched drink. "Maybe I'll make us some coffee. Would you like that better?"

"It's a myth about coffee making you sober," Troy said. "Ask any cop on New Year's Eve."

"I'm not drunk!" She whirled, and her face answered a question Troy had often asked himself. Contact lenses *didn't* stop tears. They were streaming silently down her face, making grooves in makeup that Troy hadn't known she was wearing.

"All right," he said, his angry mood dissipating. "Make some coffee. It'll do you more good than this." He took the scotch bottle out of her hand and put it down on the bar. Sunday watched him without expression, and then turned and disappeared through yet another doorway, presumably towards the kitchen. While she was gone, Troy examined the Colonial lowboy and found the wooden lever that lowered the bar back into its place of concealment.

It was almost twenty minutes before Sunday reappeared, bearing two steaming mugs of coffee. Troy was wryly amused to see that she had also managed to find a quilted robe to wear over the nightgown. She seemed to read his mind, because she said:

"I got cold suddenly. They shut off the heat in this damn building at eleven o'clock."

"Is it that late?" Troy said. "My, time passes quickly when you're having fun."

"I hope you like your coffee black. I don't have any milk or cream. I also don't have anything to offer you with it. My maid does all my shopping, and she's sick this week."

"Black is how I take it," Troy said.

"It's probably either too strong or too weak. I'm not very good in the kitchen. Or any other room, for that matter."

"What's that supposed to mean?"

"Oh, God, not you, too! Don't ever say that line to me again! I despise that line! And if you don't know what I mean—"

"I can guess. You don't like being mauled by police officers. Or just Officer William Troy. However," he added delicately, "a simple 'no, thank you' would have sufficed."

"That's the trouble," Sunday said. "I wanted to say yes. You have no idea how much I wanted to say yes. But I just couldn't. I don't expect you to understand."

"Good. Because I don't."

"Shall I try to tell you?" He didn't reply. "You said you weren't interested in Andrea's story—you wanted to hear mine."

"I'm still ready to listen," Troy said. "But I think I'll stay on this side of the room."

6 From These Roots

"I was a really *beautiful child*," Sunday Tyler began.

She was seated again, this time in the wing chair Troy had occupied before the Trouble started.

"I wasn't born on a farm," she continued. "But it was a farming community. My father ran the local savings and loan. He did foreclosures. I never understood the connection between his job and the shotgun he kept in the living-room closet. He wasn't a happy man. He drank all the time. My mother prayed all the time and made us pray with her. It would have been a lousy childhood, except for my being so *fucking beautiful. I* knew it, everybody knew it, everybody *told* me they knew it, and I grew up thinking I was the most wonderful person ever born outside of a manger.

"Then, one day, the shit hit the fan. My father became so desperate not to be hated that he let half a dozen creditors skip payments on their loans. The savings and loan found out and fired him. He got angry, he got drunk, and then he got stupid and stole a hundred thousand dollars. They caught him and sent him to prison. If that wasn't enough of a surprise for a twelve-year-old, Mama had an even bigger one. When Daddy went bye-bye, Mama moved in with the man who owned the town's hardware store. It seems she'd been slipping it to him for years without Daddy knowing. Now that he was safely behind bars, she could screw Hardware Harry in his backyard hammock whenever she felt like it. There was only one problem. She didn't think I would be happy in the new arrangement. I guessed the real reason. Hardware Harry had his eye on Beautiful Me, and I was getting riper every day. So Mama sent me to live with her sister Ursula. So much for the family that prays together.

"Ursula! When they make a movie of my life, I'm going to insist they get Margaret Hamilton to play her. But she's dead, isn't she? Doesn't matter—she'll still be perfect. Anyway, I soon found out that Aunt Ursula hated my mother even more than I did, and why? Because Mama had taken away the only man she had ever loved: my father. . . . Wait. There's more."

Sunday took a slow sip of coffee and made a face.

"God, I make terrible coffee. But I'm sure it's just as bad at the station house."

"Another myth," Troy said. "We blend our own mix of Colombian and serve croissants every afternoon. But never mind—let's hear the rest."

"Ursula hated my mother," Sunday said, "which didn't matter since they never saw each other. What did matter was that she took out all her hatred on me. I'm talking kicks and bruises here. I'm talking cheap ugly clothes and floor scrubbing and public humiliations. The only one who made my life at all tolerable was her husband, a kindly Father Christmas type with snow-white hair who bought me presents and treated me to the movies and the ice cream parlor and on my thirteenth birthday took me to a glamorous hotel in Disneyland and raped me." She laughed suddenly, not the free and easy laugh that had stirred Troy an hour ago, but a hard, brassy sound like a badly played cornet. "I know what you're thinking," she said. "Soap opera. Very bad soap opera. Well, you'd be wrong, because they'd *never* put this kind of shit on the air. It's too fucking *real*." Troy wanted to say something, but couldn't find the words.

"What do you think I did about it? Did I call the cops? I was more scared of cops than I was of Uncle Lennie. Did I tell dear Aunt Ursula? She would have blamed it on my mother's genes. No, I did the sensible thing, honeychile. I got Uncle Lennie to buy me a whole lot of *new clothes.*" She made the last statement defiantly, but still Troy didn't comment.

"Something else important happened to me that year. Remember that crap I told you about the road company coming to town? That was the only part of my story that was true. They did come to town, or at least to Charlotte, and by now I was pretty good at getting Uncle Lennie to give me almost anything I wanted. Well, what I wanted was to see the play they were putting on.

"God, I went crazy when I saw that curtain go up! When I saw those beautiful people on that stage, saying those pretty words, hugging each other, yelling at each other, making sacrifices for love, crying, laughing, fighting, dying. . . . Oh, my God, I went crazy. I wanted to jump up on that stage and be part of it, part of the story! I didn't want to *act*, I wanted to *be*! I wanted to get rid of everything I was and be one of them and live in that beautiful world forever and ever. . . ."

Sunday covered both eyes as if to hide a flood of tears. Then Troy realized she was removing her contact lenses.

"I have to take these damned things out. They're getting all fogged up. I haven't cried this much since I was Margaret O'Brien's age. You probably don't even know who she was."

"An actress," Troy said. "I own a TV set. She was the little girl who cried for five minutes in some movie or other."

"And I was the little girl who cried for a year after that play was over," Sunday Tyler said. "That's why I finally ran away from home, to see if I could find that world again. I knew where it was, of course, because even in North Carolina we knew where the *theater* was. It was in New—York —City."

"And then you met the 'bad' people?" Troy smiled. "I'm sure that part of the story was true."

"Oh, yes. Lots of bad people. But you know who were the worst? The *competition*! That's who I hated most. Not the pimps and the phonies and the press agents and the other scumbags. It was the goddam *actresses*! Every fucking midwestern little bitch with nipples and a nose-job who thought she was God's gift to Broadway! All the big-eyed throaty-voiced hip-twitching teen-agers fresh out of drama school! My God, there were thousands of them! And they all seemed to know about every job I was after. They waited until I left my house and then followed me in chartered buses. They put ground glass in my coffee to make me go hoarse during auditions. They loosened the heels of my shoes so I would trip when I crossed the stage. And then they did the worst thing of all. They told every casting director and producer in New York that I was offering wild sexual favors to anyone who had a part for me.

"Oh, but don't get me wrong," Sunday said grimly. "Little Sunday would have done exactly what was asked of her, just to set her little feet on that stage, to walk into that wonderful world of beautiful people saying beautiful things. . . . The only trouble was—*she couldn't*. I mean, she just—plain—could—not. Because sweet old Father Christmas, darling Uncle Lennie, had done more to his thirteen-year-old foster child than he intended. That was the reason he was so nice to me, and that was the reason he never touched me again. Because he terrified me so much that I still have nightmares about him and his soft, pudgy little hands that were so much stronger than they looked. . . ."

She was shaking visibly. The urge to put his arms round her was strong, but he resisted it.

"My God," Sunday said.

"What is it?"

"I just realized something. I've never told this story to anyone before. Not one person in the world. And who do I tell first? A cop!"

"Does that matter?"

"Maybe it does. Maybe it was deliberate. Maybe my subconscious thinks that a cop can go back in time and arrest all the bad people who've hurt me. Do you think that's a valid theory, Officer?"

"That's something else I'm not: a psychiatrist."

"Do you think I need one?"

"I didn't say that."

"The truth is, I tried it once. A nice Polish lady, taller than Dr Ruth. She told me I was carrying around a shitload of guilt. That I blamed myself for every bad thing that happened to me, that deep down I believed I *was* the Wicked Bitch of the South. Oh, yes, I know that's what they call me. . . . And I've never minded. I look in the mirror every day and say 'Bitch, bitch, bitch!' It makes me feel better to admit it."

"Does it?"

She gave him a thin smile. "You'll have to agree that was a bitchy thing I just did. And don't think you're the first, darling. You've just joined an exclusive club."

"I'm not sure I want to join. Since you said the membership were all assorted sleazeballs "

"There might have been some good guys. I never gave them the chance to prove it."

"Maybe they didn't know how," Troy said. "Maybe they didn't know the password."

"If it was a four-letter word," Sunday said dryly. "They knew it."

"It's a four-letter word," Troy said.

He came closer and spoke it in her ear. The word made her draw in her breath. She looked up at him in shocked surprise and her contact-lensless eyes began to melt

■ ■ ■

Gary Naughton was telling movie-star stories to Mitzo, the giggly Eurasian secretarial assistant who worked for Captain Bagley, when Troy walked into the Flushing Meadows office. He wore crepe-soled shoes, which didn't completely explain the spring in his step. Gary didn't notice anything different at first; he just asked Troy what the hell had happened to him last night. Gary had sat up until one o'clock waiting for him to arrive and had finally fallen asleep in front of the TV set. Did Troy change his mind and go home after all, despite the threat of confrontation with Fiona? Then Gary noticed the faded scratches on his cheeks, and gave Troy just what he expected. The Knowing Grin. "What happened?" he said. "She put up a fight?"

"I didn't see Fiona," Troy said. "I made other plans."

"Fiona! So *that's* the name," Mitzo said, digging for a message pad. "She called here about ten minutes ago, but I wasn't sure I heard it right." She handed it over. The name had been spelled with two "e"s. There was also a one-word message, spelled correctly: "URGENT." Troy crumpled up the paper and asked:

"Is the Captain available? I've got the stuff on 'Heartbreak Hospital.'"

"Ooh, I'm *crazy* about that show!" Mitzo said. "Do you think I could come to the shooting?"

"Jesus," Gary said. "I just offered you *Mel Gibson*. What do you want to see a goddam soap opera for?"

"That Dr Masters," Mitzo sighed. "Oh, is he a hunk. Have you met him?"

"I met the actor who plays him," Troy said.

"I just don't see why he puts up with that Bitch," Mitzo said, shaking her head. She missed the smile that flickered across Troy's face, and went into Bagley's office to see if he was available. He was, but she wondered if Troy really wanted to see him just now, considering his mood. Troy chanced it anyway, and found the captain looking ready to spit nails.

"Some day I'm going to kill that goddam bitch," he said, and Troy knew the reference wasn't to *his* bitch, but to Millicent Ludwig, the new deputy mayor who had, unfortunately, taken a special interest in the Movie/TV unit, questioning why thirty trained cops weren't spending more time fighting crime.

"I know," Troy said. "It's Friday. She made her usual Friday call."

"She just saw the new proposed budget. She's against it. She's written a memo about it. I said she could take her memo and stick it up the mayor's in-box. . . . Now what the hell is going on at that goddam soap opera? Why haven't I got that data sheet? I got five high-budget pictures in town and you're farting around with this crummy TV show."

"The data sheet is on your desk," Troy said, finding it. "As for the crummy TV show, it'll still be in New York when all five of those movie crews are back in La-La Land."

Bagley skimmed the sheet rapidly, and his face darkened.

"Next week? Next week? That's impossible! I'm stretched way out to here! The cop movie does its car chase next week, Horner is retiring, four guys are on sick leave! And I thought they were going to do this Wall Street stuff on Sunday when there wouldn't be any traffic!"

"They can't do it this Sunday, some kind of union problem. And I'm trying to find them a new location where there won't be a traffic problem."

"There's no such thing as no problem. Just little problems and big ones." Troy grinned amiably at this, and drew a suspicious look. "What the hell makes you so sunshiny bright this morning, Troy? I thought you just got a divorce."

"I never got married," Troy said.

"Uh," Bagley grunted. "That explains it."

Troy was on his way out when the captain halted him at the door.

"Look, since you're not going to be working this weekend, maybe you can give us a hand on this *Heat Wave* project."

"I'd like to help you, Captain. But I've got plans."

His sunny smile went to high noon.

■ ■ ■

When Troy arrived at Studio 22, he found the "Heartbreak Hospital" company in the midst of rehearsal, just putting the first scene of the day on its feet. It was a dinner party in the Armstrong mansion set, but there had been additions that he hadn't seen before: most noticeably, a realistic brick terrace bordered with potted geraniums. A painted backdrop created a night sky replete with moon and stars and the intermittent blinking of a small red beacon somewhere in the distance. The actors— Troy recognised only Milo Derringer, who seemed recovered from yesterday's alcoholic problem—were all in evening dress, drinking what Troy assumed was ginger ale out of champagne glasses, and the overall effect was one of convincing elegance and conviviality. There was also something else, a distinct irreverence in the air as they went through their lines, salting them with their own extemporaneous additions.

"I wonder where Andrea is?" one of the men said, glancing around. "You can always feel her absence at a party, can't you?"

A young woman said: "I saw her in the powder room, but that was some time ago."

An elegant, matronly woman with a haughty air said: "She's probably still on the toilet. She's so full of shit that she may be there the rest of the night."

The cast broke into giggles, and a voice boomed from a control room loudspeaker. Troy recognized the director, Lou Blankenship, who said: "Okay, kiddies, we've all had our fun. Now let's make this scene work."

They went back to the top, the air of levity persisting, but not as strongly. By the time they were in the third rehearsal, they were exchanging lines with sober concentration, and Troy found himself absorbed not just in their professional performance but in the content of the scene itself. Of course, he knew the answer to the question it raised. "Andrea" was in Sunday Tyler's warm bed, snuggled deep among the rumpled sheets and satin quilt, as contented as a kitten. At least, that was the way she had looked when Troy had left her apartment at six-thirty that morning. She had murmured something about having a day off, and why didn't he take one, too, but Troy had resisted the temptation and left. In a way, he was glad to be away from her, not wanting the cold light of morning to affect his mood, to alter a feeling he had never had with Fiona, with Mary Ellen Price, with Ruth Lachman, with Yvette, Jackie, Louise, Bettina and several others whose names had already dimmed in his memory. Fiona's cuteness, Mary Ellen's ripeness, Ruth Lachman's sexy braininess, all the other qualities of the women he had known had become nothing more than handy labels for his scrapbook. He would remember them all fondly, he told himself, but they would only be the prologues of his life. Because now there was Sunday. . . .

The Sunday-less scene was finally concluded. The actors dispersed, and the floor manager guided the cameras to the balcony, where an ethereal young woman in a white crinoline was gazing soulfully at a rackful of props, a Coke machine, and two technicians quietly playing Liar's Poker. Presumably she was seeing a more romantic sight, the lights of the city, the star-filled sky, and having unhappy thoughts. That was the implication of the opening line delivered by Milo, playing Dr Jonathan Masters, as he stepped out on the balcony and asked if she was "all right."

"I'm fine," the young woman said bravely. "You needn't worry about me, Jonathan."

"I feel terrible about this, Maribeth. I had no idea Andrea was going to crash the party. I hope you believe that."

"Of course I do. But she's already spoiled things. And what's going to happen when she hears the announcement —about our engagement?"

There was an anguished cry from somewhere outside the scene, and Troy turned to see Kiki holding a script, suffering a pain that didn't appear to be physical.

"What's going on out there?" the director's voice boomed like the voice of God.

"Tracking error!" Kiki groaned. "What's the matter with everybody? How could we let this get through?"

Milo looked perplexed. "I don't understand. What's wrong?"

"Patricia's line! Andrea already *knows* about the engagement! It's not a surprise any more!"

"My God," the young actress said. "That's right. That's the way we rehearsed it yesterday."

Lou Blankenship came running out of the control room, demanding explanation. When Kiki gave it, he started shouting for Phyl Wykopf; nobody knew where she was, but a bespectacled young man in a T-shirt said he thought she was off sick. Kiki had stopped groaning by now, but Blankenship took over for her.

"That's what we get for flip-flopping so many shows! I told Gene it would get us into a mess! Why didn't Phyl catch this? It's her *job* to catch things like this! Now what do we do?"

"Rewrite, of course," Kiki said briskly. She took her script and marched to the coffee table in the mansion living room. Nobody raised any objection as she slashed through the dialogue and then quickly scribbled alternative lines. Troy watched the performance with admiration, but something about it troubled him. Either Kiki was a fluent dramatist, or she already knew the lines she was adding to the script.

Gene Badger made his appearance just as Kiki was finishing her revisions, and the director filled him in on the problem. When Kiki handed the script to the producer, her manner was diffident.

"I can't write as well as Norman, of course," she said. "But we really don't have time. . . ."

"I know, I know," Badger said, skimming the emendations hurriedly and nodding. "Yeah, this'll work fine, just fine." His patented smile returned. "Okay, boys and girls, let's get back to work. We're running late as it is."

When Troy drew Kiki aside to tell her about his meeting with the captain, he voiced his congratulations at her swift response to the emergency.

"Mistakes happen," she shrugged. "When you think of all the details to remember, it's amazing that it doesn't happen more often. Of course, Phyl should *really* have caught this one. . . . Oh, by the way, there was a phone message for you just a little while ago." She smiled. "A young lady. She didn't leave her name."

Fiona, Troy thought.

He didn't let it spoil his mood. He'd call Fiona later that day, tell her that he was too busy to see her, that he had a date for the evening. To make sure it was the truth, he went to the pay telephone at the end of the studio and dialed Sunday Tyler's number; he had taken care to write it down in his little spiral notebook, a habit from his patrolman days.

The phone rang five times before it was answered, and Sunday explained:

"I was in the shower. Having a wonderful time. Wish you were here."

"I'm calling about tonight," Troy said.

"I have thirty pages of dialogue to memorize tonight."

He swallowed his disappointment before continuing. "Tomorrow, then."

"I'm busy tomorrow, too."

"Remember what I told you about resisting an officer," Troy said, but the jape sounded dull and heavy in his ear.

"My date is with an officer," Sunday said. "His name is Bill, do you know him? Tall, thin, broken nose? And sweet. Very, very sweet . . ."

Music welled up out of nowhere, a sweep of violins augmenting his feelings, but Troy wasn't completely surprised. It happened in movies, didn't it? In this case, it was happening in a soap opera. The actors had returned for another scene at the fancy dress party in the Armstrong mansion set, and a string ensemble was playing for the revellers.

"I'll be there at eight," Troy said.

"Make it seven," Sunday Tyler said. "Rehearsals start at eight a.m., so I have to be in bed early."

"I'll make sure of it," Troy said.

He hung up and turned to find himself facing a TV monitor. The party scene was trapped colorlessly in the tiny screen. A

man was anxiously pushing his way through the crowd to reach
Dr Jonathan Masters, the girl called Maribeth, and the haughty
matron. When he reached them, he said:

"Better come right away, Dr Masters. Something's happened
to Andrea!"

There was a reaction shot, and the scene faded to black.

■ ■ ■

At four-thirty, Troy, Kiki and Lou Blankenship left the studio to check out the East River site Troy had suggested for the
location shooting. It was adjacent to South Street Seaport, the
rigging of the tall ships and the towers of the tall buildings af-
fording a colorful backdrop for the proposed murder sequence.
Kiki was enthusiastic about its possibilities, but the director
seemed nervously unsure. It was almost seven by the time they
had reached agreement, thanks to Kiki's perseverance. Troy
asked her about dinner, but either because of his half-hearted
manner, or a previous engagement, she declined. Troy ate alone
in a cafeteria, pausing between entree and dessert to telephone
his own home and make sure there were no unwelcome visitors,
meaning Fiona. Then he treated himself to a movie, one in which
the Movie/TV unit had participated, and glowed in the dark when
he saw the screen credit:

With grateful thanks to the Mayor of New York
and the New York City Police Department.

He arrived at his apartment at ten-thirty and found three
messages on his answering machine. One was from Gary
Naughton, who wanted to know if he was in the mood for a
fishing weekend. Another was from his sister, asking if he had
changed his mind about attending the anniversary party. The

third was from Dan Lipschutz, and Troy wondered if the detective was upset about him sending Ramsey Duke to him for expert advice.

He called his sister first and told her that he would be there. Obviously, Daisy wasn't expecting the affirmative.

"What happened to you since the other day?" she said. "You get religion or something?"

"Or something," Troy said amiably.

The second call was to Gary. When he told his friend that he wouldn't be available that weekend, Gary said:

"You got something better to do?"

"I hope so," Troy said, trying not to sound smug.

"Oh-oh. Fiona time again, right? Some guys never learn." Troy hung up and was about to dial the third number when his eye fell on the square white envelope on top of his pillow. He knew it was from Fiona even before he broke the seal and extracted the folded sheet of paper. She had written her message in block letters to make sure of its legibility. It was only too legible.

> VERY FUNNY. NOW LAUGH THIS OFF. I AM PREGNANT. I KNOW YOU WON'T GIVE A DAMN, SINCE THE ONLY THING YOU GIVE A DAMN ABOUT IS YOUR LOUSY BADGE. BUT BETTER START THINKING ABOUT IT RIGHT NOW.

She hadn't bothered to sign it.

Troy stared at the note for a long time before he loudly pronounced the three nastiest words he knew and then crumpled the note into a ball. His loop shot at the wastebasket missed.

To release some energy, he walked rapidly up and down the room. It wasn't a very long walk. His apartment was a studio with a dining alcove and a wall kitchen. There was no way to escape the note, which seemed to fill the space like a billboard.

Finally, he sat down on the sofa whose shabby upholstery was concealed by a loose cover made by no one else but Fiona herself. As if he needed another reminder of her presence.

He began to chew his knuckle.

Was it really true? Was Fiona actually pregnant? Was it merely a ploy? Was it a threat? What was Fiona after? Was it sympathy? Was it money? Was it *marriage*?

Tune in tomorrow.

Soap opera! Troy thought.

All right. He *would* tune in tomorrow. Tonight, he would forget it. He wanted nothing to spoil the mood he had brought home.

He began to undress for bed, but then he remembered the one message still unanswered. He owed Dan Lipschutz the courtesy of a call.

The number Dan had left was at the Nineteenth Precinct, and the detective sounded rushed when Troy reached him there.

"Listen, I can call back later," Troy said.

"It's okay," Dan said. "I just wanted to talk to you about this soap opera you guys are working with."

"I guess he called you, huh? Lieutenant Savage?"

"Who?"

"The actor. Hope you didn't mind me giving him your name. I just thought you could be a lot more helpful than I was, since they're doing a murder story and you're the homicide expert."

"Nobody called me," Lipschutz grunted. "I didn't even know who the stiff was until a neighbor told me. When I heard the name, I remembered you mentioning it, and I thought maybe you could fill me in on a few things."

"Danny," Troy said patiently, "I don't have the faintest idea what you're talking about."

"I'm talking about the woman who was murdered on East 66th Street tonight. The one who was in that soap opera. 'Heartbreak Hospital.'"

7 Dark Shadows

HEARTBREAK HOSPITAL
SCRIPT #3995
PROLOGUE:
HOSPITAL WAITING AREA—JONATHAN, MRS
ARMSTRONG, MARIBETH, DONNA, DOCTOR (U/5).
As they wait anxiously to hear about Andrea,
Donna pleads with Jonathan to find out what's
happening to her sister. He's a doctor; he should
be able to learn something! He assures her they're
doing everything they can. Maribeth says: she feels
so helpless—and guilty! Nonsense, her mother
says. It isn't her fault Andrea tried to take her life!
Then a doctor is there, looking grave. He has news
about Andrea. GO TO BLACK.

Norman Levi groaned, and wished that Robin were there to share
his disdain for the cliché-laden paragraph. Wishing for Robin's
return was something Norman did a dozen times a day since the
actor had moved out of the Jane Street apartment, but no fairy
godmother had yet appeared to make the wish come true. The
godmothers were still in the closet, he thought ruefully.

He was tempted to write the scene exactly as written, with
all the standard hospital-waiting-area lines lumbering after each
other in dreary procession:

"Why doesn't somebody tell us something?"

"There, there, now, they're doing everything they can."

"If only there was something I could do! I feel so . . . help-
less."

"All we can do is wait—and pray."

Norman picked up a large glass of apple juice and sipped it
without tasting it. One thing he would *not* do, he told himself,
was end the teaser with the indicated line. The U/5—an actor
hired to speak under five lines—would either say nothing at all
as he came into the scene, or else he would say little more than,
"I have news for you, kids." It went against Norman's grain to
dangle the audience by the simple act of truncation. He sighed
and read the next scene of the outline.

> SCENE ONE:
> LT. SAVAGE'S OFFICE—RICK, CAPT. LEWIS. Rick is
> on the phone, calling for an all-points bulletin for
> some wanted criminal, when Captain Lewis en-
> ters his office, looking angry. He demands to know
> why Rick hasn't made any progress on the Mas-
> ters case. Rick says: it's harder than it looks. Dr
> Masters hasn't provided us with one clue about
> the person who struck him on the head in that dark
> hallway. It could have been anyone at all—a pa-
> tient who blamed Masters for a bad diagnosis or a
> faulty operation or just too large a bill. It could
> have been a jealous nurse upset about his engage-
> ment to Miss Armstrong. It could have been a
> mugger or an addict looking for drugs in his medi-
> cal kit. . . . Captain Lewis says: isn't there one
> possibility you haven't mentioned, Lieutenant?
> You know very well that a public threat was made
> against Dr Masters' life! Rick says: that was only
> an angry quarrel in a restaurant, Captain. I can't
> believe that Andrea Harmon meant it seriously.
> Lewis says: you're supposed to be the scholar
> around here, Savage. Don't you know the old say-

ing, "Hell hath no fury like a woman scorned"?
Andrea Harmon was in love with Masters, and he
became engaged to another woman. The phone
rings, and Rick answers it. He is startled by what
he hears and Lewis demands to know what it is.
Rick is reluctant to tell him the news: that Andrea
Harmon has made what appears to be an attempt
at suicide. There is a gleam of satisfaction in the
eyes of Captain Lewis as we CUT TO:

Just as there was a strategically placed phone call in the
script outline, the phone now rang in Norman's apartment. He
picked it up and heard Bob Neffer's voice emitting an uncharacteristic growl.

"Where the hell have you been all night?" he said. "I must
have called you half a dozen times."

"I was out," Norman said unhelpfully.

"You're out cruising and the world is coming down around
our ears! I saw Abel McFee this afternoon. He told me that Sunday wants me fired—*us* fired," he amended.

"So much for your clever blackmail scheme," Norman said
dryly. "We should have known it wouldn't work. She ran straight
to the little fat man and told him all about her porno movie."

"Listen, Norman, I want you to tell me *exactly* where you
were tonight."

The writer pulled away from the phone and stared into the
receiver.

"Why? What difference does it make?"

"It's important, believe me. If you really want to keep this
job—"

"Screw the job," Norman said, with bitterness, feeling the
day's thirteenth pang of longing for the absent Robin. "I can
always write for another show. I heard there was an opening on
'Young and Restless' just the other day."

"You wouldn't move to LA, not when Robin is working in New York." Norman said nothing to this. "Look, I've never asked you for a favor before, have I? Now tell me what you did. Were you with anybody?"

Norman hesitated. "No. I was alone."

"Did you see anybody you knew?"

"Nobody. I just had a quiet drink in a bar. I've never been there before. I don't even remember the name of the place."

"Find out the name. I was there with you."

"What?"

"I was with you," Bob Neffer said. "We got together and had a little talk about the story line. If anybody asks you, that's what I was doing tonight. Okay?"

"What were you really doing? Robbing a bank?"

"Banks aren't open at night."

"Bank machines are. You know, I always wondered what would happen if you stuck a gun at one of those and told it to hand over its cash."

"Norman, promise you'll do this for me. In case anyone asks. I mean *anyone*. Will you?"

Norman's gaze landed on a framed photograph of Robin, a head shot Norman had swiped from his portfolio.

"Sure, Bobby," he said, with his first smile of the day. "We were together tonight."

■ ■ ■

Albie, the night man, wasn't surprised to see Phyl Wykopf at the entrance of Studio 22 at, what was it, almost midnight? He checked the big counterfeit Rolex he had bought from a Colombian street vendor. Midnight on the dot, meaning he had only six more hours to go, two of which he could safely snooze away in the prop armchair he had appropriated from a library set. Albie was accustomed to seeing the producer there after hours, and greeted her with some of the jargon he had picked up on the job. "Hi, Miss Wykopf—doing a little blocking tonight?"

Phyl gave him a weary smile. "Just checking on a few things for the morning, Albie."

"Hey, I liked yesterday's air show. Nice SFX on that show. The way they burned out those windows, real nice."

"Thank you, Albie," Phyl said. She drifted past him, a big woman with long, gliding strides. Not Albie's type at all, he thought. He liked the cute little blonde playing Sunday Tyler's sister. It was too bad he didn't work the day shift, so he could get to see her and she could see him. He was, after all, a man in uniform. Then he remembered something and called after her.

"Oh, Miss Wykopf."

"Yes?"

"Just wanted you to know, so's you wouldn't get scared. Somebody else is in the studio, got here about half an hour ago. A black guy, but he's okay. I mean, he's an actor."

"Yes," Phyl said. "That makes it all right, doesn't it?"

Ramsey Duke made his presence known even before the producer saw him. A tape was playing: the music of a fusion band filling every space. The rhythm was driving, impatient, unrelenting. It was hard to imagine anyone actually dancing to it, but as Phyl entered she saw Ramsey in the centre of the studio, shirtless, shoeless, in a pair of tight blue jeans. In a standing spot he had trained on himself, sweat glistened on his naked torso. He spun and twisted and contorted his body into belligerent, even hostile, movements that managed to be graceful at the same time. It wasn't ballet exactly; there was too much anger in it. But Phyl was impressed, and when the music ended, instinctively applauded. Duke stiffened at the realization that he had an audience, and quickly reached for his T-shirt.

"Didn't know anybody was going to be here," he muttered.

"Don't apologize," Phyl said. "You were something to see."

"Thanks."

"I knew you'd been a dancer," she said. "But I didn't know you were so good. Why don't you dance on the show?" He gave her a cold look over the twisted fabric he was pulling over his head. "I'm sorry, that was a dumb remark. I mean, why don't we write something into the show that will allow you to dance?"

"I'm a cop, Miss Wykopf, remember?"

"That doesn't matter. I'm sure we can find some way to make it believable."

"Don't go to any trouble. I'm happy just playing a cop."

"This show could use some vitality," Phyl persisted. "I think it would add some color."

"Sho would, Miss Wykopf."

She blushed, and moved away from the light to hide it. "You know what I mean. Maybe there's even a story angle we could use. A cop who dances . . . I mean, I seem to remember something about cops getting ballet lessons to teach them agility. . . ."

"You're thinking of football players."

"What's the difference? The point is, I think I ought to talk to Bob Neffer about it. Maybe he can come up with something."

"I'd rather you wouldn't."

"What?" Phyl blinked.

"I said I'd rather you wouldn't," Ramsey said icily. "I realize I'm the only one on the show that's got *rhythm,* Miss Wykopf. But I'd rather not make a point of it. You get my meaning?"

"Oh, for heaven's sake. You're actually *offended,* aren't you? You think it has something to do with . . . Wait a minute. Are you upset about—Sunday Tyler?"

Ramsey, about to flick off the standing spot, paused.

"What about her?"

"That dumb statement she made on the Letterman show last night."

"I didn't see the Letterman show."

"Oh," Phyl said, this time unable to hide the blush. "Then forget it. It was nothing, really. She wasn't trying to offend anybody, it was just . . . one of those things people say."

"What was it?" When she hesitated. "You might as well tell me, since you brought up the subject."

"She was just talking about the different characters on 'Heartbreak,' that's all. About the Good Guys and the Bad Guys and the other stereotypes."

"And where did I fit in?"

"She was being satirical," Phyl said. "I mean, her choice of phrase. Letterman realized that, he said as much."

"And what was her choice of phrase?"

"She called you the show's token darky," Phyl Wykopf said. "But that's Sunday for you."

■ ■ ■

Kiki didn't like the elevator operator's smirking grin when he took her to the tenth floor of Milo Derringer's apartment house on Central Park West. It made her think of the PG Wodehouse story. Wodehouse had been a dedicated fan of "The Edge of Night," and at its twenty-fifth anniversary party Ethel Wodehouse had told her how "Plummy" preferred an apartment on the ground floor because "he never knew what to say to the lift boy." Kiki thought of a few things she would like to say, but restrained herself.

At the door of 10-D, she rang the bell six times before Milo responded, and then waited another three minutes while he fumbled with the locks, latches, and chains that protected him from the howling wilderness. When she was admitted, she saw that Chin hadn't exaggerated about the degree of Milo's intoxication. Chin was both proprietor and bartender at the Lotus Blossom, one of Milo's half-dozen "secret" hangouts. Phyl Wykopf had ferreted out most of them, and when Kiki had joined the staff of "Heartbreak Hospital" Phyl had passed her list on to her, along with several other unpleasant responsibilities. Kiki had visited each bar personally, tipped the right people from the show's petty cash fund, and given them phone numbers to call in case of "emergencies." She had stressed the last word. She didn't want to be bothered for low-level situations. When she arrived at the Chinese restaurant and learned that Milo had made his own way home, she had been irritated. Chin had exploded into an excited account of Milo's condition, but since it was mostly in Mandarin, Kiki had decided to see the actor herself. Even if there was no longer any danger of public notoriety, Milo had five scenes in tomorrow's taping.

Milo made no protest when he saw Kiki. It wasn't the first time she had come on a rescue mission. He had been drunkenly delighted on that initial occasion, making an immediate amorous lunge in her direction, only to find himself upended with his perfect profile imbedded in the deep pile carpet. When he was relatively sober, Kiki had apologized, not for her instinctive reaction, but for taking advantage of a drunken opponent. Her father had insisted on the short course in judo on the day she had relinquished her training bra.

The memory of that experience probably explained Milo's meekness. Just as she entered, he turned and headed for the bathroom, muttering about taking a cold shower. He was still fully dressed, and took so long that Kiki wondered if he hadn't fallen asleep in the tub. Finally, she heard the water splashing. Relieved, she sat on the sofa, and the condition of the coffee table suggested that Milo had been engaged in a binge of ego reinforcement. He had been reading his fan mail.

There was a lot of it. Milo Derringer's mail tally had always been the highest in the show, probably because he was the only star with an active fan club. Gene Badger called them "Milo's Monsters," but every year, on Milo's birthday, he would allow half a dozen members to come to the studio to cut a cake in front of the soap opera press corps. The fans were all female, all past thirty, all mouthbreathers with crooked hemlines. Last year's photograph was on the coffee table, and Kiki picked it up. Milo had managed to get his long arms around four of them, who looked ecstatic at the privilege. The other two were no less happy to be there, and Kiki recognized the gawky figure of Lottie Orwasher of Crown Heights, Brooklyn, the one the cast unkindly called Loony Lottie. Lottie had no eyes in the photograph. The camera's flashgun had caught the convex planes of her thick eyeglasses head-on, leaving only round white circles. With her corona of frizzy hair, she looked like Little Orphan Annie.

Kiki picked up one of the letters and read:

> Dear Mr Deringer,
> Every day I watch you on Heartbrake Hospital I mean on the days when you are on the show, to tell you the truth I don't care if I see it when you're not on. You are such a good doctor and a good person and so handsome. I really worry about you because of that Andria she is nothing but trouble and I don't think THEY are going to let you marry Maribeth even tho they talk about it all the time. SOMETHING is going to happen you wait and see the wedding will never happen you can count on it for sure!!!

Right on, Kiki thought wryly. The fans were never fooled; they were one step ahead of them at all times. Phyl Wykopf argued that it didn't matter; that fulfilling the audience's expectations was often as good as surprising them. Phyl wasn't even sure they *wanted* to be surprised. Kiki disagreed with her violently; it had got to a point where Gene Badger never invited both women to the same story conference. But Kiki was convinced she was right: they couldn't go on being so damned predictable. Although . . . she knew a thing or two that they *couldn't* count on for sure. . . .

She picked up another letter.

Dear Dr Masters . . .

Without reading any further, she knew the letter was from Lottie Orwasher. She was the only member of Milo's club who never addressed him by anything but his character name. In a sense, that made her the only member of the Jonathan Masters Fan Club.

Dear Dr Masters,

I have something very important to tell you. You are in TERRIBLE DANGER. Andrea Harmon must be going crazy because you are going to marry Maribeth. SHE WAS THE ONE WHO TRIED TO KILL YOU IN THE HOSPITAL THAT NIGHT!!! I know you won t believe me, but please, please take my word for it. I saw her with MY OWN EYES. She was hiding in the shadows and she tried to hit you with that heavy metal tray. It was lucky you moved when you did or she would have brained you for sure! And I know something else but you won't believe me either. Andrea is going to FAKE A SUICIDE at the engagement party at the Armstrong mansion. Whatever you do, DON T FALL FOR IT. She is just trying to get your sympathy and make you put off your wedding! Please please listen to me. YOUR WHOLE HAPPINESS IS AT STAKE!!! Yours as ever,

LOTTIE

There was a howl of pain from the bathroom, and Kiki whirled in alarm. She went to the door and knocked, increasing the volume until the sound of running water stopped and Milo answered her worried question.

"It's okay," he said. "I just cut myself on the damned toothpaste. "

"Toothpaste? "

"I mean the glass!" he said. "The goddam toothpaste glass! Listen, why don't you go make us some coffee? That's what Phyl always did."

"It's late," Kiki said. "If you're sure you're feeling better, I really have to go."

"At least stay until I stop bleeding."

The door opened, and Kiki reacted with further alarm, not wanting to encounter a nude Milo. But he was wearing a robe, and carrying a wet, bloodstained shirt. The rest of his clothes, his suit, tie, shoes, socks and underwear were neatly stacked on a small bathroom seat. "That cut must be pretty bad," Kiki said.

"Don't worry," Milo said, giving her his best smile. "It won't show on camera."

■ ■ ■

Abel McFee stepped out of the shower without feeling refreshed. There were times when even the pulsating massage spray failed to invigorate him. He felt the cold sweat returning even as he slipped on his terry robe and faced the bathroom mirror for the second time that day.

His evening face was different from his morning face. It was altered more by erosion than fatigue. Time was dining on him, munching away invisibly on the cells of his body. Miraculously, it made him no thinner.

He shaved again. His hand trembled so much that he nicked both chins.

When the chore was done, he put on his best Sulka pyjamas and exchanged the terry robe for a velvety number striped in alternating shades of brown. He had always believed that vertical stripes made him look taller and slimmer. He consulted the bedroom mirror, which disagreed with him.

In the living room, he started to build a martini in his Steuben pitcher, and saw that his hands were shaking even more violently. When the doorbell rang, he decided to simplify things. He poured some vodka into a glass and drank it warm. It became a hot coal in his chest as he opened the door and admitted Carol.

"Hi," she said, tossing back the white fox neckpiece she always wore. "How've you been?" she asked mechanically.

"Fine," Abel lied.

She plumped herself on the sofa and crossed her silken legs. Abel noted that she had ignored his comment at their last meeting about her makeup, and had coated her face so heavily that she completely concealed the fresh young skin underneath. Never mind. Carol would never change, so why bother?

"How's business?" she said. "Can I have a drink?" He knew she meant a diet orange, and had it ready for her. She gulped half of it quickly, put down the glass, and stood up. She removed her light satin topcoat and dropped it on the sofa. Then she unbuttoned her blouse, revealing her braless figure. She was just unzipping her trousers when the doorbell rang again, and Carol looked annoyed. "You didn't tell me it was a party," she said.

"It isn't," Abel said hastily. "Look—maybe you better go in the bedroom."

Carol shrugged and gathered up her coat and blouse. "Don't be too long, huh? I've still got one more call to make."

"I'll be right there," Abel promised.

Carol was gone a moment later, but her perfume wasn't. Hoping to dissipate it, Abel fluttered his hands feebly in the vicinity of the pungent floral scent, to little avail. Then he answered the door, and was more irritated than surprised to see Gene Badger's forced smile.

"What are you doing here?" Abel said. "Why didn't you call if you wanted to see me?"

"I did call. I left a message on your machine."

"You did?" He glanced at the device on his desk. "I forgot to check the damned thing." He did that now, flipping the switches and pressing the rewind button. When he started the tape, he heard Gene Badger's voice saying:

"I've got to see you, Abel, tonight. It's very important. Call me back at the apartment if you can't make it. Otherwise I'll see you sometime after ten."

Abel flicked off the machine. "I would have called you back," he said. "I . . . have some things to take care of."

"You look like you're ready for bed."

"It can't be that urgent, can it?"

"Let me put it this way," the producer said, unsmiling. "It's the most urgent meeting you and I have ever had."

Abel swallowed hard and turned away from the answering machine. "All right," he said. "What is it?"

Gene Badger said: "I've just killed her."

■ ■ ■

Why water? What was the primal magnetism that brought the troubled-in-mind to the water's edge? Was it some Freudian connection to the womb, or just the soothing, hypnotic palliative flow of the current? Troy didn't know the answer. His footsteps just took him eastward when he left the building on East

66th Street. He found himself on the walkway fronting the East River, but no one was walking. Only the late night joggers were out, grunting their way past him with sidelong suspicious glances, wary of muggers. Nobody looked at him for long. He looked like a mugging victim himself, dazed, violated, stripped of all his valuables, left to wander the streets without hope of reparation.

He leaned against the railing, thinking of nothing and glad of the vacuum. Nature abhorred it, so debris rushed in, scraps of songs, broken shards of sentences, and finally, a word. His word-loving mother had taught it to him. It was "serendipity," the gift of finding agreeable things. The word had occurred to him before, when Morgan died. His brother had just made the transition from elder brother to friend, at a time when Troy, facing the lonely prospect of adulthood, had needed one. Then Morgan was killed for the contents of his wallet. It was serendipity in reverse.

It wasn't the last example in his life. Two years later, his pride crushed by failure at college, he had found Mary Ellen Price, whose features were so perfect that he forgot what she looked like between dates. She was cute, funny, chaste, and everyone envied him. He enjoyed the envy so much he didn't object to the chastity. Mary Ellen gave him back his ego. Then she took it away, by admitting she was sleeping with his best friend.

Now there was Sunday.

He closed his eyes and had no trouble remembering what she looked like, sitting on the plump cushion of her sofa and pouring out the pain.

Then he remembered her in his arms. Remembered her upturned face. Remembered the smooth, perfect fit of her body next to his. Remembered her eyes gleaming like a cat's in the darkness. Remembered her breath on his cheek, her whisper in

his ear, her sweetness flowing into him like cool water. Serendipity, serendipity. He had found the other half of himself, and
someone had performed unnecessary surgery and now he was
less than half. Sunday was dead, he told himself, Sunday was
gone. Serendipity in reverse. Serendipity without the pity. Play
on words. His mother would have approved.

To Detective Dan Lipschutz, words were blunt instruments.

"Somebody chopped her," he had said. "I mean, the woman
wasn't just stabbed. She was chopped. With this."

The weapon was lying in a crumpled newspaper, which
seemed like an odd way to preserve any possible prints, but Dan
told him that it was found just that way, a chopping knife with a
ten-inch stainless steel blade, a trademarked feather etched into
the metal. There was so much blood left over from its recent use
that only a few words of newsprint were still legible. Troy could
read several of them. Fire. Mayor. Storm. Controversy. Taxes.
White House. Slaying. Garden Vegetables.

"We think the paper was used to wipe off prints," Dan was
saying, "If it worked or not, we still have to find out."

"Is that all you have?" Troy said numbly. "I mean, just the
weapon? Didn't anyone hear anything, see anything? If she was
cut up so bad, she must have screamed, struggled—something. . . ."

"No," Dan said flatly. "So far, there's nothing. It's what I
call a Three Monkey case. Nobody saw any evil, heard anything, or can tell us anything. At least for the moment. But . . .
we just started, right?" He said the last sentence gently, as if
sensing Troy's need for reassurance.

Troy didn't view the body. He didn't ask to see it. He talked
to Dan Lipschutz in the entrance hall of Sunday's apartment
and averted his eyes from the living room, now as brightly lit,
as heavily trafficked, as any studio set. It was a chilling irony,

the resemblance between Sunday's final scene and the scenes she had played for a livelihood. It helped Troy past the initial shock, dulling its reality.

But now, facing serene waters beginning to lose their sedative power, reality was starting to creep back into Troy Wayland's consciousness. And another word clanged in his brain like a fire bell.

Why?

8 Search for Tomorrow

The hushed, businesslike ambience of the network conference room had always oppressed and intimidated Abel McFee, but this morning he took comfort in it, in the neatly squared rows of clean yellow pads and even yellower pencils with well-sharpened points and pristine erasers, indicating that no judgments had yet been made, and no mistakes. He arrived several minutes before the appointed time, to make sure he wouldn't be seated at the head of the table by default. Abel had no desire to chair this meeting. Sheldon Greenway, vice-president of programming, had suggested the conference, and Abel was only too happy to let him carry the ball. Unhappily for him, by the time the "Heartbreak Hospital" people started to arrive, Sheldon's secretary informed him that Mr Greenway, regretably, had been called away on what was obviously more urgent business. Wherever Abel chose to sit, the ball was in his court.

Ophelia Utley arrived first. The associate head writer was clearly unimpressed by the surroundings. She wore the same ash-stained green sweater and baggy jeans she worked in, dined in, and, some people thought, slept in. She had gained weight since Abel had seen her last, at the "Heartbreak" Christmas party four months ago. With her helmet of black, stringy hair she resembled her literary idol, Ayn Rand. Ayn Rand with the mumps.

Her boss, Bob Neffer, arrived a few minutes later with scriptwriter Norman Levi in tow. They had dressed in a manner befitting either a business meeting or a wake, which seemed appropriate in the circumstances. Phyllis Wykopf was right behind them, looking gaunt and hollow-eyed; her appearance reminded them of their desperate need for coffee and Abel dispatched his secretary Irma on the errand without waiting for the two missing participants who were already twenty minutes late. It was uncharacteristic of Kiki Carney, who was noted for her punctuality, but she had promised to pick up Gene Badger, a notorious slow-starter. When they finally arrived, Kiki looked crisp and bright-eyed, and even Badger seemed energetic and properly executive, carrying a neat leather attaché case.

When they were all seated, Abel reluctantly made the opening remarks.

"I guess we all know why we're here," he said, looking as if he didn't. "We've never had a situation like this on the show, and the network thought we should all put our heads together to decide how best to handle it. This will be, uh, what you might call a brainstorming session. Meaning we should just open up, be real loose, say anything that comes to mind. . . ."

"About what?" Ophelia Utley said, in her froggy baritone. "The press has said everything there is to say, if you ask me."

"Did you see the *New York Post?*" Norman Levi asked. "They're doing a three-part series, for Chrissakes!"

Bob Neffer grunted. "The *News* had the best headline. SOAP STAR KILLED OFF. I wonder how many of their readers understood that 'off.'"

"The *Times* ran the story for three days and then quit," Ophelia said, lighting a Gauloise and blowing choking fumes into the center of the table. "If we all just wait a while, there'll be another sensational story and everyone will forget there ever was a Sunday Tyler."

"What I don't understand," Kiki said, "is why there's so little TV coverage. It seemed like a natural to me, but only one week after that poor woman gets murdered, absolutely nothing."

Abel cleared his throat. "I don't know about the other networks, but I can speak for this one. It was a policy decision. We didn't want to milk the story until we knew the effect it would have on the show."

"What the hell does the *show* have to do with it?" Phyl Wykopf said. "I thought you had such an independent news division. Isn't it a hot story?"

"Not without some movement in the case," Bob Neffer said. "And from what we've heard, there isn't any. Isn't that right, Abel?" He looked at the executive searchingly. "The police don't know a damn thing more than they did when they found her body, do they?"

Abel shrugged his narrow shoulders. "Why ask me? I'm not getting any inside information. I suppose they're still sticking to their original theory. The interrupted robbery and so forth."

"Only there wasn't any robbery," Phyl said. "The news stories say that nothing was taken."

"Look, guys," Bob Neffer said. "We get so used to the kind of police crap we put on the air that we get it mixed up with reality. First of all, the cops never tell the public the truth, at least not all of it. You can be sure they're holding back just enough so that when they find the maniac who chopped up Sunday they'll be able to pin it on him."

"Wait a minute here," Abel McFee said. "This isn't the kind of brainstorming I was talking about. We've got enough people handling the PR on this. What we need is some kind of consensus on what to do with The Story."

"You know what we've already done," Gene Badger said. "We wrote Andrea out for the next two weeks. Bob and Ophelia and Norman did one hell of a job at very short notice. Am I right about that?" He glanced round, looking for commendation. The only response came from Ophelia, who blew a smoke ring and said:

"Damn right."

"And, of course," Neffer said, "we've been talking about the long term, and we have some preliminary thoughts to discuss. For instance, we think that if we can write in some kind of off-screen accident or illness for Andrea, then we can vamp until we're ready to make a decision about the character."

"Wait a minute," Kiki interposed. "Isn't that the *first* thing we should be doing? Deciding whether we kill off the character or recast?"

"That's the hard part," Norman said worriedly. "How many times have we said that Andrea *can't* be recast? That Sunday Tyler is indispensable?"

"I still feel that way," the head writer said. "If we're taking a vote, I'll give you mine right now. Let's make Art imitate Life for a change. Let's rewrite this murder story making Sunday the victim."

The suggestion silenced the room for a moment, and then they were all talking at once.

"It would work," Ophelia said. "1 mean, let's face it, everybody hates Andrea, she's a born murder victim. We can still do our False Accusation story, only Andrea is the one who gets it in the neck and that poor *shlemiel* Jonathan gets arrested."

"—lousy publicity," Phyl Wykopf was saying in counterpoint to Ophelia's baritone. "Everyone will say that we're exploiting Sunday's murder."

"I agree with Phyl," Kiki said. "Don't you remember what happened on 'Edge of Night'?"

"—recasting may not be such a terrible problem," Gene Badger said. "There's something you guys don't know—"

"What happened on 'Edge'?" Norman asked curiously.

"They were doing a story about a youth cult," Kiki said. "It was called 'The Children of the Earth,' and it was run by one of these charismatic guys that people will do anything for—even kill themselves, if he says so."

"Jonestown," Abel McFee said. "They stole the idea from that story in Guyana. All those people who drank poisoned Kool-Aid just because Jim Jones wanted them to—"

"Wrong." Kiki shook her head. "The projection was written long *before* Jonestown. You know how much lead time we need before a story actually gets on the screen. By the time *this* one hit the air, the Jonestown business was just coming to light, and it looked as if we were following the headlines, day after day. Naturally, the complaints started to come in. We were accused of exploitation, cheap theatrics, all the rest of it."

"What did you do?" Norman asked.

"Killed the story, of course. Just cut it off and went on to something else. All I'm saying is, we're liable to get an equally bad reaction if we have Andrea murdered. I say it's dangerous and we should avoid it."

"Frankly," Abel said, "I think the network will feel exactly the same way. They'd rather the public forgot the murder, not be reminded of it for the next six months."

Phyl Wykopf managed a weary smile. "Why don't we send Andrea upstairs to do her homework? Like we did with little Davey?"

"We don't have to lose the character," Gene Badger said. "I say we recast. And I know how we can do that just as soon as we want."

He opened his attaché case and removed an 8x10 glossy, the headshot of an attractive woman who bore a faint resemblance to Sunday Tyler, or at least to Sunday Tyler as she had appeared in the role of Andrea Harmon. He flourished the photo like a conjurer with a white rabbit.

"Anybody remember this lady?"

"It's Julia Porterfield," Abel said. "The first Andrea."

"And if we can agree on terms," Badger smiled, "the next one."

"We thought she disappeared!" Phyl Wykopf said. "Nobody's heard about her for almost three years."

"I heard she was in Italy," Norman Levi said.

"I thought she was dead!" Bob Neffer snatched up the picture and examined it incredulously.

"She's alive," the producer assured him. "Alive and well and living in New York City. Actually," he added casually, "right on East 66th Street, by an odd coincidence. In Sunday's building."

The silence that followed differed from the first. It was heavier and more palpable. Phyl broke it by saying:

"God, this is awful. We're sitting here talking about replacing Sunday as if she was a bad set of tires. You complain about the press ignoring that horrible murder—how about us?"

Abel McFee said: "We all feel terrible about it, Phyl, you know that."

"We went to her funeral," Badger said. "What more could we do?"

"I even sent *flowers,*" Ophelia Utley grumbled.

"We can't bring her back," Norman Levi said. "Life has to go on." Then he looked shamefaced. "Sorry," he added. "I've been writing soaps too long."

"Maybe . . ." Kiki looked embarrassed, but said it anyway. "Maybe we should have a minute of silence or something."

The third quiet break of the meeting followed, but it lasted less than ten seconds. Irma, Abel's secretary, sailed into the conference room with a brazen indifference to the pious moment she was interrupting. She carried a sheaf of Xeroxed pages, each one ruled into three vertical columns divided by a dozen horizontal lines, the resulting squares filled with handwritten numerals.

"You said you wanted these right away, Mr McFee."

"My God, I forgot," Phyl Wykopf said. "It's Thursday."

"Thursday, Bloody Thursday," Norman muttered darkly.

The sheets passed quickly from hand to hand. Now there was the silence of total absorption as they skimmed the Nielsen ratings, their eyes diving like seabirds to the box reserved for "Heartbreak Hospital."

"Will you look at this?" Gene Badger said, open mouthed.

"We're up," Kiki said elatedly. "We beat both networks! We haven't done that for seven months!"

"Eight!" Abel said excitedly. "And that was a Freak Week—Christmas, New Year, I forget which—"

"We're up two-and-a-half rating points!" Bob Neffer crowed. "And look at the share. A *twenty-eight share*! We haven't broken twenty-seven for the last two *years*!"

"Hot shit," Ophelia Utley grinned. "This is the first time that bitch ever did the show some good. Let's dig her up and kill her again."

■ ■ ■

He was supposed to be on the Brooklyn Bridge. It was a nice day for it. The city was in the dog days of August, but the morning felt more like April. April was beguiling. Wasn't that a line from a song? He remembered his mother singing it in her small, clear voice. Troy's parents were firm believers in Families Singing Around Pianos. Theirs was a massive Steinway that filled one third of the living room. His father had a lusty tenor, and his sister Daisy was the pride of her high school glee club, but when Troy was asked to produce pear-shaped tones, what emerged sounded more like small sour apples. . . . He pushed away the intrusive wave of nostalgia and tried to think of the present. He should have been on the Manhattan side of the Brooklyn Bridge half an hour ago, for the final day of shooting of *Heat Wave*. Bagley had assigned him to the detail after the indefinite postponement of the soap opera's remote, but Troy was still at home, lying on top of an unmade bed in pants, an unironed shirt, no socks or shoes. He didn't realize he was barefooted until he answered the doorbell, and saw Dan Lipschutz looking at his feet. "Your toenails need cutting," he said.

"Did my mother send you?" The question had once had more relevancy when they had been growing up in neighboring brownstones in Sheepshead Bay. But then the possible significance of the detective's visit struck him and drove out all flippancy. "What is it, Danny? Have you got something? Have you found the son of a bitch?"

"Relax," his friend said. "I just came to talk. Maybe you can help me a little."

"For Pete's sake, that's what I told you days ago! That I can help you on this case, that I've met some of these people!"

"I know, I know," Dan said.

"Let me work with you, Danny. It doesn't have to be official, I know you can't arrange that. But I can take a leave of absence from the unit, I can take some vacation time—"

"Yeah," Dan said gruffly. "You look like a guy could use a vacation. You look burned out, kid. Maybe I *should* call your mother."

"That won't be so easy. They don't live in New York any more, they live in Dutchess County."

"You never told me that."

"My mother retired. Pop teaches in a hick college. The old days are dead and gone, Danny." Troy was alarmed to feel the stirring of long unused tear ducts. He turned away and said: "Come in and I'll make some coffee."

It was a measure of Dan Lipschutz's concern that he didn't object to the result of Troy's offer, a bitter black brew made from the leavings of two different brands of Instant. It was the first time they had seen each other since Sunday Tyler entered the Homicide files, and despite daily calls to the detective, Troy was only as well-informed about the case as any newspaper reader. His resentment was as bitter as his coffee, as if he had been a husband or blood relation whose interests had been ignored by the authorities. How could he have explained to them the wonder and mystery of the bonding which had taken place between him and the dead woman in the short span of twenty-four hours? How could he convince them that he was entitled to share in their confidences, that the only possible anodyne for his pain was the primal satisfaction of the Hunt, the Capture, perhaps even the Kill of the beast who had taken all of Sunday Tyler's life and so much of his?

"It's still a Three Monkey case," Detective Dan Lipschutz said. He was a stocky man just turned thirty, his round fleshy face saved from homeliness by dark, thickly-lashed eyes that earned him the station house nickname of "Valentino." Troy couldn't see the eyes now, as he stared at the chipped rim of his coffee mug. "It's what, seven, eight days since the murder? And we haven't found one witness in a building with sixty-eight apartments and maybe two hundred and fifty tenants. Could be a few explanations for that. The most obvious being, the killer was somebody your friend Sunday knew, someone she let into the apartment herself."

"What about the 'interrupted burglary' theory? That's what I read in the papers."

"Forget that," Dan growled. "Nobody in the Department said anything about a burglary, some reporter just printed that because he had nothing else to write about. You can't 'interrupt' anything unless you go out and come in again, and as far as we can tell, Sunday Tyler didn't leave her apartment all day."

"Is there a doorman in the building?"

"You were there. Don't you remember?"

"No—I don't."

"There's your answer," Dan said dryly. "There are three of them, working in shifts. But practically every tenant we talked to says there's no real security. The doormen are always putting away packages, or using the john in the basement, or on the phone in the inside hallway where they can't even see the front door. They're supposed to announce visitors, but most of the time they don't. Anybody can walk across the lobby to the automatic elevators, get off at any floor, ring anybody's doorbell. Whether they get admitted or not is up to the occupant—every front door and every service door has a peephole."

"And if they're a professional burglar, and ring the bell and nobody answers, they assume the apartment's vacant and try to jimmy the door open. *Criminal Trespass and Burglary Handbook*, Page One. And if the doormen are so lax about people coming in, what about people going out? How can you be sure Sunday didn't leave?"

Dan sighed. "I came to ask you questions, not the other way round." Then he shrugged and took out the familiar small spiral notebook. "The ME puts the time of death between seven and nine p.m. In fact, the wounds were so fresh when the body was found, he can almost pinpoint the hour as eight. Even if we didn't have medical evidence, there's this." He flipped the book. "At six-fifteen, Miss Tyler made a phone call to a man named Abel McFee, the executive producer of her TV show. McFee said she talked to him for a good fifteen, twenty minutes, about business, he said. He's sure about the time because his TV set was on, a local news program; he recognised the six-thirty station break a few minutes before they hung up. Then she made another call, to an agent named Honey Raider who lives on East 57th Street. Apparently, she called Mrs Raider frequently, even though she hasn't represented her for the past three years."

"What was the subject of that call?"

"Mrs Raider said it was the same as all the other calls she made to her. To complain—about her present agent, her producer, the writers of the show, the story, the dressing room toilet, you name it. The call went on for about half an hour, even though Raider tried to cut it short. What finally got her off the hook, literally, was the doorbell."

"Hers, or Sunday's?"

"Sunday's. She told Raider that someone was at the door, that she would get rid of whoever it was because she had a fat script to memorize that night."

"Yes," Troy said, his own memory painful. "She told me that, too. That she had thirty pages of dialogue to learn."

"We found the script," Dan said carefully. "It was lying near the body. I doubt she had time to memorize it."

"You think whoever was at the door—killed her."

"Seems likely to me. But we can't be sure."

"According to your arithmetic, the time would then have been seven o'clock, a little after."

"That's right."

"And if the murder took place almost an hour later, that means her visitor was there for some time. Is that why you think it was somebody she knew?" Dan nodded slowly. If only out of politeness, he accepted a refill in his coffee mug. "But if it was an intruder with a weapon, a total stranger, she could have been forced to accept his company, right?"

"As a matter of fact, that's Rivera's pet theory."

"Who?"

"Carl Rivera. Another homicide detective assigned to the case. You didn't think I was the only one?"

"How many are there now?"

"Five. There'll probably be ten if we don't crack it soon," Dan said ruefully. "We won't be able to get out of each other's way."

"And what does this Rivera guy think?"

"That it didn't have to be someone she knew. That it was a whacko who picked her at random or saw her on the tube and decided she could use disembowelment. But then, Rivera's been working up a serial killer case for the last six months. "

"Serial killer," Troy echoed blankly.

"Not daytime serial. Somebody who commits random murders, one after another. Like the Boston Strangler, the Hillside Slayer, people like that. Rivera's collected what he considers four identical unsolved cases since last October. But he's the only one convinced that they're identical. One was a bag lady down in Soho, cut up with a meat ax and left in a supermarket delivery cart. Another was a young woman who worked at an all-night bookstore in the Village. Dragged into an alley, stabbed a couple of dozen times. No sexual abuse; the guy got off on gore, apparently."

"Yeah," Troy said. "That case I remember."

"The third one was the Swenson case—you ought to remember that one, too. Girl found murdered in Queens, another knife job?"

"But there was an arrest in that case, wasn't there? Her uncle, the guy she had accused of rape?"

"There was a warrant out for him, but it was never served. The guy did a disappearing act. When he was finally found, he was in a motel bathtub with his wrist open. That pretty much closed the case, except that Rivera figures his guilt about the rape was the reason for the suicide, not the murder."

"I'm not sure I buy this theory, Danny. The only things these cases have in common are knives and women."

"Exactly what the Chief thinks. But Rivera keeps trying. His fourth case is only ten days old, the Claudine Potter case? You familiar with that?"

"No," Troy said.

"Woman in her late twenties, would-be actress, came to New York only a month ago, rented a small furnished apartment in midtown Manhattan. Cut to pieces by an unknown assailant. No real clues there, either. And the fact that she was an actress, like Sunday Tyler—"

"Danny," Troy said somberly, "don't talk to me about what you *don't* believe is true in this case. Tell me what you think really happened."

"You want my opinion? Okay. I don't think your friend Sunday was killed by some disinterested fruitcake. I don't think it was a random homicide. I think she was murdered by someone she knew, for reasons she knew. I think she had enemies. I was hoping you might tell me who some of them are."

9 When a Girl Marries

They ordered a pizza, everything on it but anchovies, and opened two Heinekens. It was almost like the old days in Brooklyn. Only this time they didn't discuss the merits of the Met infield, the possibility (remote) of buying a secondhand car with joint funds, the odds for or against "getting somewhere" with Shirley Shuster or Louisa Watts. This time, they talked about murder suspects.

"I don't *know* these people," Troy warned him. "I met some of them, but that doesn't mean I know them. I listened to them talk, about themselves, about each other. And I listened to Sunday talking about them."

"It's more than we have now," Dan said encouragingly. "All we have is names on a list, most of them straight out of her own address book. We've interrogated them all, naturally. They all said they were shocked as hell. They all had alibis for that night, some of them good, some of them shaky. One thing I know for sure: you may be the only person in this town who *liked* the woman."

"I know," Troy said. "Sunday went out of her way to make enemies. I think I can guess some of the reasons, but don't ask me to analyze her. I'm not a psychiatrist."

"I'm not asking for an analysis," Dan Lipschutz said. "For one thing, you didn't know her long enough."

"I knew her long enough," Troy said flatly.

The detective flipped a spiral page.

"Abel McFee," he said. "Age, fifty-three. Married three times, divorced twice, no children. In the process of separating from his third wife—"

"Hold it," Troy said. "I never met the guy. All I know about him is what Kiki Carney told me. He's the executive producer of the soap, works for the network—"

"Carney," Dan said, skimming his list. "The name wasn't in Tyler's address book."

"She wasn't a friend of Sunday's, that's for sure. She's the associate producer, works with a woman named Phyllis Wykopf."

"Did this Kiki Carney say anything about Miss Tyler's relationship to McFee?"

"Relationship?" Troy blinked once.

"I don't mean business. I mean like humping him. Making zum-zum. How would you like me to put it?"

"No," Troy snapped.

"Don't take it personally. I'm just asking the question."

"Kiki didn't imply any such thing."

"Of course, you don't know *her* very well, either."

"She said a lot of other unpleasant things about Sunday. I don't see how she could have resisted telling me that, too. Assuming it's the truth." He looked up from his beer glass. "Is it?"

"I don't know," Dan shrugged. "At least two of the people we talked to hinted that Sunday Tyler was McFee's girlfriend, or at least his pussy in the corner. They implied that was the reason for her inviolable position on the show. Hey, how do you like that word, kid? *Inviolable.* Tell your mother my vocabulary's improving."

"It's your judgment I'm worried about."

"I didn't say I believed it, did I? I'm sure your friend was a virgin. A thirty-five-year-old virgin."

"Thirty-five? Sunday wasn't that old."

"That's what the birth records say. She just knew how to look younger, that's all." He was back at the notebook. "Okay, so you don't know about Abel McFee. But since he just *might* have been, uh, romantically involved with the victim, we can't scratch him off as a suspect, can we?"

"You said he was on the phone with her."

"Right," the detective nodded. "And maybe the conversation inspired him to pay her a visit. He had plenty of time to get over there by seven or so. And because his building has a very *conscientious* doorman, we also know that Abel McFee *did* leave his apartment house at approximately—" checking the notebook "—six forty-five."

Troy sat upright. "Did he say where he went?"

"He took a long walk." Dan smiled. "It was the first warm night of the year. He walked downtown, he says. Stopped to have a crepe or a quiche or something at one of those gourmet carts. He's dieting, he says, his theory is that if he eats standing up the food won't make him fat. Then he walked back home. He was going to retire early for the night, but he had a visitor."

"Who? "

"A man named Gene Badger. Do you know him?"

"He's the producer. Sunday was on *his* shitlist, that's for sure."

"Badger doesn't deny it. He says he would have been surprised if the cops *hadn't* talked to him. It would have shaken his faith in our competence."

"Funny man."

"He comes off like Mr Nice Guy. I thought he was trying too hard, myself. His alibi isn't too bad, however. He says he worked late at the studio, then walked home to a *pied à terre* he and his wife maintain on the East Side. His home is in Greenwich, but when he works late, he stays at the townhouse apartment."

"And his wife?"

"She was in Connecticut. She confirms that her husband called her from the apartment around seven-thirty, that they talked for a good twenty, thirty minutes."

"How did she know it was from *their* apartment?"

"She can't prove it. And, of course, she's the man's wife, so we can't be sure she isn't simply supporting an alibi. However, there's another kind of proof available to us."

"The phone bill," Troy said. "It was long distance. That means time and length of call were recorded."

"If they check out, it means Badger would have been on the phone at the same time Sunday Tyler was being chopped up for hamburger meat. Sorry." Dan flushed. "I keep forgetting that—"

"Skip it," Troy cut him off gruffly. "And I still wouldn't take the story for granted. Someone else could have made that call. Maybe there's some kind of conspiracy—"

"I'm not taking anything for granted," Dan said. "Anyway, Badger says he continued to work at home after the call, and then decided to discuss what he was working on with the executive in charge of the show, Abel McFee." He made a wry face. "Apparently, these soap opera people work days *and* nights."

"What time did he show up at McFee's place?"

"Around ten. We questioned McFee about Badger's state of mind, and McFee says he was kind of agitated, but nothing unusual. He claims they talked about show problems for about half an hour, and then Badger left. Badger himself confirms the time span, but he was vague about what kind of problems they were. Not that it would mean much to me."

"It might mean something to the investigation," Troy said.

"Meaning what?"

"The problem they were *always* talking about was Sunday Tyler. About some new story line she wanted them to use. If Badger came to have a *serious* discussion about it, then he wouldn't have known that the problem had been solved. By murder."

"It's a point, I guess. Unless—it was Badger's way of covering up the fact that he *knew* the problem was solved. And how."

"Yes," Troy admitted. "That's possible, too. . . . Listen, do you have a guy named Neffer on your list? The show's head writer? He was the one who was in the most imminent danger from Sunday, and so was a scriptwriter named Norman Levi."

"What kind of danger?"

"Sunday wanted them both fired. And in case you didn't know, the head writer was earning half a million bucks a year. The scriptwriter wasn't getting nearly that much, but it was still a lot of money to give up."

The detective frowned. "So they had a mutual interest."

"Right," Troy said.

"Well, they also had a mutual alibi. Neffer and Levi told us identical stories. They met around seven-thirty and did some bar-hopping or pub-crawling or whatever it is you *goyim* call it these days. Naturally, the spots they picked were so dark and crowded they didn't see anyone who can confirm their story. One of them, by the way, was a gay bar." A glance at the book. "It's called Oranges and Lemons." He looked up questioningly.

"I never met Norman Levi," Troy said. "As far as Neffer goes, he seemed straight to me. In fact he was just divorced."

"Maybe that was the reason."

"I wouldn't know."

"All right," Dan sighed. "Let's go back to the address book. There were only three women listed. Miss Tyler didn't have loads of girlfriends. One was an actress on the show named Rima

Walters. She was at a private dinner party with friends that night, so we can scratch her from the suspect list. Another was a maid, cook, cleaning-lady type who also checks out harmless. The other was listed as—" notebook "—Phyl, spelled P-H-Y-L Wykopf."

"A producer," Troy said. "Second in command to Badger. Do you have a line on her?"

"Nothing," Dan said. "She lives alone. She can't name a single witness to account for her whereabouts between seven and nine. But she has two witnesses after that. She went to the studio at ten, to do some preparatory work for the next day's taping. The night man saw her, and so did an actor named Ramsey Duke."

"I know the actor," Troy said. "I had lunch with him. He filled me in on a few things about the show."

"And about Sunday Tyler?"

Troy hesitated. "There's one more name I think I'd better mention. It's a friend of Ramsey Duke—the guy who plays one of the male leads in the show. His name is Milo Derringer. "

"He's on the list," Dan said quickly.

Troy showed his surprise. "You mean Sunday's list? Her address book? I thought she hated the guy."

"He wasn't in the book. But we put him on the list because of the connection."

"What connection?"

"Didn't she tell you?" Dan Lipschutz said. "He was her husband."

Troy couldn't have been more startled if his friend had announced that Sunday Tyler had been brought back to life. In a way, she had. In a portion of his brain, Troy saw a tiny square shaped exactly like a TV monitor, and there was Sunday's monochromatic image, and right behind her, the jutting jaw and too-sculptured nose of Milo Derringer, nuzzling her neck. He felt a surge of nausea, but swallowed hard just as the doorbell rang.

He was grateful to have something to do. He opened the door, and barely recognized the woman in the too-dark sunglasses and too-large raincoat.

"Hello, Daddy," Fiona said archly. "Did I catch you at a bad time?"

■ ■ ■

Dan Lipschutz didn't make any excuses for his prompt departure. He simply pushed aside beer and pizza and went to the door, flinging his topcoat over his shoulder and telling Troy that he would talk to him later, adding a promise to send him a copy of Carl Rivera's "serial killer" file. In truth, he was glad to be leaving. Half an hour before, he had realized that he wasn't going to learn much from Troy's truncated opinions of Sunday Tyler's friends and enemies, of whom only Troy himself seemed to be the former. It didn't matter. What had really brought him there was Guilt, what Dan called the Jewish mucilage; it kept people stuck together but without the deadly permanence of superglue. There was a lot of mucilage between him and Troy, especially after Troy had opted to follow in Dan's footsteps—almost literally—by joining the New York City Police Department three years after Dan himself had followed a family tradition dating back to the La Guardia years. By that time, Dan was resting his feet at a desk, having been promoted to detective due to several heroic exploits on the meaner streets of Manhattan.

Dan hadn't encouraged Troy's decision; but he hadn't done much to discourage it, either, despite a suspicion that it was more insurrection than career move, a rebellion against what Troy regarded as his family's academic tyranny. He knew Troy was troubled about being a "disappointment" to them; about preferring detective novels to Dickens, TV to Tolstoy. He was embittered over his failures at Columbia, about his inability to live up

139

to the scholastic standards set by his elder brother. There was nothing Dan could do to untangle the snarl of emotions Troy brought with him to the Police Academy, but he felt responsible just the same. What worried him now was the new emotion he had just discovered. Troy was mourning a dead woman as if she had been his long-loved wife.

Fiona Farrar wasn't as discerning. She had a different diagnosis for the pain she saw in Bill Troy's eyes. She watched them focus on her midsection as she stripped off the raincoat, and then she laughed.

"No, I'm not showing yet. But I wasn't lying, if that's what you're thinking. I've got the lab report in my purse. Want to see it?"

Troy shook his head.

"Aren't you going to ask me any questions?"

"Yes. Did you take my *King Kong* tape? I can't find it anywhere."

Fiona frowned and removed her sunglasses. "What do I have to do to get your attention? Climb the Empire State Building?" Her eyes were puffy. She had made no attempt at cosmetic improvement, as if it no longer mattered, as if she had a beauty secret far more alluring than all the tricks she had employed before. She had also shed all the little-girl cuteness that had been her trademark. Without it, Troy realized, there was nothing left.

"Let's get one thing straight right away," she said. "I'm not getting rid of this baby."

"I thought you were pro-abortion."

"I am. For other people. The whole idea scares me to death. So if you thought that was the solution, forget it."

"I didn't think anything," Troy said wearily. "Are you allowed to eat pizza?" She had folded a piece and crammed the end into her mouth.

"I'm leaving Durolabs. They don't know the reason and I'd rather they didn't. I might went to come back one of these days, and I don't want them to know about the baby."

"You're leaving New York?" Troy tried not to sound hopeful, but it must have come through.

"Don't get excited. I called my mother and told her what happened, and she wants me home. She lives in Englewood Cliffs. That's in New Jersey, right across the George Washington Bridge."

"Do you want some beer?"

"No alcohol," Fiona said firmly. "My mother's being terrific about the baby. The only thing that worries her is the money. She has a bad back so she can't work, but the welfare people don't believe her so she hardly gets a dime. I don't mean she's an invalid or anything. When she has a couple of drinks she's a lot of fun. You'll like her."

The last sentence reverberated ominously.

"Look, Fiona," Troy said. "I'm really sorry about this. I don't know how it happened—"

"You don't?"

"I mean, I could swear you told me you were on the Pill."

"Nobody's perfect," she said sententiously. "I might have skipped a day or two. But if you're going to try to put all the blame on me—"

"I'm not talking about blame," Troy said. "Just tell me how you want to handle the situation, and I'll help in any way I can. We're not the first people to have this conversation."

"No," Fiona said. "That was Adam and Eve. Only she couldn't go home to her mother."

"I think it's a sensible solution," Troy said. "And if money is a problem—"

"It's a problem, all right, but it's not the only one." She wiped her mouth delicately and came over to the couch where Troy sat squeezed into the corner. She sat next to him and took one of his hands. "You see, baby, not everybody is *People* magazine material. Some of us have different values, old-fashioned values. Like my mother, for instance. Like me."

"Meaning what?"

"We really had something special, didn't we? Even though we broke up, God knows what for. I mean, I don't even remember what we were fighting about, do you?"

"It's what we always fought about. My job."

"Job! What a funny word for being a cop. But never mind. If you love it, you love it. If you want to keep it, you keep it."

"Thanks," Troy said dryly.

"Cops have babies, too, I guess," Fiona said, moving her leg up against him, but failing to create any pleasurable sensations. "Cops have families. You see them at the funerals on TV. My mother has absolutely no prejudice against cops, really she doesn't. Besides, I told her you'll probably go into politics some day. Didn't you mention something about that?"

"Never," Troy said. "You're the one who mentioned it. And you've also mentioned your mother three times now. Why do you keep talking about your mother?"

"I guess because I'm going to be one myself," Fiona said, with a hint of a giggle. "I guess that's the time a girl appreciates her own mother. She's dying to meet you, Troy, I told her all about your cute little broken nose."

She tweaked it, and batted her eyes in tribute to the cute little-girl tactics she had used to get herself into her present condition. Troy tasted cheese, tomato sauce and pepperoni trying to make their way back from his digestive system. He had been wrong about what Fiona wanted from him. It wasn't sympathy, money, or marriage: it was all three.

10 For Better or Worse

(SCENE: JONATHAN'S OFFICE. JONATHAN IN CONSULTATION WITH MRS ARMSTRONG)

JONATHAN

Of course, the decision is yours, Mrs Armstrong. But I strongly recommend that you have the operation as soon as possible.

MRS ARMSTRONG

But only last month you told me there was no hurry. Why must I have it now?

JONATHAN

Because I need the money.

Norman Levi gave a short, barking laugh and then turned a guilty face towards his boss. On Gene Badger's office sofa, Bob Neffer looked up only briefly from his story notes, untroubled by his colleague's writing noises. Norman, unaccustomed to Badger's Kaypro, had to search the key board for the DELETE key. When he found it, he wiped out the final speech in one quick stroke. Then he substituted:

JONATHAN

Frankly, it's as much for your daughter's peace of mind as your own. Maribeth is quite worried about you.

MRS ARMSTRONG

If you want the truth, Jonathan, I'm just as worried about *her.*

JONATHAN

Why is that?

MRS ARMSTRONG

Because of you, of course.

JONATHAN

If you're worried about the . . . wedding postponement, let me assure you . . .

MRS ARMSTRONG

Postponements have a way of becoming permanent, doctor. That's what I believe and it's what
Maribeth fears.

JONATHAN

But I've assured her—

MRS ARMSTRONG

(over)

I'm sorry to say this, Jonathan, but your assurances
don't mean very much as long as Andrea Harmon
is around!

(PHONE BUZZES. HE PICKS UP)

JONATHAN

Yes, Lydia, what is it? . . . No, I don't want to be
interrupted. . . .

(surprised)

Are you sure it was her? . . . Yes, all right. Bring it
right in.

(HE HANGS UP)

You must have second sight, Mrs Armstrong.

MRS ARMSTRONG

What do you mean?

JONATHAN

Andrea was just in my outer office. She left an
envelope for me. Said it was . . . urgent.

(THE NURSE ENTERS. SHE HANDS THE ENVELOPE
TO JONATHAN AND GOES OUT. HE LOOKS AT IT, AND
THEN STARTS TO PUT IT INTO HIS TOP DRAWER.)

MRS ARMSTRONG

No. Go ahead and open it. I can see that you're
anxious.

JONATHAN

Very well.

(OPENS IT)

It's just . . . odd that Andrea would do such a thing. Drop off a letter in the middle of the day . . .

(HE BEGINS TO READ IT, AND HIS FACE DARKENS)

MRS ARMSTRONG

It's not bad news, I hope.

JONATHAN

(grimly)

You wouldn't consider it bad.

(JONATHAN READS ALOUD)

"My darling . . . I've done nothing but think since our last meeting. And I've decided that there is only one right thing to do, for your sake as well as mine. As painful as it will be, we must never see each other again. . . ."

MRS ARMSTRONG

(dryly)

Sounds to me like another one of Miss Harmon's grandstand plays. . . . I'm sure she doesn't mean a word of it!

JONATHAN

Listen to the rest.

(reading)

"I know there is only one way we can make this decision mean something . . . only one way for me to resist the temptation to see you again. By the time you finish this letter, I will be on my way to the airport. I won't tell you what flight I'll be on, or where it will land. Just be sure that it will be very, very far away, my darling. . . . I'll need many miles between us if I'm to have any chance at all of forgetting how much I love you. . . ."

"My God," Norman Levi said aloud. "She's really gone."

"Is that the last line of the scene?" Bob Neffer asked.

"I guess it is," the scriptwriter said wryly, tapping at the keys again, speaking the words as he wrote them. "'*Jonathan:*

My God, she's really gone....'" He hesitated. "No, there should be one more speech . . . '*Mrs Armstrong: 1 certainly hope it's true, Jonathan. Believe me this was the only cure for you both. Surgery! One swift cut of the knife!'*"

"No," Bob Neffer said.

"No, what?"

"That last line. Get rid of it. We don't need any reminders about knives."

"Oh," Norman said, gloomily. "Yeah, that's right. I'll just end it with Mrs Armstrong touching his hand sympathetically. There won't be a dry eye in Televisionland." He made the alterations and removed the floppy disk. Then he looked round the head writer's office, but there was no sign of a printer.

"Badger doesn't have one," Neffer said. "Take it home and print it on your Epson. It can wait until morning."

"Whatever you say, boss." Norman yawned, and picked up his coat. It was military cut, full of straps and buckles and grenade hooks. He was just making the last closure when Milo Derringer entered, preceded by a cloud of wine fumes .

"Kiki said you were rewriting my scene for tomorrow," he said, with the air of truculence alcohol always produced in him.

"That's right," Neffer said amiably. "But don't worry. We've only changed a few lines, and most of them are written down."

"Are you telling me I can't remember lines?"

"It's a letter," Norman said quickly. "A letter from Andrea. It arrives when you're in the office with Mrs Armstrong. It's her valedictory."

"Her what?"

"Her farewell speech," Neffer said. "She leaves town, never to return. Unless, of course, we recast the part."

"That's a rotten idea. Whose rotten idea was that?"

"The Badger's," Neffer said pleasantly. "It seems that Julia Porterfield is back in town. He thinks she can step right into the role. . . . Listen, if you're worried about the changes, Norman can send a copy of the new scene to your place tonight. Would you do that, Norman?"

"Sure, why not?"

Norman went out, looking cheerful. He was thinking about the paella he was going to make that night. He saw himself in the kitchen, de-veining shrimps, with Luis coming in and admiring his skill. He smiled at the thought of Luis. Robin wasn't the only one who could find a Latin lover. Revenge was sweet.

At the studio exit, he saw a tall, thin-faced man with a broken nose identifying himself to Albie, the night guard.

He looked vaguely familiar. Then Norman remembered he was a cop, and hurried by him without a word.

Bill Troy wasn't thinking like a cop. His purpose in searching out Milo Derringer at Studio 22 had nothing to do with the police case in which he now felt entitled to deal a hand. It wasn't anything Dan Lipschutz had said. The mere fact of the detective's consultation had been a tacit invitation, even if Dan hadn't intended it as such. But at the moment, Troy's investigation was strictly personal. He wanted the kind of answers that only a jealous lover needed to hear.

He knew he had found Milo when he heard the raised voices coming from the production office. At first, he thought it might be a rehearsal for a "Heartbreak Hospital" stanza, but the illusion didn't last.

"Andrea is *dead,* for Chrissakes!" Milo was saying heatedly. "She died when Sunday died, don't you know that yet? You can't just have somebody walk in and take her place!"

"Sunday took *Julia's* place, didn't she? Don't forget who had the part first."

"Julia Porterfield isn't *bitchy* enough, hasn't anybody thought of that?"

"We'll *write* her bitchier!" Now Troy recognized the second voice as Bob Neffer's. He knocked loudly on the half-open door and walked in. They stopped at once, almost guiltily, as if caught in the midst of an intimate domestic quarrel. Milo said nothing, but Neffer greeted Troy with a nervous smile.

"Didn't expect to see you around here again, Officer. I mean, since the remote's been canceled."

"I just thought I'd come by and say hello." Troy looked at Milo, and realized that he was seeing him with new eyes. Before, there had been something unreal, even alien about the actor. Now he was solid flesh, flesh that had once been pressed up against Sunday Tyler's warm, living body.

Neffer seemed glad of the opportunity to break up the meeting. "Sorry I can't stay," he said, pushing back his chair. "I've got a date with a word processor. If you want to come to the meeting, Milo, I'm sure Abel wouldn't mind. It's at the agency, at six o'clock."

"Who's going to be there?"

"Besides Abel? The writers, Gene, Phyl, Kiki . . . And Julia, of course." He smiled pleasantly. "It'll be a nice opportunity to see how you two look together." At the open door, he paused to ask Troy about progress on the Case, but appeared only mildly interested in Troy's noncommittal reply.

But the exchange seemed to disturb Milo. When they were alone, he said uneasily: "I didn't know you were assigned to the murder. I mean, you're a different sort of policeman, aren't you?"

Troy made a strategic decision. "I was asked to help out Homicide," he lied. "Because of my prior involvement with the show and all that."

"I see," Milo said, not happily. "And is that why you wanted to see me? I've already talked to the police, you know. I told them exactly what I was doing the night Sunday was killed." He tilted an eyebrow, *à la* Cary Grant. "Same thing I do every night, luv. Didn't she tell you?"

"She?" Troy's heart tripped over itself.

"Your friend Kiki. My guardian angel. My Cerberus. You know who Cerberus was, don't you? The three-headed dog who guarded the gates of Hell, which I do my best to enter every evening."

"Are you saying Kiki was with you that night?"

"She came to my rescue, as she always does. I was at the Lotus Blossom, having one too many Chinese firecrackers. . . . Of course, I don't need to establish an alibi, do I? Since I had absolutely no motive for wanting poor Sunday dead."

"Everyone on this show seems to have had a motive," Troy said gruffly. "From what I've heard, she was a threat to everybody's job."

"Not mine," Milo said disdainfully. "Hasn't anyone told you that? I'm the *star,* baby. Check the Q ratings."

"Yes," Troy said. "I know you were pretty secure. . . . But of course, you could have had a quarrel with Sunday that wasn't career-oriented. Maybe it was domestic."

He had the satisfaction of seeing Milo stiffen.

"Obviously, you've heard that Sunday and I were married. If that's what you call it."

"Does it have another name?"

"There are all kinds of marriages," Milo said. "The knot that held ours together was tied by an accountant, not a minister. We would have gladly undone it years ago, if either one of us could have afforded it."

"You know so much about Greek mythology—didn't someone *cut* a knot that couldn't be untied?"

"That wasn't Greek mythology, just a Greek. It was Alexander the Great. And he used a sword, not an ax."

Troy felt outclassed by the actor's swift responses; after a thousand scripts, he was better at taking cues. "Sorry," he said. "I didn't mean that to sound like an accusation."

"That's all right. I suppose murder's a fairly popular way of getting rid of an unwanted spouse. But it wouldn't have made much sense in this case. You see, Sunday wanted a divorce much more than I did. The marriage was a burden to her."

"And what was it to you?"

"A convenience." He smiled, showing perfect teeth. "It's very useful for a man to have a wedding ring on his finger when his ladyfriends start making demands. But you don't have to take my word for it. Speak to our attorneys. They'll tell you that Sunday was always the aggressor whenever we talked about our . . . knot."

Troy was beginning to feel better, the dull ache of jealousy beginning to subside. He would have concluded the interview right there, but Milo wouldn't let well enough alone.

"But if you're still having doubts about me," the actor said. "You can always talk to Cerberus about that night."

"I've already talked to Kiki," Troy said flatly. "She said you left the Lotus Blossom before she arrived. That it was at least an hour before she caught up with you at your apartment. Theoretically—just theoretically, you understand—you would have had plenty of time to call on your wife to talk about 'knots' or anything else."

Milo looked as if a page in his script was missing.

"She said an *hour*? That woman has no time perception."

"She also said you were in pretty bad shape. That you cut yourself on a piece of glass and got blood all over your shirt. Did she get that wrong, too?"

"No," Milo said. "I did cut myself. See?" He held out his left hand. There was a thin red welt on the fleshy part of his palm, not more than an inch long. "But I didn't get blood 'all

over' my shirt. Just a few drops. And if you'd like to get it ana-
lyzed," he said with heavy sarcasm, "you're too late, Mr Holmes.
I've already sent the shirt to the Eagle Hand Laundry. Do you
think they really wash eagle's hands?"

"Well, maybe I didn't hear Kiki right."

"Oh, you probably did," Milo said sourly. "She must have
been delighted to cast a little suspicion on me. I'm not one of
her studio pets."

"You don't like each other?"

"Do you know what I call Kiki Carney? Blonde Ambition."

"Anything wrong with ambition?"

"Depends on how many heel marks you leave on people."
Now he watched Troy's eyebrow lift. "Hang around the studio
for a couple of months and watch her work the room. Watch the
way she keeps finding mistakes in Phyl Wykopf's work—tracking errors, mostly. Of course, Kiki always has instant solutions
ready."

"I don't get your meaning."

"Phyl is supposed to make sure the plot is tracking right,
that things don't happen out of sequence. But Kiki proofreads
the scripts *after* her, and somehow, mistakes creep in. . . ."

Troy frowned. "Are you saying that she's tampering with
the scripts?"

"Sunday caught her at it more than once. Deliberately setting up errors so she could make herself a heroine on the set."

"And how did Sunday manage to catch her?"

"Because Sunday saw the scripts even before she did. Star's
privilege. That's how she realized that Kiki was giving poor
Phyl a royal screwing. And of course, she knew why."

"Because she wants Phyl's job?"

"Kiki wants *Badger's* job. But the rules say she has to knock
off Phyl first. After that, I suppose she'll want to be president of
the network, and then on to the White House —who knows?"

He grinned at Troy's reaction. "Shakes you up, doesn't it? All the pretty little women, acting just like nasty men. You and I were born in the wrong era, Troy."

Troy worked on his expression, not wanting the actor to see how affected he was by this new portrait of Kiki Carney. He switched gears and said:

"Tell me something, Mr Derringer. Do you have any theory about who may have murdered your wife?"

Milo wasn't daunted by the question. "Talk to the last man she slept with," he suggested amiably, "who was probably Abel McFee, according to popular wisdom."

"Popular wisdom is usually wrong," Troy said, more bitingly than he intended.

He turned, sensing Milo Derringer's eyes on his back. The sensation lasted all the way to the studio exit. On the street, the sunlight was hard and relentless against the steel angles of the buildings. For what he was feeling, the city landscape was altogether too harsh and too real.

■ ■ ■

It is midnight at Hartford Hospital. Dr Jonathan Masters heads for Andrea's room, when he meets MARSHA, a nurse who is madly infatuated with him. She makes advances, but Jonathan, his mind on Andrea, rejects her rudely. She is livid as he brushes her aside and goes into Andrea's room, closing the door quietly behind him. He leaves the room dark, and tells her: he has just learned that her suicide attempt was faked, and now realizes that their love is hopeless. . . . He is going to marry Maribeth. . . . Outside, Marsha listens at the door, but hides quickly when Jonathan emerges, looking shaken. We CUT BACK TO Andrea's room. A

man who has been hiding there all this time steps
out of the shadows and goes to the bed. His hands
reach out for Andrea's throat. . . .

Abel McFee sighed as he slipped the single-sheet document
into a folder labelled STORY-LINES and placed it on the coffee
table next to *Great Painters of the Renaissance.* The artbook
had been there since the apartment was furnished, and nobody
had yet cracked the cover. Abel's own reading was limited to
People, Ad Age, and STORY-LINES. God knew he had read too
many of the latter in the last three months.

When the house phone gargled, he glanced at his watch and
wondered if Carol had got the message changing the time of
their appointment. In a way, he hoped she hadn't. It was only
five; his meeting at the agency was at six. Time enough for something quick and tension-relieving. . . . But the doorman disappointed him by announcing the arrival of still another police
officer. Would the damned cops never leave him alone?

This was a new one: lean, sad-looking, broken nose, not
very good casting. Abel would have okayed him for the part of
an idealistic young college professor, not a cop. But he had a
badge, all right, and there was something familiar about his name.
There was also something familiar about his questions, and Abel
bristled when he heard them.

"Look, I don't think I have to say this over and over," he
told Bill Troy. "You guys have my statement. I *did* talk to Sunday that night, on the phone. I *did* leave my apartment at six-
forty-five, but I was only gone for a little over an hour."

"And then you had a visitor, right?"

"Yes. The producer of the show came over, Gene Badger.
To talk about the story." His eyes strayed to the folder on the
coffee table, and Troy followed them.

"Yes, we know that Mr Badger was here."

"Then what else do you have to know?"

"It was something you said in your statement, concerning you and Sunday Tyler. You described it as a business relationship, but most of the people we've talked to think it may have been . . . friendlier than that."

"It was *show* business, don't forget," Abel said stiffly. "Show people are different, they like to keep business friendly. Hugging and kissy-face and all that."

Troy managed a smile. "And you were on a kissy-face basis with Miss Tyler?"

"That's right."

"No more intimate than that?"

"If you mean was I sleeping with her, the answer is no. I thought you said you read my statement?"

"Yes. And I've also read the visitors' book."

Abel blinked at the unexpected reply. "What book?"

"Your building security system is very good. Didn't you know that the front desk, the concierge, keeps records of all deliveries and all visitors? That's how we were able to check out your statement about the night of the murder. That's how we also know that Sunday Tyler was in your apartment at least half a dozen times in the month before her death."

Abel looked a bit less tanned than usual.

"Sure, okay, I guess I knew that. I always see them scribbling in that book of theirs. Only don't give the little suckers too much credit. We've still had two or three burglaries."

"Of course the system isn't perfect. They can't possibly know what goes on in the apartments after people arrive. Miss Tyler's visits could have been strictly business, as you say."

"Business, social, what the hell's the difference?" Abel said irritably. "We were both adults, both unattached—"

"But not unmarried."

"Sunday liked to come by and *complain,* that's why she was here so often. I'm the executive producer, the buck stops here! She'd sit where you're sitting and drink my booze and tell me all her troubles, and that was it."

"Did she ever talk all night?"

"What's that supposed to mean?" Abel frowned and shook his head. "Boy, I'm glad she's not around to hear me use that line."

"Pardon?"

"That line drove her crazy when she saw it in a script: 'What's that supposed to mean?' No," Abel said. "Sunday didn't stay the night. We weren't lovers, no matter what people think."

"Then there must be some tracking error," Troy said.

"What?"

Troy reached into his pocket for a scrap of paper. For the first time, he regretted not having a little spiral notebook.

"You and Miss Tyler returned here one night in early July. You were in evening clothes, as if you'd been to a party. You were still celebrating. . . . Miss Tyler didn't leave the building until the following morning. She was wearing the same evening dress."

Abel was staring at him. "Tracking error," he said. "Now I know who you are. You're that cop from the mayor's office."

"I'm with the Movie-TV unit, yes. But at the moment, I'm assisting Homicide." It was the literal truth, anyway.

"Son of a bitch! So that's how you picked up all those rumors about me and Sunday. Only they're all lies! We had nothing going, absolutely nothing! That night she spent here, she just passed out from too much alcohol. . . . She never let me touch her. She was like a wildcat if you touched her. . . ."

Troy knew it only too well.

"I swear I had nothing at all against Sunday! Hell, I was the only one who *wanted* to keep her on the show when everybody

155

else was looking for ways to kill her off ! That's why Gene Badger came here that night. He was coked to the eyeballs, and he had this new story line—" Abel stopped.

"What story line?"

"He said he found a way to kill off Andrea. . . ." The producer's eyes strayed towards the folder, and Troy reached for it without asking.

"It doesn't matter now," Abel said dully. "I mean, I remember thinking that night, after I heard what happened to Sunday, she didn't have to be killed off on the show, she was killed in real life. . . . Only Gene didn't know that, of course."

Troy was skimming the single-page synopsis.

"No," he said thoughtfully. "It doesn't sound as if he knew it."

Abel smiled crookedly. "I guess it establishes an alibi for Gene, doesn't it? If he had killed Sunday that night, he wouldn't have had to write her out of the show."

"No," Troy said. "Unless he *wanted* to establish an alibi."

"What?"

"Never mind," Troy said. He finished reading Gene Badger's account of Andrea Harmon's death by strangulation, and then glanced at the next page in the folder. It was apparently different, despite the similarity of the opening sentence.

> It is past midnight at Hartford Hospital. Dr Jonathan Masters is just coming off duty after six- teen long hours. . . . He bids goodnight to a young intern. . . .

"What about *this* story line?" Troy asked. "Did this come from Gene Badger, too?"

"No," Abel said. "That was Sunday's own contribution."

"Was everybody a writer on this show?"

"Everybody thought so." He pursed his lips and reached for the folder, but Troy pulled away from his small grasping fist. "That's confidential material," Abel said nervously. "It has nothing to do with the police. . . ."

But Troy was skimming it rapidly, and the implication of the final lines jolted him:

> "The young intern, alerted by the cry, dashes out into the parking lot. He stoops over the body and says: 'My God, it's Dr Masters. And he's been murdered. . . .'"

Troy stared at Abel.

"Does this mean what I think it means? That Sunday wanted Milo Derringer killed off?"

"And if she had lived," Abel said gloomily, "she would probably have succeeded. Sunday always got what she wanted on this show."

"So Milo's job *wasn't* a hundred percent secure, was it?"

"There's no security in this business," Abel growled. "That's why you have to save your pennies. That rainy day is bound to come." He glanced through his picture window at the glooming skies. "Looks like it's already on the way. And I've got to go to a meeting. . . . Is this going to take much longer?"

"I have just one more question," Troy said. "Do you know if Milo Derringer was aware of what his—of what Sunday Tyler was trying to do? Kill him off the show?"

"Of course he was aware of it. Sunday wouldn't have missed the opportunity of telling him. She hated his guts and vice versa. Typical American marriage." For the first time, his clouded features brightened. "Hey, how about that? I just gave you a *mo-*

tive, didn't I? Maybe her son-of-a-bitch husband gave Sunday those forty whacks! Maybe he thought he could plead self-defence if he got caught. 'Your Honor, I killed her off before she could kill me off. . . .'" He was actually chuckling.

"Something tells me you're not too fond of Milo yourself."

"He's been a bone in my throat ever since I've worked on this show. . . . I must tell him about our little chat. I'll enjoy seeing his face when he hears about it. . . ."

Abel McFee was still absorbed in happy anticipation when they shared an elevator down to street level. He offered Troy a lift, but Troy opted for a separate taxi. He was already in Bleeker Street when he realized that "home" was no longer a safe haven; the odds were very good that Fiona was still there, rehearsing some cozy domestic scene. He had managed to put Fiona and her problem—*his* problem—out of his mind for the past five hours, but that didn't mean it had gone away.

Sure enough, he spotted her little red Mercedes, parked five feet too close to the fire hydrant. He rapped hurriedly on the scratched plastic panel that separated him from the driver and told him to stop. Gary would just have to put up with him for one more night.

He didn't get the chance to test the limits of Gary Naughton's hospitality. He arrived at his front door at eleven, after killing the intervening hours in a bookstore, a cafeteria, and a movie theater. Gary wasn't home. Either he had pulled late duty, or got lucky with one of his girlfriends. Troy had to make a hard choice. He could risk going home, or he could try to use an already overcharged credit card to find himself a hotel room. He decided against both alternatives. He did what he used to do in his first year after dropping out of college. He found his car, a twenty-year-old Volvo, parked on Prince Street within two blocks of his apartment house, and crawled into the back seat. For a few minutes, by the dim illumination of the roof light, he read the paperback crime novel he had purchased, but soon rested it on his chest and began to ponder the only crime that really mattered to him. But even the gory image of Sunday Tyler was soon crowded out of his mind by the bloodless but even more chilling vision of Fiona Farrar on his living-room sofa.

He might have been relieved to know that Fiona was no longer there. Fiona was gone. So were his Herbie Hancock album, his James Bond videotapes, his Elmore Leonard collection, his Sony Walkman, the new issue of *TV Guide* and everything else left at his front door. He would never see any of them again. For that matter, he would never see Fiona again.

11 For Richer, For Poorer

I t might have been worse. The day of Troy's requalifying
physical was still three weeks away; if it had been that morning, he would have been packed off with a disability pension.
Every bone ached, and every muscle complained about its treat-
ment in the back seat of his Volvo. But Troy still had reason for
elation: when he reached his street, there was no sign of Fiona's
little red two-seater or of Fiona herself. Inside his apartment,
however, there were clear signs of her recent departure. A sinkful
of dirty dishes, an empty cardboard container from a pastry baker,
and a disarray among his books, tapes and records which should
have warned him that Fiona hadn't reformed her larcenous habits. Troy was too grateful to assess the extent of his loss. He
took an icy shower, and the waters of Lourdes couldn't have
effected a more miraculous cure. He felt wonderful. So he called
the Movie-TV unit in Flushing Meadows and said he was sick.

He didn't feel guilty about the deception. As far as he was
concerned, he had a new police assignment, and it was far more
important than securing the perimeters of a movie set.

When he entered his old precinct house, Troy was struck
with a sensation of *déjà vu* that had nothing to do with his own
career on the force. Then he recognized the source: the squad
room set in Studio 22, an effect heightened by the presence of
the fictional Lieutenant Rick Savage, seated at Dan Lipschutz's
desk.

"You guys know each other, right?" Dan grunted.

The actor, Ramsey Duke, put out his hand. "Lieutenant Lipschutz finally had some time to talk to me," he said ruefully. "Only I'm not sure I need his technical help now, since there might not be any homicide investigation on the show."

"You mean they're dropping the murder story?"

"It wasn't just a murder story. It was the good old False Accusation of Murder story. Andrea Harmon gets accused of killing somebody, goes on trial, hero traps killer, Andrea goes free, and everybody's happy. Same old bullshit."

"Bullshit is right," Dan grunted. "How many times has something like that happened?"

"About fifty thousand," Duke grinned. "At least in soaps. But it won't happen in 'Heartbreak Hospital,' since we don't have Andrea Harmon any more."

"You might," Troy said. "I heard that they're about to recast the part."

"With Julia Porterfield?" When Troy nodded, Duke aimed his grin at Dan Lipschutz. "Now if I were writing *your* script, Detective, that's somebody I'd put on top of my suspect list."

Dan looked surprised. "I never heard of her. What did she have against Sunday Tyler?"

"Sunday took over her role when Julia went to Hollywood, and she did a better job than Julia ever did. That's reason enough for any actress to commit murder." Dan wasn't impressed. "Hollywood didn't treat her well, so Julia came back here. And guess where she moved? Into the same apartment house where Sunday Tyler lived."

Troy glanced at Dan, who was busy writing something in his ubiquitous spiral notebook. The sight made Ramsey Duke uneasy.

"Hey, I'm not accusing anybody, you know, that was just a joke. I don't *really* think Julia Porterfield killed Sunday."

"Nobody said she did," Dan told him blithely. "But we wouldn't be doing our job if we passed up any leads, would we? Any more suggestions—Detective?"

"I'm not a detective—I just play one on TV." Duke was smiling, but there were fresh drops of sweat on his upper lip.

"Come on—I can use some technical help myself. If you were a *real* cop, who would you pick as the murderer? And why?"

"I don't think I want to play this game." He looked to Troy for help, but Troy's face remained impassive. "Well, what the heck," he said. "I've thought about it, of course. And my guess is that the killer is someone in the show."

"Like who?"

"I don't know for sure. Someone who knew her, someone she was close to, someone who hated her. . . ."

"Pick a name," Dan said. "If this Julia Porterfield isn't on top of your list—who is?"

"I don't have any evidence!"

"I'm not asking for evidence, I'm asking for an opinion."

"Look, this isn't right—"

"A name, goddammit!"

"*Phyl*," the actor said, blurting it out exactly the way Dan had intended him to do. "Phyl Wykopf would be my first choice, okay? But like I said, I don't have any evidence. Maybe it was just the way she looked that night. . . ."

"You mean the night of the murder?"

"Yes. I told you guys that I saw her at the studio. She came to do some work, she said."

"And what were you doing there?" Troy asked.

"I was rehearsing. Sort of."

"Rehearsing all by yourself?"

"It was a dance routine, okay?" Duke looked indignant. "I told you that I used to be a dancer, with the New York City

Ballet. Every once in a while I like to see if I can still make the moves."

"But you weren't there the whole evening, were you?" Dan flipped pages of his notebook. "You actually didn't arrive until about nine. What I mean is," he said cordially, "you haven't exactly established your own alibi, have you— Detective?"

"Hey, man," Duke jived, grinning toothily, "you ain't just talking to the po-lice. You're talking to a *black* man. Everybody knows that black men don't kill no white chicks on TV. . . ."

"But this isn't television, is it?" Ramsey Duke's mocking grin went away. Dan permitted himself a thin smile, and dropped his hand on the actor's arm. "No sweat, Mr Duke," he said. "I'm not leaning on you. I'm just looking for all the help I can get."

"What about Phyl Wykopf?" Troy reminded. "Why do you think she might have done it?"

"I'm sorry I ever started this," Duke said miserably. "All I know is, Phyl came into the studio looking scared. In fact, she's been looking scared for a long time, and I can't help thinking it had something to do with Sunday Tyler."

Dan said: "How well did she know Sunday?"

"I don't know. I just figured they must go back some ways. But only because of the accents."

Now Troy made the connection. That night in her apartment, when Sunday let down her inhibitions and her acquired speech habits, he had heard the echo of Phyl Wykopf's voice.

"There's no such thing as just a Southern accent," Duke said. "I've got family all over the South. When they get together, you can pick out Georgia from Virginia from Mississippi, same way you can separate Cockney from Yiddish. . . . First time I heard those two together, I knew they were both from North Carolina. One day, I asked Phyl, and she told me she was from Charlotte."

"And Sunday Tyler?"

"I never talked to her. Sunday wasn't too approachable."

Troy cleared his throat. "I can confirm it," he said. They both looked at him. "Sunday told me herself that she was born on a farm in North Carolina. . . . But it's a big state, of course."

"Well, it's interesting," Dan said. "Particularly since Miss Wykopf has no alibi at all for the time of the murder. . . . Mr Duke may be on the right track."

"Hey, wait a minute," Duke said, worried. "I don't *really* have any idea who killed Sunday. For all I know, it was just some psycho who came to her door selling eggbeaters. . . ."

"Don't worry so much," Dan said reassuringly. "Nobody's going to quote you, Mr Duke. And I wasn't just playing with your head. I'm really looking for ideas. If you get any, or if you hear something at the studio you think I ought to know, give me a call."

"Sure," Ramsey Duke said uncertainly. "I'm supposed to be a detective, anyway—right?"

"Right," Dan grinned.

When the actor left, Troy shook his head.

"I guess that answers my question. You still don't have a break on the case. If you had, you wouldn't be appointing Junior G-men."

Dan looked pleased with himself. "I've been telling every body on the show the same thing. You never know when one of them might come up with a lead."

"I thought the same thing yesterday, when I talked to Abel McFee."

He told the detective about his meeting with Milo Derringer, and its aftermath in Abel's apartment.

"Milo was lying to me," Troy said. "He knew what Sunday was trying to do, that she was plotting to get him fired from the show. And I mean 'plotting' in every sense of the word."

"Assuming Abel McFee was right, that Sunday told her husband about the new story line."

"But if he *did* know, we'd have the one thing Milo claims we don't have—a motive."

"Sounds like you've made up your mind about this case already. "

"No," Troy said glumly. "I wish I could. But there's something . . . unreal about these people, about the world they live in. It's as if they're just shadows on a screen. Maybe I ought to have a script when I talk to them."

"Who said you should talk to them?"

"What the hell," Troy said. "If you can deputize a TV detective like Ramsey Duke, why can't I play, too? How would you like me to talk to Phyl Wykopf, for instance?"

The detective looked off into the middle distance.

"I didn't hear a word you just said."

■ ■ ■

At the studio, the director named Lou Blankenship told Troy that Phyl Wykopf was taking an early lunch, as she needed to be back at her post by one for an SFX rehearsal, whatever that was. Troy crossed the street to the Green Grotto, where he had first met the production staff of "Heartbreak Hospital." There were only a few patrons as yet, so he had little trouble determining that Phyl wasn't one of them. But before he could retreat, Kiki Carney's familiar voice called his name. He responded reluctantly, especially when he saw the unfamiliar woman at Kiki's table. As he came closer, he was struck by her slightly off-center resemblance to Sunday Tyler. By the time Kiki introduced them, he had already guessed that he was meeting the newest addition to Dan's ever-lengthening suspect list, Julia Porterfield.

"This is a sort of 'welcome home' lunch for Julia," Kiki said, a little too bubbly in the circumstances, Troy thought.

Julia managed to look demure, but it seemed merely obligatory. There was an air of crisp professionalism about her; every move she made would have looked good in front of a camera.

"Of course, I don't really start on the show for several weeks," she said. "The writers still have to figure out how to get Andrea back into the story."

"And how will you explain her change of appearance?"

"We never do," Kiki said. "Never apologize, never explain—soap opera rules. We simply make an announcement at the top of the show that the part of Andrea Harmon is now being played by Julia Porterfield. They'll accept it; they always do. It's part of that covenant between the show and the audience."

"Or conspiracy," the actress said, with an easy laugh. She lifted her glass of white wine with delicate, porcelain fingers. At that moment, Troy irrationally decided that Julia Porterfield wasn't Dan Lipschutz's ax murderer. If she had murdered Sunday Tyler, she would have done it with a knife and fork.

"Actually, I was looking for Phyl Wykopf," Troy said, when Kiki asked if he cared to join them. "There were a couple of questions I wanted to ask her."

"About the murder?" Kiki said cheerfully. "Don't tell me you think *Phyl* had anything to do with it? Well, at least that lets you off the hook." She looked at Julia archly. Seeing Troy blink, she said: "Julia was all upset when she found out that Sunday was living in the same apartment house. She didn't know until the meeting yesterday. Ophelia Utley was gauche enough to mention it."

"What meeting was that?"

"At the agency. Didn't Abel McFee mention it? He certainly mentioned you."

"Me?" Troy said, surprised. "What for?"

"He said you'd been assigned to investigate Sunday's murder. And he seemed to think you were about to pin it on somebody, but he didn't say who. . . . Was he right?"

"Let's just say the investigation is continuing," Troy told her.

"Well, you can have my alibi right now," Julia Porterfield said lightly. "I wasn't even home the night poor Sunday was killed. I went to see that *Iceman* revival in the Village. The O'Neill play."

"What more could you ask for?" Troy said, smiling in return, feeling as if he were running lines with her. "Couple of hundred witnesses."

"Well, more like forty or fifty," the actress said. "It isn't exactly a smash. But I did the play at Long Wharf, so I wanted to see it. Unfortunately, I didn't run into anyone I know, so I don't suppose they'll qualify as witnesses."

"You're in luck, Officer," Kiki said. But she wasn't refer ring to Julia Porterfield's flimsy alibi; she was looking at the entrance where Phyllis Wykopf had appeared. Troy excused himself and went to intercept her. He couldn't help but observe the look of alarm that flickered in the producer's eyes, but he decided not to interpret it.

Phyl seemed less than happy about having her lunch delayed by Troy's interrogation, but he promised not to stay longer than it would take to eat a breadstick. He chose a table well out of earshot of Kiki and her guest, a decision Phyl clearly appreciated.

"I thought you were all through with us," she said, her eyes and lips betraying the nervousness Ramsey Duke had cited. "Abel told us you practically had the murderer under lock and key."

"Abel is giving me too much credit," Troy said. "There's still a lot we don't know, especially about Sunday herself. Her background, I mean."

"If you want her biography, talk to Little Miss Muffet. That's her department."

"Little Miss Muffet," Troy smiled. "I suppose that means Kiki Carney?" Phyl didn't reply. "Funny—everybody seems to have different nicknames for Kiki."

"Different strokes for different folks."

"Only in this case, you and Sunday seemed to have the same nickname. Is that a coincidence?"

"I don't know what you mean."

"How close were you to Sunday Tyler? Were you friendly? I mean, outside the studio?"

"We used to be, when she first came on the show. In fact, I was the one who arranged her audition, when Julia Porterfield first decided to leave us. But then Sunday became the Big Star, and that was the end of that."

Troy decided on a frontal assault.

"Actually, you knew Sunday before she came to New York, didn't you? Back in North Carolina?"

The hesitation wasn't long. "Yes. I knew her. We met at a theater group Nancy Nixon put together in Charlotte. I was trying to be a director then, but I wasn't very good at it. She was only about sixteen, living with her Aunt Ursula. At first, she was only a scenery painter, but then I gave her a few walk-ons and then some small parts. . . . She was in the group for about three months before her aunt found that she wasn't in school where she was supposed to be. One day, Ursula walked into the theatre and dragged Sunday out by the hair. That was the last I saw of her before she came to New York and started getting stage work."

"So you got her the job in 'Hospital' and she wasn't any too grateful, is that it?"

"Exactly what do you mean by 'it'?"

"I mean your reason for disliking Sunday so intensely."

"Enough to kill her?" Phyl said dryly. "Is that what you're getting at?"

"You're way ahead of me. I'm talking about the day you sat right *there,* at that table near the potted palm, when I heard you and Gene Badger and Bob Neffer plotting to kill Andrea Harmon. It was only too obvious that you didn't care for your friend Sunday."

"Have you met anyone who did?"

Troy decided not to mention Abel McFee's sole defence. "No," he said. "I guess Sunday wasn't very good at making friends."

"But terrific at making enemies," Phyl Wykopf said. "That's why there were so many people at her funeral. Like somebody once said, 'Give people what they want and they'll come.'" Her eyes widened, and Troy quickly determined why. Kiki Carney had left her table and was coming towards them. She gave Phyl a wicked little smile, but addressed her question to Troy. "Do you have a Japanese girlfriend?"

"Do I what?"

"I just spoke to Lou at the studio—another tracking problem, I'm afraid. Anyway, he mentioned that some Japanese girl was trying to reach Mr Troy."

"Probably Mitzo," Troy said, half to himself. "Only how the hell did she find me?"

"I'll take care of the tracking problem," Phyl Wykopf said, rising. "I don't think I have much more to say to Officer Troy anyway. . . . Why don't you pull up a tuffet and sit down?"

Troy had a debate with himself as he left the restaurant, and curiosity won the point. He entered a phone booth and called the Flushing Meadows office.

"I thought you were sick," Mitzo said accusingly. "I called your house and no answer, so I called the TV studio."

"Some friend," Troy grunted. "You trying to make points with the captain?"

"Captain isn't here, he's got a meeting with a big movie director, Scorberg or Spielese, I forget which. . . . It was somebody else looking for you, I'm afraid to say the name. If I get it wrong it sounds awful."

"Come on, Mitzo, what's this all about?"

She said the name and got it wrong. But Troy knew who she meant and dialled the precinct number with fumbling fingers, hoping that Dan Lipschutz was going to tell him what he was aching to hear, that Sunday's killer was sitting in the cooler. But Dan had more unexpected things to say.

"I've got more bad news for you. Your friend Fiona was in an accident last night and got herself killed."

Troy didn't know how to respond. He hoped Dan would regard it as a "stunned silence." But he wasn't stunned at all. A dozen thoughts crowded into his mind all at once, and he didn't dare pick and choose his reply from among them. Finally, he simply asked a question.

"What should I do, Danny? Should I go to the hospital, the morgue, what? Tell me what to do."

"I think you should come down here," the lieutenant said. "You might as well give us your statement as soon as you can."

"A statement? Why a statement?"

"Fiona was evidently in your apartment just before the accident. She left around ten-thirty, hit a parked truck on Spring

Street about ten minutes later. Judging from the force of the impact, she must have been killed instantly. Some people like to know things like that."

"Then why do you need a statement from me? I didn't even see Fiona last night, Danny, and I sure wasn't in that car."

"We have another statement," the detective said. "That's why we need yours. It's from Fiona Farrar's mother. She's with me right now. Better get down here, Bubby."

■ ■ ■

The moment he entered the interrogation room, and saw Fiona's mother sitting like a tightly-wrapped package in the wooden swivel chair, Troy felt disgraced by his own thought. But it entered his head just the same.

There, but for the grace of God, sits my mother-in-law.

Violet Farrar was barely past fifty, but she had managed to add a decade to her appearance by an overwrought attempt to look younger. Her lips were too red, her hair too orange, her eyeshadow too blue. But deeply set within those iridescent circles her eyes burned with obsidian intensity.

"She called me twice," Fiona's mother said. "She called me at Bill Cosby and then she called me again at the Channel Five News. She said she was waiting for *him* to come home." She looked at Troy accusingly, as if he had already been an errant husband. "We talked for about ten, fifteen minutes. She was fixing herself something to eat, she said. Not that there was much in the house, you know the way *they* are."

"They?" Dan said politely, probably aware that she was categorizing all bachelors, or perhaps all cops.

"When she called me again at ten, she said she wasn't feeling well, that she was having cramps. I got real scared for her, on account of I lost three myself."

"Three what?" Dan asked.

She ignored this question, too.

"Anyway, she was feeling real bad, she thought it might have been something she ate. I said to her, maybe it was something spoiled, out of the fridge, you know? Some old piece of meat or fish *he* left uncovered, but she said no, she only had some soup and stuff out of cans, and a piece of lemon chiffon pie. . . . She sounded real panicky, so I told her to get herself to the hospital as fast as she could, the emergency room, you know?"

"Wait a minute," Troy said. But Dan stayed in charge of the interrogation.

"Is that where she was heading, Mrs Farrar? To someplace like St Vincent's?"

"I don't know. Maybe she was trying to drive home. I mean to my house in Jersey. Fiona was always scared of hospitals ever since I took her in for her tonsils." The childhood memory loosened a backwash of tears and she gulped hard and sobbed out the next sentence. "Whenever she needed help, she came to her mama. She always acted so independent, but she never stopped being my little girl."

"I just want to ask one thing," Troy said. "When she went out to get that pie, why didn't she buy herself a sandwich or something?"

"I told you, she didn't go out," Violet Farrar said, not deigning to look at him. "She never left the apartment on account of she was waiting for *him* to get home. Fiona was a good driver," she said pleadingly. "She never had an accident in her whole life. It must have been the cramps she was having? Don't you see? She must have been in terrible pain, and she lost control of that car because of it."

"It sounds likely enough, Mrs Farrar," Dan said in a conciliatory tone. "But it's not the only possible explanation."

"Yes," the woman said bitterly. "I suppose it ain't. She could have been losing it, the way I lost mine. The baby I mean."

Troy was almost relieved that the word was finally spoken. But apparently it wasn't for the first time.

"Yes," Dan said. "You told me that your daughter was pregnant." He was trying hard not to look at Troy. "And it was confirmed by the hospital. Your daughter was in her third month. But there was no sign of spontaneous abortion, so those cramps you described might well have been a stomach ailment."

"That's what I want to know," the woman said, and her voice, shrill and furry before, now had a hard, metallic edge. "I want to know how come she got so sick. My Fiona had a stomach like iron. She never got sick, never. Maybe sniffles now and then, everybody gets colds, right? But she could eat anything, she had an appetite like a horse."

Troy, who had fed that appetite on several occasions, could have vouched for the statement. Instead he said: "Look, Mrs Farrar, if you're trying to blame me for Fiona's illness because I left some spoiled food around, let me tell you this. I never invited your daughter to stay in my apartment; she was there because she happened to have a key to the place. In a way, she was a trespasser."

"I knew it," Violet Farrar said, rocking in the swivel chair. "I was expecting that. Blame the victim, right?"

"And I still say that she must have gone out to eat, especially if she had some lemon meringue pie, because there sure wasn't anything like that in my refrigerator."

"Lemon chiffon," Fiona's mother said flatly. "And it was there, all right, ask the lieutenant."

"The container was there," Dan told him. "It came from a bakery upstate that sells pies and cakes to a supermarket chain."

Now Troy recalled seeing the remains of the cardboard carton in the kitchen wastebasket.

"So Fiona went shopping in the supermarket. There's one right around the corner."

"No," Dan said. "They don't carry it. She would have had to travel. The chain that sells the pie doesn't have branches in the Village. The nearest one is on Twenty-third Street."

"How do you know all this?" The temperature of the room seemed to drop suddenly. "Have your guys been in my apartment?"

"We had to check out Miss Farrar's movements," Dan said, still avoiding his eyes. "Don't worry, it was all legal. We didn't even have to bust your lock. The building super had a duplicate key."

A little switch clicked in Troy's head.

"Let me try to understand this. You think there might be something *deliberate* about this? That I *wanted* Fiona to get sick?"

"She told me how you acted about the baby," the woman said. "You went all green, like you were going to puke yourself."

Dan, clearing his throat, said: "I'd say that was a fairly normal reaction most men would have, Mrs Farrar, wouldn't you?"

Instead of answering him, Violet Farrar turned her head and drove her obsidian eyes into Troy's.

"Only *some* men would do things other men wouldn't."

The phone on the desk chirped. Dan Lipschutz picked up the receiver and listened to what somebody had to say to him, and his own skin color underwent a change. His dark eyebrows collided beneath a furrowed brow as he looked at Troy.

"That was Bushin at the ME's office," he said. "They've established cause of death. It was a severe brain concussion." But he didn't give Troy any time to feel relief. "They also found a healthy dose of arsenic in her body. I guess that's what you might call the secondary cause."

12 The Edge of Night

In the space of an afternoon, the policeman became afraid of the police.

When he spotted the prowl car on his corner, he crossed the street and entered the dry-cleaning store which still had possession of his blue suit, the one he planned to wear to his parents' anniversary party. He didn't have the claim ticket with him, but he fumbled in his pockets as if he did, keeping his eye on the police vehicle all the time. When it pulled away, he muttered something about returning with the ticket, and left the store. He wasn't home safe yet. Two cops he had matriculated with at the Academy were just coming out of a camera shop, grinning over an envelope of newly developed photos. They were too preoccupied to notice him, and he made it to his front door without further encounters with the law.

He expected to find vestiges of the police search when he walked into the apartment, but he recognized only his own, and Fiona's, disorder. The relief he felt made him more conscious of his paranoia. There was no reason to panic, he told himself. There was obviously a question mark about Fiona's death, but it wasn't necessarily hovering over his head, too. Wasn't that the message implicit in Dan Lipschutz's parting speech? He ran over it in his mind, examining the words for all the reassurance they contained.

"Don't worry too much about this, funny things happen to people. Maybe your girlfriend was taking some medication. Maybe we've got another one of those Tylenol maniacs around, poisoning things in the supermarket. There could be all kinds of explanations besides . . ."

Besides what? Dan had never finished the sentence, but it wasn't too difficult to finish it for him. Fiona's mother had already implied premeditated murder without putting it into so many words, and for all Troy knew she was doing exactly that right now at the offices of the Manhattan District Attorney.

But Dan was right. It was foolish to worry about it. Maybe Troy had an obvious motive, but its very blatancy was a kind of defense. Maybe he couldn't prove his whereabouts last night, but the fact remained that he had spent it alone, curled up in the back seat of his Volvo. He hadn't left a lemon chiffon pie laced with arsenic in his refrigerator. Fiona had bought it herself; she always did have a sweet tooth. He used to think that the reason she bolted her food so quickly was her haste to get to the dessert. Besides, people didn't go to prison for crimes they didn't commit, that was bullshit. He spoke the word aloud, but it had no resonance in the small room. He remembered Dan using the word, reacting to Ramsey Duke's description of the new story line on "Heartbreak Hospital." The old False Accusation of Murder story. "*Bullshit*!" Troy said again. That wasn't going to happen to him. This was real life, not a soap opera. Life doesn't imitate Art, no matter what Oscar Wilde said.

He had succeeded in making himself feel better. Imbued with new energy, he began to restore order among the spillage of books and records on the living-room floor. That was when he discovered Fiona's last larceny, the missing Bond tapes, the Elmore Leonard paperbacks. He swore at her under his breath, forgetting that he was castigating a dead woman. Maybe that was the reason she died. Maybe Fiona had stolen one thing too many. Maybe there was a boyfriend Troy knew nothing about who had got angry enough to feed her that fatal dose of arsenic. He began to compose an optimistic scenario. The boyfriend would turn out to be the real father of the baby she was carrying; she had threatened him the way she had threatened Troy. He would confess at the first interrogation by the police, blubbering out his guilt. Troy saw the whole scene like the denouement of a TV crime show. The tough cop was played by Ramsey Duke, the killer looked like a younger Milo Derringer. The murder was solved, the theme music played, and the screen faded to black. . . .

Troy's appetite was restored. He went into the kitchen, and all the good feeling he had been generating for the past half hour melted away at the sight of the garbage bag tucked into the trash container near the sink. The garbage bag was new. The old one, containing the white cardboard container, was gone. He knew where it was, of course: in a police laboratory, the remains of a lemon chiffon pie being scrutinized under a microscope.

The doorbell rang. Coming at that moment, it induced a panic response, but Troy quickly subdued it. He also did something he rarely did: he checked the peephole. The face in the tiny aperture was young, Latino, and vaguely familiar. It also made him think "cop," and he hesitated before opening the door. Then he stopped thinking and turned the knob.

"Hey, how's it going?" Luis Campos said. Troy didn't recall the name until his visitor repeated it. "You remember, Fifth Precinct, vice squad."

"Yeah, sure," Troy said, connecting him with something, with sudden violence, a memory of pain. Then it flashed on him. A wet Village street, a hooker with the face of a Botticelli angel. . . . Campos had been his partner the night Troy was stabbed.

Troy let him in and offered him a drink, but Campos said he'd better not, he was on duty, only it wasn't vice squad duty, he was in Narcotics now. The quick career summary relaxed Troy; at least he wasn't there to arrest him on a homicide charge. Then what accounted for his nervousness? Campos was showing more apprehensiveness than Troy was feeling.

There wasn't any reminiscing. Troy and Campos had been paired less than a week when Troy had misjudged the malevolence of the young prostitute he was arresting. He did remember that Campos had done all the right things. He had taken care of his wounded buddy, the culprit second. But there was something else about the guy, something he had forgotten, or decided to forget. . . .

"Tell you the truth, I kind of lost track of you after you left the hospital," Campos told him. "I mean, I heard later that you were okay, that you got reassigned. Something to do with the mayor's office."

"Yeah, something," Troy said. "Movie-TV unit."

"Yeah, good deal," Campos grinned. "Only now you're doing something else, right? For Homicide?"

"Who told you that?" Troy asked guardedly.

"I just heard it around. That you were working on the soap opera case, the actress who got murdered. I don't remember her name, but I've seen her on the show. I don't watch it regular, I just saw it once or twice. There's this guy I know." He stopped, and there was a tinge of crimson over his dark features. "Maybe I better explain."

"You do that," Troy said.

"Like I said, I'm with Narcotics, I do undercover stuff. I hang around these places, find out what's going down. One place, it's called Oranges and Lemons, we picked up leads on half a dozen good arrests."

"I know the place," Troy said, watching the blush deepen. Now he remembered what was different about Luis Campos, and probably what made him an effective cop.

"Yeah, it's a gay bar," Campos said, apparently relieved to have it said. "Anyway, last week I met this guy, he was working on that show, whatever it's called—"

"'Heartbreak Hospital.'"

"Yeah, that's the one. He's a writer on the show. He was pretty stoned the night I met him, all broken up about something. He boasted about having all kinds of shit in his apartment, coke, crack, you name it. So I decided to go back with him. Turned out that all the shit was in his head, all he had was a couple of joints. The guy was really a pussycat, even when he got high it was on Amaretto on the rocks, you know what I mean?"

"Sure, I get the picture," Troy said. "What's this pussycat's name?"

"It's Norman. Norman Levi. Only it's not him I came to talk about. It's about something he told me."

Troy felt his throat tighten. "About the murder?"

"I better explain something else," Campos said. "I never told Norman I was a cop. We sort of became friends, and I didn't want him to think I was hassling him. I mean, I'll tell him sooner or later, but not right now, okay? Anyway, it was about this guy he works for, a writer named Neffer. You know him?"

"Yes," Troy said. "I know Bob Neffer. What about him?"

"Like I said, Norman was worried about this woman who got killed. For some reason, he thought it might affect his job. He's a real insecure kind of guy, Norman. On the other hand, he's also kind of ambitious, you know? And he said, maybe he's being stupid not telling the cops about Neffer. Because if Neffer was out of the picture, Norman might get *his* job. He didn't know what was the right thing to do, that's why he talked it over with me."

"Are you saying Norman knows something *incriminating* about Bob Neffer?"

"Right. That's when he mentioned you, that you were working on this case. And what the hell, I figured I owed you something."

"You got that backward," Troy said. "You're the one with the IOU. You're the guy who put me in that ambulance."

"I don't know, I always figured that little *puta,* she could have shoved that pigsticker into me instead of you, am I right? Anyway, what's the difference? I got to tell somebody about this, and I figured a buddy is the best person."

"Go ahead, then," Troy said.

"What happened was, this guy Neffer phoned Norman the night the actress was killed. And he told Norman that he needed an alibi."

"An alibi for what?"

"He didn't say. But he was all nervous and excited, and he wanted Norman to swear he was with him that night, that they went out drinking together, you know? I mean, what could Norman say? He worked for the guy, he could put him out of a job. So he said okay, he would back him up. So I ask myself, what does a guy need an alibi for, unless he did something wrong?"

All the tension left Campos's body as he leaned back in the armchair. Then he grinned loosely and said:

"What the hell. A beer couldn't hurt."

■ ■ ■

Troy learned three more things in the next twelve hours. One was the fact that Bob Neffer was no longer living in his bleak West Side hotel; he had checked out a week ago, without leaving a forwarding address. The second was that it was perfectly possible to drink half a bottle of vodka and retire with your dignity intact. The third was it was impossible to drink half a bottle of vodka and wake up feeling like anything human. Outer space aliens had slipped into his bedroom during the night and taken up residence in his head and stomach. But despite the fact that they were now cutting their way out with laser beams, Troy phoned the Flushing Meadows office to say he was reporting for work.

Mitzo made a little sound of surprise. Mitzo was very good at conveying her emotions in bursts of sound, and this one had another element that Troy couldn't recognize. Was it embarrassment?

"Uh, I think maybe you better talk to the captain," she said.

"I can't talk to anybody," Troy groaned. "Not for the next couple of hours. Just tell him I'll be there around eleven."

"No, you better talk first. Wait, wait!"

He waited. Then Bagley was on the phone, his bullhorn voice threatening to explode Troy's brains right out of his ears.

"Don't come in, Troy," the Captain said. "I just got a call from downtown, and you're under temporary suspension. "

"I'm *what?*"

"You heard me. You're suspended, pending a review of your case by Internal Affairs. Don't ask me what it's all about, nobody tells me shit. Or maybe you know already. Do you?"

Troy didn't recall whether or not he answered Bagley's question. The next thing he remembered was lying full length on his sofa, wondering when the aliens were going to make their breakthrough. Then he put the phone on his chest and dialed Dan's number. He got the precinct switchboard, and learned that Detective Lipschutz wasn't available, did he want to leave a message? He didn't. He hung up, just in time for the phone to ring with an ear-splitting vibrato. He reminded himself to get a phone that chirped, especially if he planned to drink again.

His sister Daisy said:

"I just wanted to make sure you remembered. About tomorrow night."

"Tomorrow?" he echoed blankly.

"Oh, God, he forgot," Daisy said. Daisy was always complaining to God about her brother. "The anniversary party," she said, with exaggerated patience. "Mom, Pop, our parents, remember? Now don't tell me you're busy, because I don't want to hear it."

"No," Troy said. "I'm not busy. I won't be busy for days, maybe weeks. I've been suspended."

"Did you buy a gift? I hope you didn't get something stupid like last year."

"No, I haven't had a chance to shop yet. I'll get something today."

"Make it something nice for a change. A clock, or a silver picture frame."

"Daisy, did you hear what I just told you? I'm suspended! They think I poisoned somebody, a girl I knew!"

"Oh, God," she wailed, not asking for details. "Just don't spoil the party by *telling* them about it, okay?"

"What, me spoil a party? Not on your life," Troy said, trying to hold down the hysteria he was beginning to feel.

In respect for his hangover, he eased the phone noiselessly into its cradle and tried to make his aching head work. There was no doubt that the suspension was due to the investigation into Fiona's death. It didn't necessarily mean that an arrest was imminent; her mother's complaint alone was enough reason for the Department to put him on the shelf. Police politics were delicate mechanisms, as complex as Talleyrand's. He wasn't going to be panicked by it, he told himself. Hell, it was a blessing in disguise. Now he could pursue Sunday's killer without restraint. And for all he knew, the pursuit might have reached its terminal point, if he could learn the whereabouts of Bob Neffer.

He spent the morning trying. He did the obvious first: he called Directory Assistance to inquire about a new listing in Neffer's name. There wasn't any, not in the five boroughs. He called Studio 22, but nobody there knew Neffer's new residence; few seemed to know his original address. Kiki Carney might have been helpful, but she was taking a vacation day, according to a production secretary named Ginny. He could have called Norman Levi—his number was in the phone book—but out of regard for Luis Campos's confidence, he decided against it. But the open directory gave him an idea. Neffer had a wife, an ex-wife rather, and just possibly she was a Manhattan resident still. His fingers walked down the listings and found: *R. Neffer.* It was worth a call.

R. Neffer's voice was pleasantly modulated until he mentioned the head writer's name. Then it changed to fingernails on a blackboard.

"Of course I don't know where he is!" the woman said, her voice raspy with rage. "Wherever it is, I'm sure he's got Harpo with him. Are you a friend of his?" She didn't wait for an answer. "Then tell him I know it was him! I know exactly what he did, and he isn't getting away with it!"

"With what?" Troy asked.

"You tell him I'm going to the police! Do you hear me?"

"I hear you, Mrs Neffer, and I *am* the police. So why don't you tell me what this is all about?"

"Don't give me that! He asked you to call me, didn't he? He wants to find out exactly how much I know. Well, I know plenty and I'm doing something about it! You tell him I've got

Liebowitz and Adams working on it, and he's going to jail for what he did!"

The phone clicked off, and he winced at the sound. Then he reviewed the one-sided conversation. and extracted more questions than answers. Did the ex-Mrs Neffer know something about the crime Neffer had committed? Who were Liebowitz and Adams? Lawyers, private detectives? And who was Harpo, apart from one of the late Marx Brothers? And why did Bob Neffer have Harpo with him, wherever he was hiding, assuming he *was* in hiding?

That question, at least, was answered. The phone rang, and Ginny, the production secretary, told him:

"Mr Neffer just walked into the studio, Mr Troy. Do you want me to have him call you?"

"Uh, no, it's okay," Troy said, thinking fast, an accomplishment in his condition. "I'll reach him later."

"It's no trouble. He's in Mr Badger's office—"

"Forget it," Troy said. "It wasn't very important."

He hung up, and leaped into action. Hangover and all, he was dressed and ready to leave his apartment in six minutes.

■ ■ ■

"Here's how it works," Bob Neffer said, rattling the paper in his hand. "Andrea is living all by herself somewhere— Chicago, LA, it doesn't matter. She's depressed, moody, doesn't know how to go on with her life. Then one day, she decides to go for a walk. She passes this church, and on an impulse goes inside. . . ."

"Andrea in *church?*" Gene Badger said skeptically. "You're really jerking this character around."

"It's just an *impulse.* She's role-playing. You know. She goes into the confessional—"

"A Catholic church, yet?"

"She talks to this priest, a real character. She tells him what a rotten life she's led, but now she's made the biggest sacrifice of her life, she's given up the man she loves so that he can be happy with someone else. . . . She gets a kick out of it, see? Especially when the priest tells her what a terrific martyr she is. She eats it up! But then—something happens. When she starts to leave the church, she sees that there's a wedding about to take place. A young couple, real sweet kids. She's got to watch it, of course. But what she sees is *Jonathan and Maribeth coming down the aisle!*"

Badger was beginning to smile.

"Hey—not bad. It's a way to have the wedding without really having the wedding. Not bad at all!"

"The point is, the hallucination changes her mind. Right in church, right after confession, right after she's been acting saintly, Andrea reverts to her old bitchy self. She makes a sacred—no, an *unholy*—vow: to stop Jonathan's marriage at any cost!"

Now Badger looked worried.

"In church? Like at the altar, with all those candles and statues and stuff? Won't the audience think that's kind of . . . blasphemous?"

"It's not blasphemous coming from Andrea. It's *bitchy*. It'll give Julia Porterfield a flying start, right from the beginning of her role."

"Yeah, she'll need a kick in the behind." He leaned back in his padded leather chair and locked his hands behind his head. "I really like it, Bob. I like it a lot. You really came up with a winner this time."

Neffer glowed under the praise. He decided not to mention that it was Norman Levi's idea. He let the Badger slap him on the back, and then he folded the paper and went out of the studio, eager to get Ophelia Utley working on the daily breakdowns.

He was feeling sanguine about the future; the threatening past was behind him. So was William Troy, but Neffer was too absorbed to notice.

August was relinquishing its smothering hold on the city. There was actually a light breeze now, a tantalizing promise of Fall with its cool, wine-flavored air. Neffer decided to walk home. To his new home. That was another reason for his good humor. He had been paying the rent on the garden apartment since May, when the divorce action was finally winding down, but he hadn't dared move in, fearful that his estranged wife, Rosalind, would discern his intentions. The garden would have been a dead give-away.

Troy, whose only surveillance assignments had included two other cops, kept as much space as possible between himself and the writer. At one point, he was almost "made." Neffer, heading uptown, reversed himself suddenly and ducked into a small *bodega* on Ninth Avenue. He emerged carrying a brown paper bag that revealed the corner of a bright blue box.

Neffer smiled when the four-story brownstone came into view. He clutched the box close to his side, thinking about how Harpo was going to react when he shook it in his face.

Troy watched the writer let himself into the building. He waited five minutes before approaching it, checking the four names adjacent to four doorbells. WINSTON, SANDERS, GREENE and GOLLUB. No 'Neffer.' Was he using a pseudonym? It was one more indication of guilt. The name that seemed most recently installed was "Gollub," so Troy pushed the button and hoped he was right. Sure enough, a buzzer sounded as the front door lock opened.

He found himself in a small interior hallway, facing a row of mailboxes, four more buttons, and still another locked door. He pushed "Gollub" again, and this time a voice emerged from the speaker embedded in the wall. To his dismay, the voice was female.

"Hi, baby," it said. "You're late. Better get up here fast, he'll be home in an hour."

Troy smothered the impulse to giggle, and said: "Then let me in—baby."

The buzzer gargled, and the inner door lock yielded to his push. He was inside a dim hallway, still not knowing where to find the pseudonymous Bob Neffer, only certain that he wasn't calling himself "Gollub."

There was just one apartment on the ground floor. He was about to knock on its door when he became aware of another light source. It came from a diamond-shaped window cut into a door at the end of the corridor. He could make out very little through the frosted glass pane, but a blur of green hinted at the presence of a garden.

Bob Neffer didn't mind the fact that the "garden" was little more than a blighted tree and a plot of dirt that seemed to be cultivating a crop of beer cans and cigarette butts. He was blissfully happy watching the small brown dog thrashing about ecstatically at the sight of the blue box and its bone shaped biscuits. He released the catch that secured the animal's leash to the tree, and Harpo bounced four feet off the ground in an attempt to lick his face. There was no sound of joyous barking, because basenjis rarely barked; it had been one of the selling points when he and Rosalind had chosen a pet. Now Neffer was more grateful than ever that the mute animal didn't give away his presence.

The cool air was condensing into rain, and he decided to take the dog inside. When he opened the garden entrance door and saw the police officer in the hallway, he failed to recognise him in the incongruous setting. Then Troy said:

"Harpo. I get it. Because he doesn't talk."

"What are you doing here?" Neffer tried to sound indignant, but the reading was unconvincing. "Who gave you this address? I haven't told anybody where I was living."

"Especially your wife," Troy said.

"My *ex*," Neffer said harshly. "Don't tell me *she* sent you to look for me! I thought you were a cop, not a private investigator."

"Would you mind telling me why it's such a secret?"

"That's none of your business!"

The basenji proved it was capable of sound by starting to growl. Troy looked uneasily at its bared teeth, and said.

"Look, can we go inside and talk about this? Unless you'd rather do it some other way—like at headquarters?"

It was a bluff, of course, but it made Neffer's resistance collapse. He pulled the dog away from dangerous proximity to Troy's pants cuff, and went to the apartment door. When Troy was inside, the animal suddenly decided to turn friendly and playful, but Neffer was as sullen as before.

"All right," he said. "What's this all about? What did you do, follow me from the studio?"

"Not because of your ex-wife. I'm not working for her. I'm working on the Sunday Tyler case, haven't you heard?"

"Yes, I heard. Abel McFee said you were hot on somebody's trail." His eyes rounded. "Not on *mine,* for God's sake?"

"Do you remember what you told the police about the night of the murder? About where you were?"

"Of course I remember. I was with Norman Levi, he writes scripts for me. We were hitting a couple of bars, talking about the show."

"What if I told you that we've asked around in those bars you supposedly hit, and nobody remembers seeing either one of you?"

Neffer bristled. "It's so fucking dark in those places, how would anybody know who was there and who wasn't? Look, if you have any questions, speak to Norman."

"I have a question for you. Who are Liebowitz and Adams?"

"My wife's divorce lawyers, why?"

"She said something about setting them on you. . . ." The word reminded him of the dog. He looked at Neffer's pet, and a couple of jigsaw pieces interlocked in his head. "Wait a minute. Does *Harpo* have anything to do with all this?"

"It's got nothing to do with the police!"

"That's not what your wife says. She threatened to call them, because of 'what you did.' The question is, just what is it that she thinks you did?" The basenji had decided to lick his hand, and Troy fondled the smooth skull. "If it's something less than what I'm thinking right now, maybe you better tell me."

Neffer looked at him appraisingly, perhaps trying to read his mind. Then he gave a heavy sigh and said:

"Okay. I guess I can trust you—since Harpo does. I wasn't telling the truth about that night. I wasn't with Norman. I was someplace else."

Troy waited. Harpo took his wrist into his wet mouth and held it gently.

"I was at my old house in New Canaan," Neffer said. "My wife had all the locks changed, but there's a broken window at the back that I was supposed to have fixed but didn't. . . . I knew she would be out, because we had *Phantom of the Opera* tickets for that night. We bought them way in advance. I gave her both tickets in the property settlement. She took her mother. I only hope the chandelier fell on her."

"You went there to steal the dog, is that it?"

"She got Harpo in the property settlement, too. The court awarded him to her because I was living in a hotel at the time.

They didn't allow pets. She didn't *want* the dog, she just knew that I did. It was pure spite. So I decided to take him back."

"And that's why you needed an alibi?"

"When I left the house, I also left the back door open so it would look as if Harp might have run away. I took this apartment months ago, so I'd have a place to keep him. Then all I needed was someone to say I was someplace else the night Harp disappeared."

"And, of course, you picked the same night Sunday Tyler was murdered."

"That's how it turned out," the writer said, with just a hint of a smirk now. "So if you had me on top of your list, officer, I'm sorry to disappoint you. I've got a real alibi. I was committing an entirely different kind of crime."

Troy, not liking the smirk, fixed his mouth in a thin line. "Do you? Remember, nobody saw you dognapping that night. You did a good job of concealing your actions. Maybe too good a job."

Neffer paled. "Hey, it's all true," he said. "I swear it is. I only write about murders, I don't commit them."

"You might not have been writing them on 'Heartbreak Hospital' for very much longer, if Sunday Tyler had lived."

Harpo was getting worried by his belligerent tone of voice. The small, sharp teeth began to apply more pressure to Troy's wrist.

"Nice doggie," he said, forcing a smile. Harpo looked dubious at this change of mood, but loosened his hold. Troy removed his hand carefully and stood up. "You don't have to worry about one thing," he said. "I won't give you away about the dog. You can straighten that out with Rosalind, Liebowitz and Adams. But I'd advise you to tell Detective Lipschutz the whole story."

"Lipschutz? I thought you were handling the case. That's what Abel McFee told us."

"Who, me?" Troy said. "At the moment, I'm just an interested civilian."

He started for the door, but the sight of a bookcase filled with videotapes caught his attention. Neffer watched him examining the titles, and grinned crookedly.

"Remember books?" he said. "They're about to become an endangered species."

One of the tape boxes was labelled crudely with a felt pen: SUNDAY S FINALE. Troy plucked it out of the case, and Neffer said: "It's a tape of Andrea's last show. I only save the good ones. . . . If you'd like to borrow it, go ahead."

"I don't own a tape machine."

"Play it on somebody else's." The grin widened lasciviously. "It might bring back happy memories."

"You really hated Sunday Tyler, didn't you?"

"I wouldn't have kicked her out of bed. Not that I had much chance of getting her there, especially the way she swung."

"Meaning what?"

Neffer flicked his forefinger across the tapes until he found one labelled: PEACHES. He removed it and handed it to Troy.

"You might enjoy her performance in this one, too. Just don't forget to return them."

■ ■ ■

He spent an hour in Bloomingdale's looking for an appropriate wedding anniversary present. It might have been the tapes he was carrying that steered him to a digital VCR that performed all sorts of visual tricks. His father would enjoy all the gadgetry and the complicated instruction manual. His mother would enjoy anything to do with television. It was her secret vice.

Back in his apartment, it took him almost as long to find the dry cleaner's receipt, which turned out to be one of those tricks of fate that determine human destiny. If he had located the ticket five minutes earlier, he might have missed Dan Lipschutz's call, gone out to dinner and a movie, and not felt obliged to make a stop at the precinct house.

There were fewer friendly greetings when he crossed the squad room towards the detective's desk. The news of his suspension, like all station house gossip, had spread quickly. He didn't get much of a greeting from Dan himself, for that matter.

"Sorry I missed your call," Dan grunted. "I'm juggling three dozen cases today."

"Including mine?" Troy asked lightly.

"I know you got suspended, but that wasn't my idea. Mrs Farrar swore out a complaint, accusing you of her daughter's murder. I'm sure that doesn't surprise you."

"And that's all it took, huh? Just the word of one hysterical woman?"

"A little more than that. A little corroborating evidence. There *was* arsenic in that lemon chiffon pie, Bill. Probably from a bottle of weed-killer. When the lab report went to the DA's office, there was at least one hotshot there who wanted to issue a warrant for your arrest. He agreed to wait until the investigation was further along."

"And how far along is it?"

"We've been talking to your neighbors," Dan said. "We can't really prove that Fiona Farrar didn't leave your apartment before ten-thirty."

"If she didn't leave, then she had the pie with her when she got here. There's no other explanation."

"There's one," Dan Lipschutz said. "We got some testimony from a woman who lives on your floor, a Mrs Babcock. She says she was leaving her apartment when she saw the groceries and stuff at your front door."

"What 'groceries and stuff'?"

"She couldn't describe them exactly. Just a brown paper bag with groceries, along with one of those freebie community newspapers, and a copy of *TV Guide.* She remembered wondering if there was anything perishable in the bag, if she shouldn't maybe refrigerate it for you, like a good neighbor. But she decided to mind her own business, and left. When she got home later that night, all the stuff was gone."

"Maybe Fiona ordered the groceries by phone."

"Not from your neighborhood she didn't. We checked out all the food markets in the area, and none of them had any record of a delivery to your building that night."

"So what's your theory?" Troy said. "That I left Fiona a nice poison pie for dessert?"

"I don't have any theories," Dan said, and the look of pain made Troy aware of his friend's dilemma. "I was hoping you might."

"I've got three of them," Troy said. "One, somebody's made a terrific mistake. Two, somebody's trying to frame me. Three, this is all a dream, and I'm going to wake up in about two minutes and go brush my teeth."

"Scratch one and three," Dan said gruffly. "Then talk to me about two. Who else might want to poison your lady friend?"

Troy felt a sudden fatigue, and took the seat alongside Dan's desk, the chair usually occupied by suspected felons.

"I don't know," he said wearily. "I never did know much about Fiona. The only people she ever introduced me to were the people she worked with, at a company called Duro labs. They do some kind of film processing. But she could have had another boyfriend, Dan. Maybe he was the jealous type. Maybe he wanted to knock her off and implicate me. Two birds with one stone."

"You're just guessing now, right?"

"Yes," Troy said miserably. "Just guessing. But one thing I know for sure. I didn't lace any lemon chiffon pie with weed-killer and leave it at my own front door. Somebody else did that, but don't ask me who or why."

"So far, there's no evidence of another boyfriend. Fiona's mother swears there was no one but you. She also insists you were the father of that baby she would have had. and I haven't heard you deny it, either."

"I don't deny it. I can't. The fact that she was pregnant didn't make me happy, but it didn't make me think of murder. "

"So you're asking us to find another killer and another motive. You're asking us to explain how somebody gets poisoned in somebody else's apartment."

"She wasn't supposed to be there. She was trespassing, for Pete's sake! I didn't invite her, Danny, she just made herself at home."

"And yet this hypothetical killer of hers found her anyway?"

Troy looked up and studied Dan's features. He didn't see them clearly. His vision was no longer stable, as if cataracts had formed instantaneously. The whole world seemed hazier, less solid, less secure.

"Hey, you know something?" he said. "Maybe it had nothing to do with Fiona. Maybe that lemon pie was a present for me."

■ ■ ■

Dutch Boy Pictures Presents
A Walter B. Geary Production
LADIES IN WADING
Starring
AURORA DAWN

with
Tammy Cummings * Mona Lowe * Amber Light
Peaches Paree * Nikki Nukey
written and produced by
WALTER B. GEARY
directed by
PHILIP W. MORGAN

Troy, in his darkened living room, felt a combination of pleasurable anticipation and inexplicable embarrassment. He had never been able to sit through a porno film in a public theater, concerned that the audience would be observing *him* rather than the gymnastics on the screen. This unlikely possibility shouldn't have troubled him during a private showing, but he didn't shake it off until the film was five minutes into the essential action. Then he realized that *Ladies in Wading* was an All-Girl Band, and his shocked reaction had nothing to do with prudery. Was this what Bob Neffer meant? That Sunday Tyler had been a lesbian?

He discounted the notion almost as soon as it occurred. Sunday was an accomplished actress, but not *that* damned accomplished. Her response to him on their one night together had been the full-blooded response of an all-woman woman. But curious to see her perform, he sped through the tape until he found the young woman listed in the credits as "Peaches Paree." She had been a pale, fragile redhead then, long-limbed, thinner than the Sunday he remembered, almost scrawny. To his relief, she also made an unconvincing lesbian, touching her lover with a tentativeness bordering on distaste. She delivered her few lines in a thick Southern drawl, but so did all the other ladies of the cast. Troy speculated that the beach setting was in North Carolina— Roanoke Island, perhaps.

When "Peaches" had played her last scene, he stopped the videotape and stared at the blank screen, wondering why Bob Neffer had the film in his possession. Surely Sunday wouldn't have wanted her career in porno films to become public knowledge?

No, Troy reasoned, there had been spite in Neffer's expression when he had handed him the videotape. It must have been the writer's private discovery. Could it also have been used as a blackmail weapon, if only a defensive one? Blackmail, Troy speculated, was a crime that often had its sequel in murder. . . .

But he had already scratched Bob Neffer as a likely suspect. Unless he and his ex-wife were involved in an elaborate conspiracy, which seemed unlikely, it would be easy enough to establish the validity of his alibi. R. Neffer would remember the date of Harpo's abduction, and Troy felt certain it would coincide with the date of Sunday's demise.

The trouble was, he thought grimly, his suspect list was shrinking every day. Despite the magnitude of the I-Hate-Sunday Club, he felt no closer to the solution than he had been on the night of the murder, and he doubted that Dan or any of the detectives assigned to the case were faring any better. Did that mean his initial conclusion was wrong? That Sunday hadn't been hacked to death by someone connected to "Heartbreak Hospital"?

In a way, it would be a relief. It would mean that Troy's newest theory was incorrect: that the instrument of Fiona's death hadn't been intended for him; that the arsenic-flavored lemon pie was a deadly gift from someone outside the world in which Troy had been living for the past few weeks.

"They had a meeting at the ad agency," he had told Dan. "The same day I saw Abel McFee. McFee told them I was working on the case, that I practically had the murderer nailed. He meant Milo Derringer, of course."

"Because he knew Derringer was your chief suspect?"

"Yes. And because McFee hated him the way everybody else hated Sunday. He couldn't resist trying to make him nervous."

"Who else was there besides Derringer?"

"Gene Badger, Kiki Carney, Phyl Wykopf, Bob Neffer, Norman Levi, a scriptwriter named Ophelia Utley, and the new actress playing Andrea, Julie Porterfield."

"And you think one of them got scared when he or she heard you were close to the truth. . . . So they went home and baked a lemon chiffon pie with one extra ingredient. . . ."

"I know it sounds far-fetched." Troy had squirmed in the hot seat beside Dan's desk. "But it makes more sense than somebody trying to kill Fiona that way. Especially if that someone is *me*."

Troy ejected the porno tape and pushed it back into its slipcase. Then he shoved the tape labelled SUNDAY'S FINALE into the slot of the video player, and pressed PLAY.

When Sunday appeared on screen, in the role of Andrea Harmon, the contrast between porno princess and soap star was striking. Andrea Harmon was a sculptured beauty, flawlessly tinted, coiffed, clothed, her voice as mellow as a stringed instrument without a trace of regional origin. And yet, there had been something more appealing, more affecting in the thin, vulnerable Sunday who had been "Peaches Paree" than in this plastic rendition of a woman devoid of character or compassion. Troy wondered: which role was really pornographic?

He removed the tape, and then carefully restored the VCR to its pristine condition in the original box. Or rather, he attempted to restore it. For some reason, the styrofoam packing now refused to fit the contours of the machine. Cursing all modern technology, Troy finally managed to get the device back into its box. He threw away the excess material.

He opted for an early bedtime. But his head was on the pillow no more than a minute when it began buzzing with the echoes of soft, drawling syllables. Why were they haunting him, the voices of those giggling, naked Southern belles?

Then he remembered. Phyllis Wykopf. Gentle, doe-eyed, and—let's face it—mannish Phyl Wykopf. She had met Sunday at a "theater company" in North Carolina. She had mentioned a name with political resonance, but he couldn't remember what it was. He tried to recall other names, the list of credits—if that was the word—for *Lady in Wading*. Made-up names, of course. "Mona Lowe." "Amber Light." . . . Could one of them have been a stage name for the producer? He tried to visualize a face or form that might possibly have been Phyl in earlier years, but it was hopeless. And, of course, it might not be of any significance. . . .

That night, he dreamed of Sunday for the first time since her violent death. It was strange that she had eluded his unconscious for so long, but she gained entry that night. She was standing directly in front of him, smiling, little crinkles around her luminous, blue-shadowed eyes. She was helping him dress. She was knotting his tie for him, slipping it under his collar, but so tightly that it hurt. He had seized the tie, and felt the roughness of hemp. Then he realised it was a hangman's noose, and he choked and gagged until a cough woke him. It was four-thirty. He didn't fall asleep again until six, and when he woke again it was after nine, which meant that Studio 22 was open for business.

13 One Man's Family

"It's not a good day," Phyl Wykopf told him. "Besides the taping, we've got a delegation from the Milo Derringer Fan Club on our hands, and guess who's been elected hostess?"

"I thought Kiki handled that sort of thing."

"She's supposed to," Phyl said caustically. "But it seems there are a couple of horrendous tracking errors in today's script, and Kiki is going over them with Norman Levi. So . . . I'm the one who has to deal with Loony Lottie and all the rest."

"I'd really like to talk to you for a few minutes. My schedule's pretty flexible, so you can name the time and place."

"Well, maybe after five, for a drink or something."

"I'm due upstate at an anniversary party at six-thirty," Troy said. "Look, I'll call you this afternoon and see how you're doing. . . . Oh, just one more thing. You mentioned a name the other day, a woman who ran a theatrical company in North Carolina."

"I don't know if she's still involved with it. Charlotte isn't exactly Broadway."

"Her name is all I want."

"It's Nixon," Phyl said. "Nancy Nixon."

His expectations were low when Troy called 1-704-555-1212, but he was happily surprised when Directory Assistance immediately obliged. He was even happier when a sweet Southern voice answered his second ring and turned out to be Nancy Nixon herself. If she was at all perturbed about receiving a call from a New York City police officer, she kept anxiety out of her reply.

"Yes, of course I remember Sunday, I was shocked when I heard what happened to her. . . . But you do understand it's been almost *twenty years* since she left the Playhouse. I didn't think there was much point in—well, getting in touch with anyone."

"Of course not," Troy said. "But I was hoping you wouldn't mind answering a few questions by phone."

"No, not at all."

"Did you hear from Sunday after she left the company?"

"No, but I didn't expect to. I'm afraid we didn't part on the best of terms."

"You mean you had some sort of quarrel?"

"I have a tendency to give advice," the woman said wryly. "Even when people don't ask for it. Sunday didn't care for my objections to her new career plan."

"You mean the porno film she made?" There was a silence he had to fill. "We do know about *Lady in Wading,* Mrs Nixon. Was that her maiden effort, if you'll pardon the expression?"

"I really don't know. But I'm sure she tried to forget the whole experience after she started getting more . . . legitimate work. And who knows?" she said. "Maybe I was partly responsible for it. She met the director of the movie in my theater company."

"The director? And how about the other ladies in the cast? 'Tammy Cummings' and 'Mona Lowe' and so forth?"

"No," Nancy Nixon laughed. "Sunday was the only one, I'm sure. Not that I know much about the movie. I've never seen it, and I don't intend to."

"I can understand that."

"It's not because I'm a prude. I *did* see a porno film once, in New York City. I was visiting with these three lady friends? We all had lunch and went to this theater in Times Square? Well, about half an hour into the movie we all started wondering if we'd gotten the salad that was included in the lunch."

"Just one more question, okay? What can you tell me about Phyllis Wykopf?"

"Phyllis who?"

"Wykopf. She was in your company, too. A friend of Sunday's. She used to direct for you. Now she's one of the producers of 'Heartbreak Hospital.'"

"I'm sorry," Nancy Nixon said. "But the name is completely unfamiliar to me."

"Are you sure? It was a long time ago."

"I remember *everyone* who ever set foot in the Playhouse, and there was no such person. Sorry."

Troy was still staring at the telephone receiver ten seconds after Nancy Nixon had broken the connection. Why had Phyl Wykopf lied to him? Obviously, she hadn't anticipated that Troy would actually take the trouble to check out her story about Sunday's career origins. But why concoct a falsehood? He knew he couldn't wait until afternoon to get the answer.

The first person he saw at the studio was Gene Badger, striding through the lobby with his head lowered like a charging bull, a sheet of paper gripped tightly in his hand. His glowering expression seemed connected to the document he carried. That was Troy's instinctive guess, and it proved correct. Badger, clearly in need of someone to vent his spleen on, seized him by the arm and said: "Look at this, will you? Can you imagine the *balls* of these women, to hand me something like this? Who do they think they are?" He shoved the paper at Troy, who read:

> PETITION TO THE PRODUCERS OF
> HEARTBREAK HOSPITAL
> We, the undersigned, members of the Milo Der-
> ringer Fan Club, do hereby demand that the writ-
> ers and producers of Heartbreak Hospital cease and
> desist in their persecution of Dr Jonathan Masters
> at the hands of Andrea Harmon; that they take the
> opportunity afforded by the recasting of the role
> of Andrea to reform her wicked personality and
> allow Dr Masters to find peace and happiness in
> his marriage to Maribeth Armstrong. If these de-
> mands are not met, the Milo Derringer Fan Club
> will do everything in its power to have the current
> production and writing staffs of Heartbreak Hos-
> pital removed by the network and sponsors.

There were a dozen signatures scrawled underneath the edict, and for some reason Troy noticed that "Loony Lottie's" wasn't among them.

Badger made an effort to display his indifference. He chuck-led weakly and said: "One of the crazy ladies had her lawyer-husband draw it up. They've also sent a petition to the network and a letter to Julia Porterfield, warning her not to be as much of a bitch towards Milo as Sunday was. . . . Funny, huh?"

"Are they still here?"

"Milo's Monsters? I told Phyl to get them out of the studio before I committed mass murder. She took them to the Green Grotto for coffee."

"Thanks," Troy said.

It was only a few minutes past eleven, but the ladies of Milo Derringer's Fan Club had decided to forego the coffee in favor of Mimosas and Bloody Marys. When Troy entered the bar area, there were half a dozen of them clustered round a table, show-ing no signs of the belligerent mood expressed in the petition.

They were making happy, clacking noises, like partying geese, but there was no sign of their gooseherd. Then Troy spotted Phyllis Wykopf emerging from the powder room, her fresh make-up not doing much for her martyred expression.

"What is this?" she bristled. "I told you I had no time to talk to you."

"I'm afraid it just couldn't wait."

"How many questions do I have to answer, for God's sake?"

"I don't have any more questions," Troy said. "But I think I may have some answers."

A frozen moment passed between them; even the ladies in the bar fell silent in that brief interval. Phyl must have seen something in his eyes that warranted immediate action. She strode purposefully over to the table and announced:

"Ladies, I'm sorry, but we have to cut our meeting short. Your bar bill will be paid by the show, but if you decide to order lunch, the tab is all yours." Then she turned to Troy and said, just as crisply: "I have to walk over to my doctor's office to pick up a prescription. If you want to come with me, that's up to you."

"Sure," Troy said. "I can use a walk."

As they left the restaurant, he asked: "What happened to Loony Lottie? She didn't sign the petition, and I didn't see her with the other girls."

"They said she was sick," Phyl answered. "They haven't seen her for a couple of weeks." That was the last word she spoke until they reached the traffic light on the corner. Then she said:

"You talked to Nancy Nixon, didn't you?"

"I didn't have any trouble reaching her," Troy said. "It's funny sometimes, how easy it is to find people you expect to be inaccessible. Guy I knew in Missing Persons, he looked for a bigamist named Hofstitcher for a year and then found him in the Brooklyn phone book."

"I thought about it two seconds after we hung up. That I shouldn't have given you her name. There's probably a neat psychological explanation why I did. I'll have to ask Dr Linhardt about it."

It occurred to Troy that the physician with the prescription was a psychiatrist.

"Maybe you just got tired of hiding the truth. Cops see it all the time, people yearning to talk about their sins. Not that I'm suggesting there's a sin involved in what you did."

"And exactly what is it you think I did?"

They were walking uptown now. The streets looked strangely deserted. There was a late summer haze in the air, like microscopic flecks of gold. It made the atmosphere unearthly, which coincided with the way Troy felt.

"For one thing," he said, "you killed a man named Philip Morgan."

Phyl smiled and touched his elbow, steering him down a side street.

"Don't worry too much about Phil Morgan, he was no loss to society. Even his family was glad he was gone. He was a complete embarrassment."

"And not a very happy guy, I assume?"

"No," Phyl said sadly. "Not very happy. Full of anger. He loathed and resented everyone, himself most of all. That's why he did some of the things he did, like directing porno films. Bad porno films at that."

"But then you put him quietly to sleep. And . . . Phyllis Wykopf was born."

"That was probably the most perverse thing I did, when I decided to change sexes. Calling myself 'Wykopf.' It was my middle name, from my mother's side of the family. She hated me using it, but my father was so relieved that I wasn't calling myself 'Morgan' that they eventually forgave me."

"You've seen your family since?"

"Just once," Phyl said. "My mother gave me her old clothes." She laughed. Then she stopped at the foot of a flight of brownstone steps and said: "I haven't told anyone about my transsexual operation. It makes some people uncomfortable. It's not, however, against the law."

"I don't have any intention of telling anyone," Troy said. "I'd just like to know if anybody *else* knew the truth. Someone who may have been . . . blackmailing you about it."

"You mean Sunday, I suppose."

"Or anyone else."

"Sunday didn't exactly blackmail me. She just kept reminding me. Every once in a while, she'd send me an old snapshot of Phil Morgan, so that I wouldn't forget my humble origins."

"I think I've seen one of those," Troy said. "The day I had lunch with Ramsey Duke."

"Sunday always made sure her 'friends' remained friendly. Maybe now you understand why it was so hard to like her. Although something tells me you did. Very much."

"I still want to find her killer, if that's what you mean."

"I can help you in one way," Phyl said. "You can scratch me off your list. That night, just before I went to the studio, I was right here, in this nice brownstone, lying on Dr Linhardt's couch and crying my little trans-sexual eyes out. I didn't tell the police my alibi because . . . well, because Dr Linhardt specializes in people like me. I wouldn't have kept my secret much longer."

"Maybe that's your real problem. Keeping the secret."

"You sound just like Dr Linhardt," Phyl Wykopf said. "Now if you don't mind, I'd like to get my prescription. I need at least one really good night's sleep."

■ ■ ■

There was a brown manila envelope lying outside his apartment door. He recognized the familiar imprint of the NYPD, and a chill rippled down his back. But it was only a file folder crudely marked: SERIAL KILLER. It was stuffed with badly photocopied police files and memoranda, most of them from Detective Carl Rivera, the cop who was pursuing the "serial killer" theory to explain Sunday Tyler's murder. There was a Post-It note on the folder from Dan Lipschutz that read: "Better late than never."

Troy glanced through the folder without enthusiasm. He had even less faith in the theory than Dan, but he had to admit that he had failed to come up with a likelier solution. For the next hour, he read about the bag lady in Soho who was dispatched with a meat cleaver, her killer displaying a grisly sense of humor, perhaps, by leaving her remains in a supermarket food cart. He read about the slaying of a young woman in an all-night bookstore; the savage butchering of a girl in Queens; the young would-be actress hacked to pieces in a midtown Manhattan apartment. . . .

One document was from the DA's office, concerning the disposition of the third case, the district attorney being sufficiently convinced that the killer was the girl's uncle, a suicide. The other cases remained open, but whether they were linked in any way, and whether they had any relevance to Sunday Tyler, Troy simply didn't know. In truth, he was weary of thinking of death and retribution, of Sunday, of Fiona, of his own fuzzy future. He remembered the family party that night, and found himself actually longing for the comfort and security of their embrace.

He was showered, shaved and dressed by five. The VCR was handsomely wrapped in some old Christmas paper; he hoped they wouldn't notice the holly leaves. By five-thirty he was in his car, heading for the Triborough Bridge.

■ ■ ■

Noel's shiny maroon Jaguar was parked in the middle of the driveway, so Troy had no choice but to pull up behind it, shaming his old, abused but beloved Volvo by comparison. Daisy's husband, a financial analyst, never kept a car more than a year. He had also changed houses twice since their marriage, and his job three times. Once, when Daisy was being particularly irksome, Troy had reminded her of Noel's fickle nature, suggesting that wives might be his next category. She had taken his remark more seriously than he had intended, and Troy had never mentioned the subject again.

Daisy greeted him first, giving him an uncharacteristic hug; Daisy was rarely demonstrative. "Pop's in the basement with Noel," she told him. "Showing off the new playroom. Only for God's sake, don't call it a playroom, you know how Pop is about *words*. He insists on calling it a recreation room."

"And where's Mom?"

"In the kitchen, where else? Making her little boy's favorite dish."

"I don't have a favorite dish."

"It had better be honey-glazed ham and mashed potatoes, kid, because that's what she thinks it is."

Troy grinned. "I remember now. I once said I used to like it at camp. Of course, I was fourteen years old then."

"You'll always be fourteen to her. My God, who would think a woman with a PhD could be so darned . . . maternal."

"When are you going to start being 'maternal'? You always told me that you wanted to have a kid before you were thirty."

She tugged at the pearls round her throat. "Noel doesn't think it's a good year. He's thinking of changing jobs again. The west coast, maybe."

"What's wrong with New York? There's plenty of finance to analyze here."

"Never mind. What was that ridiculous story you told me, about someone accusing you of murder? That was a joke, right?"

Troy hesitated. Then he heard the counterpoint of male voices coming up the stairs and said: "Sure, Daisy. Just a joke. "

His father gave him a well-coordinated handshake and two manly slaps on the back. The greeting, along with the neartly trimmed beard, the tweed jacket with reinforced elbows, the well-thumbed pipe, were all part of the collegiate image Eric Troy had cultivated in his twenties. It was affectation then; now it was just a natural feature of the landscape.

Noel Earnshaw hadn't settled on his persona yet. He wore a banker grey suit and grew his hair down to his shoulders, as if undecided whether his heart was in Wall Street or Greenwich Village. He greeted Troy heartily, and made a joke about his illegal parking. Troy was spared a forced laugh when his mother came out of the kitchen and gave him the coolest greeting of the evening, and yet it was obvious that she was the one most affected by his visit.

"I hope you brought a big appetite," she told him. "I'm making your favorite dish."

"Are you kidding? I'm sure you don't even remember my favorite dish. Honey-glazed ham and mashed potatoes?"

"Mashed sweet potatoes," his mother corrected. Then she looked triumphantly at her husband. "There, didn't I tell you?"

At the dinner table, he tried to steer the conversation to the occasion of the celebration, but nobody seemed very interested. All their questions were addressed to him, and it was soon obvious that the anniversary party had been a ruse to get him into the witness chair. Troy had managed to remain outside the family circle ever since his transfer to the Movie-TV unit, and they were pointedly curious.

"Do you see many movie stars?" Daisy wanted to know. "Not that I'd recognize any movie stars, they're all *kids* these days."

"I used to see a few," Troy said, toying with the over-sweetened ham. "But my most recent assignment wasn't a movie. It was a soap opera."

Eric Troy made a sputtering noise, halfway between amusement and contempt. "Interesting, interesting. They've got a fellow up at the school, sociology professor, actually takes all that nonsense seriously, gives lectures about soap operas. Always draws a crowd."

"Your father doesn't like them," his mother smiled. "He almost filed for divorce when he found out I watched them."

Daisy looked heavenwards, undoubtedly imploring God silently. His father swirled gravy into his potatoes and said:

"Surrogates, surrogates! That's all they are. Substitutes for real life. Don't like your family? Turn on the TV—there's a whole new family for you. Living together, too, if not in the same house, then right next door."

"I think it's *nice* to see families together," his wife said, taking the gravy bowl from him and passing it to Troy.

"Want a new husband? Turn on a soap opera, there's a big handsome guy always treating his wife like a queen. . . ."

Daisy grimaced. "Usually cheating on her with her best friend, Pop, you don't know these shows."

"That's okay, too. Surrogate infidelity. Fantasy life made easy. Don't even have to daydream any more—just turn on the TV."

Noel turned a toothy grin at his mother-in-law. "You don't really watch the soaps, do you, Mom?"

Troy's mother hid her disdain for both her daughter's husband and his question. "Well, why not? Now that they've 're-tired' me from teaching, I don't have that much to do with my afternoons."

"But you've got all that charity work," Daisy said. "Aren't you still running that women's club?"

"Oh, yes. We meet right here every Tuesday and Thursday, and what do you suppose we do, after we get all the important gossip out of the way? We watch 'Heartbreak Hospital.'"

Troy cleared his throat. "That's the show," he said.

"What?"

"That's the show I've been working on. They were going to do an outside taping, but then things got a little complicated."

"I should say things got complicated!" his mother said. "Ever since they killed Andrea Harmon. That was a terrible thing, wasn't it?"

"Andrea wasn't killed," Troy said. "It was the actress who played her. Sunday Tyler."

His mother shrugged. "I always think of her as Andrea. I've been watching her practically every day for the past two years."

"You know what you are, Mom?" Troy's sister said. "You're hooked!" Daisy had always felt overshadowed by her mother's intellect; this new confession obviously pleased her. She glanced slyly at her father, who gave her a conspiratorial wink.

"Your mother seems to think these people are real. One of them was dying in a hospital once. Sat in front of the screen with tears in her eyes. Surprised she didn't send flowers. "

"They *do* seem real to me. I see more of them than I see of my own family!" She frowned at Troy. "Anyway, I hope your police friends are going to find the person who killed her."

"They haven't yet," Troy said.

Daisy said: "Do they have any idea why she was killed?"

"No. Not really."

"Well, it's perfectly obvious to me," Troy's mother said, filling his plate for the third time. "All you have to do is watch the show. The woman made a career out of making enemies. I'm surprised something like this didn't happen before. "

Daisy blew an exasperated breath. "It wasn't the character who was killed, Mom, it was the *actress.*"

"Well, maybe," her mother said. "And maybe not. I hope you people are saving some room for dessert. It's banana cream pie."

She sailed off towards the kitchen.

And maybe not. The words seemed to remain suspended above the dinner table.

"Daisy tell you what we're planning on doing?" Noel said. "There's a big mutual fund out on the west coast looking for a financial wizard. . . ."

And maybe not.

"What did you say?" Daisy asked, seeing his lips move.

"I don't know about you," Eric Troy grumbled, "but I don't think I want to see another honey-glazed ham for a long, long time. . . ."

His mother came out with the pie on a large silver platter, holding it before her like an Olympic flame.

"And maybe not," Troy said aloud.

They were all staring at him, but he wasn't aware of it. He had suddenly realized that he might have been pursuing not only the wrong culprit but the wrong victim.

14 Love is a Many-Splendored Thing

"You want what?" Kiki said.

He had expected incredulity, but not quite so much shock.

"An autographed picture of Milo," Troy repeated. "I'm sure there must be one lying around. It's for our secretary at Flushing Meadows."

"Well, we might have some glossies in the office, but I don't know if any are autographed. Besides, doesn't she want him to personalize it?"

"What the hell—I'll do that myself."

"Isn't forgery a crime?"

"I've got friends in the force."

Kiki shrugged and left him in the waiting area. Deliberately casual, he strolled towards Gene Badger's vacant office, and studied the adjacent bulletin board. He flipped through the fan letters pinned to the cork surface until he found the one he wanted. As he jotted down the return address, the studio guard walked by and looked at him suspiciously. The man had good instincts, Troy thought. He seemed to sense that Troy was there under false pretences.

Kiki was back five minutes later, clutching a manila envelope. "You're in luck, Milo had a stack of these prepared for yesterday's meeting of his fan club. There's only one problem. It's not autographed."

"But it's worthless without it. . . . And you're sure Milo won't be in today?"

"He won't be in for a week. He's got a movie out."

"A what?"

"It's a clause most contract players ask for. If they get a chance to do a movie, or a commercial, or something like that, they're entitled to time off. Milo's auditioning for a pilot."

"Damn. I hate to break my promise."

"You won't have to," Kiki said cheerfully. "Who do you think signs Milo's autographs when he's too drunk to hold a pen?" She removed a ballpoint from her purse and opened the envelope.

"Now who's the forger?"

"I can write his signature so well that even Milo can't tell the difference. . . . Okay, what's your secretary's name? Is this the Japanese girl?"

"She's Eurasian. But don't write her name—I have no idea how to spell it. Just write: 'Get well soon.'" When Kiki looked up, he explained, "She's down with the flu. I thought it would cheer her up a little."

Kiki shrugged, and obliged. Troy didn't let her hear his sigh of relief.

He decided not to buy the flowers until he got to Crown Heights; the thought of holding a bouquet on the subway didn't appeal to him. There must be florists in the borough of Brooklyn, he reasoned. His only problem would be finding the right train to take him there. Troy's grasp of the underground system was sketchy at best.

Luckily, a change booth clerk was able to guide him. He squeezed into a seat between two well-fed lady passengers, and sneaked a look at the envelope's contents. Milo Derringer's eyes met his accusingly, and he pushed the photo out of sight.

The walk from the subway station wasn't very long, but Troy was forced to take a lengthy detour to find a florist. He chose what he thought Milo himself would have chosen: white roses. They were showy and virginal at the same time; he felt sure the convalescent would like that.

Number 435 turned out to be a narrow brownstone five storys tall. Something warned him there would be no elevator, and that the apartment he sought would be on the fifth floor. He was nearly right. It was on Four.

Well, there was the door. Go ahead, he told himself. You decided to do it this way. Do it.

He rang the doorbell.

It took him a few moments to realize that the bell was inoperative. He resorted to his knuckles; after three tentative and two forceful rappings, he heard sounds behind the door. He was sure he was being warily scrutinized through the peephole, so he tried to look agreeable and harmless. He must have passed the inspection. A bolt was drawn, and the door opened just enough to expose a heavy chain and one round, bespectacled, inquisitive eye.

"Yes?"

"Miss Orwasher?" he said. "Hi! I'm from the Studio. 'Heartbreak Hospital'? My name is Troy, and I'm the assistant floor manager."

She looked baffled. At least the Eye did; it was still all she was willing to expose. Troy decided to strengthen his appeal.

"I'm here on behalf of Mr Derringer. He had to go out of town, but he wanted to make sure you got these today."

He waggled the bouquet in front of the Eye. The effect was immediate, but Troy assumed it was the magic of the name, not the bouquet. The chain slid away and the door opened, and now he saw that the woman had *two* round, pale blue eyes behind the flat planes of her spectacles. Her nose was pink as a rabbit's, but it seemed to be a natural condition, not the result of any respiratory illness. She wore a bathrobe three sizes too big. Her bare feet poked out underneath like two white fillets of sole.

It was an apartment that could be generously described as a two-and-a-half, the half being a wall kitchen with a sink glutted with unwashed dishes. It was cramped and unlovely. The only ornamental touches were a single vase filled with faded flowers and a wall covered with photographs arranged without any sense of symmetry. Incongruously, there was a collection of oversized furniture of good quality, probably heirlooms from a less lonely past. But the most dominant object in the living room was an enormous console television pushed against the farthest wall. More photographs, in wedding-ring frames, sat on top of the set, and a love seat, two identical armchairs and a coffee table were grouped around the thirty-inch screen as if it had been a fireplace. The analogy was probably apt, since it provided the only constant source of warmth in the woman's life.

"I tried to call first," Troy said. "But I couldn't locate your number." Neither mentioned that she had no telephone. "Miss Carney thought you wouldn't mind if I called on you personally."

"No," she said, pulling the collar of her bathrobe closer around her neck; if she was fearful of revealing cleavage, she had little to worry about. "It was very nice of you," she said. "You see, I've been sick. . . ."

"Yes, your friends told us. That's why Mr Derringer wanted me to come here today and . . . give you these."

He handed her the flowers. She gathered them into trembling hands.

"White roses," she murmured. "How could he know? My absolute favorite! I just hope I have something to put them in."

She found something, by the simple expedient of dumping the wilted contents of the vase into a wastebasket. Troy waited until she filled it with fresh water and had the roses arranged to her satisfaction. Then he presented her with the signed photo. It was obviously not the first one she had received; half of the pictures on the wall were of Milo Derringer. He wondered how many of the autographs had been forged by Kiki Carney.

"'Get well soon,'" she read. "Get well soon!" She closed her eyes blissfully, absorbing the poetry of it. "Oh, to think that he would take the *time*. To think that he would *care*. I can't tell you how much this means to me, Mr . . ."

"Troy," Troy said.

"The only thing I don't understand is . . . Well, I know he has to use *that* name on the screen. He explained it to me a long time ago, about the name. But why did he use it now?"

"I don't know what you mean."

"Why, this name, this 'Milo Derringer.' He never signed it that way before. You see?"

She was looking behind him, at the wall of photographs. He turned, and saw at once that Milo had signed each picture "Dr Jonathan Masters." In some cases, simply "Jonathan."

For Troy, the quotation marks explained the conceit, but apparently they didn't have the same significance for Lottie Orwasher.

"Well, never mind," Lottie said. "He must have been in a hurry, especially if he had to leave town. . . . Will he be gone for very long?"

"Just a week or two," Troy said. "He said he'd be in touch when he returns. He hopes you'll be completely recovered by then."

Her body sagged within the oversized robe. "I don't know," she said miserably. "I don't think I can ever feel really well again, considering . . ."

"Considering what?"

"I'm sure you know. Bringing that woman back! I don't know why they did that. I don't know *how* they could do it!"

"Oh," Troy said. "I suppose you mean Andrea."

"Is it really true?" Lottie asked, her eyes pleading for denial. "It's in all the magazines, that they're bringing her back. Can they really do that, even though she's . . . you know. "

"I'm not sure I do."

"Even though she's . . . *dead*?"

She became suddenly cautious. She squared her shoulders, and started to play hostess. "Can I get you anything?" she asked. "Coffee or tea? I was just going to have some tea myself."

"That would be fine," Troy said.

"Please . . . won't you sit down?"

"Thank you," Troy said, conscious that they were playing a scene she had watched a hundred times on "Heartbreak Hospital." But he must have made a mistake in stage directions. When he went to sit in the nearest armchair, Lottie said: "No, not that there. The other one's much more comfortable."

Troy watched her move to the wall kitchen to heat the water in the aluminum kettle.

"Everybody really missed you at the meeting yesterday. . . . I suppose you know about the petition?"

"The what?"

"We noticed that you didn't sign it. . . . The petition asking the show to treat Dr Masters more kindly. Or maybe you haven't seen it yet, since you've been ill."

"No," Lottie said dully. "I don't know about any petition. I haven't been in touch with any of the girls. And I haven't talked to Dr Masters for more than a month. : . ."

"What did you talk about?"

"We talked about *her,* of course. I told him how awfully she was treating him, that I could hardly stand to watch the show any more. And he said that . . . it might even get worse."

"In what way?"

"Oh, you know," Lottie said impatiently. "You work at the studio, you must have heard what they were planning!"

"They don't tell us *everything* at the studio. You know the way the front office is."

"She was trying to get him off the show! That's what Andrea was doing! There was actually some plan to kill him!"

"You're not serious."

"I am! Andrea was going to *murder* poor Jonathan! She was going to hit him with an ax, right in the hospital parking lot! Oh, he was so terribly upset. I thought my heart was going to break. . . ." She caught a sob in her throat.

"Well," Troy said, clearing his own throat, "Andrea won't be able to hurt him any more, will she?"

"Yes. That's what I thought," Lottie Orwasher said bitterly. "I thought he was finally safe from that woman. But now they say she's coming back! How is that possible? Andrea is dead! This woman they're talking about, she's a fake, an imposter!"

"Is that why you didn't come to the studio yesterday? Because of her?"

"I don't know what to do any more," Lottie said, twisting her hands together. "I don't know what else I can do to help him that I haven't already done."

"You must care a lot for Dr Masters," Troy said.

"He knows how I feel about him, I'm sure he does. I told him I would do anything for him, anything at all. That's what love is all about it, isn't it? It says it right here. . . ."

She turned to the other wall, and Troy realized that not all the framed objects were photographs; there was an embroidered sampler and a hand-lettered sentiment in a gold leaf border.

"'Love never reasons,'" Lottie quoted from memory, "'but profusely gives . . . gives like a thoughtless prodigal, its all, and trembles then lest it has done too little. . . .' Isn't that true?"

"Yes," Troy said. "I suppose it is."

A sensation of *déjà vu* made him rise from the chair to examine the sampler. It read:

Tomorrow shall be my dancing day,
I would my true love did so chance
To see the legend of my play,
To call my true love to my dance.
Sing, oh! my love, oh! my love, my love, my love,
This have I done for my true love.

"I've seen this before," Troy told her. "Did you ever send Andrea Harmon a present?"

"Yes," Lottie said. "I sent her the same sampler at the studio last Christmas. It's from an old carol, it's about . . . Jesus, about what he suffered. . . . I thought it might help her change, help her *repent*. But it didn't do any good."

"I don't remember seeing these last two lines. . . . What do they mean to you?"

"Just what it says. There's nothing the Lord wouldn't do for those He loved."

"And . . . nothing a woman wouldn't do?"

"No!" she said defiantly. "Nothing!"

"Even murder, Lottie?"

There was no reply.

"You said 'nothing.' That would include murder, wouldn't it?" Troy slipped the wallet out of his back pocket and let it fall open. "You see, I don't really work at the studio, Lottie. I'm a police officer, and we know just what you did to help Dr Masters. You killed Andrea Harmon before she could kill him, and you used the same weapon."

"No," Lottie Orwasher said calmly. "It wasn't an ax. It was just a knife, a sort of chopping knife, about this long."

She spread her hands, and measured a distance almost exactly the length of the blade that had killed Sunday Tyler.

15 Hidden Faces

"It was the feather that clinched it," Dan Lipschutz said. "It was one of those details we withhold to make sure we get the right confession from the right person."

"What feather?" Troy asked, wishing his coffee was hotter and his mood more elevated. He had felt depressed ever since poor Lottie Orwasher had been transported from two-and-a-half rooms in Crown Heights to a cell in the detention center. Troy and the detective had a good view of the grim grey building from the coffee shop window. and Troy kept imagining Lottie within, looking bewildered and self-satisfied at the same time, as if uncertain whether she was going to be punished or rewarded for her actions.

"It was on the knife blade," Dan said. "A trademark of the company that made the cutlery, Quill Manufacturing."

"Yes," Troy said. "I remember that. The bloody feather . . ."

"There aren't too many knives like it around, since they went out of business twenty years ago. Lottie Orwasher owns a complete set. Short of one piece, of course. The one she left behind in Sunday Tyler's apartment. Then there was the script, lying near Sunday's body. We never mentioned it in the press. But Lottie mentioned it."

"She's not responsible, you know." Troy put the coffee mug down. "She's a mental case, Danny, I hope I made that clear."

"We don't decide these things, kid. We just pick 'em up and lock 'em up. The rest is up to the courts."

"She's out of touch with reality. She thinks the people she sees in 'Heartbreak Hospital' are real. She wasn't killing Sunday, she was killing Andrea Harmon, a woman who never existed."

"But it was Sunday Tyler we buried, wasn't it?" Dan squeezed Troy's arm. "Don't worry so much. I'm sure you're not the only one who understands what happened here. I'll bet you dinner at the River Cafe that Lottie winds up in the funny farm."

"I know who *ought* to go to prison," Troy said grimly. "The guy who started this."

"You mean Derringer? Put it out of your mind, Bubby. We don't have anything to charge him with. He just cried on her shoulder, inspired her sympathy. That's not the same as asking her to kill his wife. We're not dealing with Charles Manson here."

"He could have suggested it, indirectly. He must have known he was talking to a madwoman, someone who couldn't tell reality from fantasy."

"She claims it was her own idea," Dan said. "Her own inspiration. She wanted to help the guy because she loved him. . . . You're not happy about this collar, are you?"

"Not exactly."

"If it makes you feel any better, there are a dozen Homicide cops who feel the same way. They'd all like to kick your butt for doing what they couldn't do. . . . Come to think of it, I'm one of them." But he grinned and swallowed a mouthful of cold coffee.

They returned to the station house together, and on the way, Dan said:

"I hope you realize this may be bad news for you, too. "

"In what way?"

"I mean the Fiona Farrar case. . . . You kind of shot yourself in the foot when you pinned the Tyler murder on Loony Lottie.

You thought the poisoned pie might have been intended for you, that someone on the show had sent it to your apartment because they thought you were breathing on their neck."

"Yeah, I spoiled that theory, didn't I?"

"Pretty much," Dan said.

"Which leaves what?" Troy asked. "The police theory? That I murdered Fiona because I didn't want to be a daddy?"

Dan said nothing more until they entered the station house. There was a line of messages on the detective's desk. He picked one up, and looked at Troy with a peculiar grimace.

"Uh, you remember this lady producer on the show, this Phyllis Wykopf?"

"Of course," Troy said, remembering the "lady."

"Hope you didn't develop a thing for her, too," Dan said. "On account of she put herself to sleep last night."

"Say that again?"

"She committed suicide. Overdose of sleeping pills. If you hadn't nailed Loony Lottie, this might have made her a likely candidate for the Sunday Tyler murder."

Troy picked up the scrawled message, but the words blurred on the pink paper. His stomach churned; he felt as if he had swallowed a revolving door.

"No," he said. "That wasn't her reason. I think she was hurting about killing someone else."

"Huh?"

"It doesn't matter now," Troy said.

■ ■ ■

There was a life preserver hanging above the bar at Oranges and Lemons, with the legend: BERMUDA QUEEN. Luis Campos stared at it as he sipped his beer and waited for Norman Levi to keep their lunch date. Norman was never less than half an hour late, dismissing his failing as GPT, Gay People's Time. Now he was close to a record hour and fifteen minutes. But when he finally strolled in, he was confident in his excuse.

"First suicide we've ever had on the show," he said. "Kind of surprising when you think about it. Everybody who works on a soap feels like cutting their throat sooner or later."

"I thought you guys specialized in stabs in the back."

"That, too," Norman said. "Let's eat."

The special menu was Mexican. When the order was placed, Norman told him about the tragedy. As it happened, Luis already knew about Phyl Wykopf's suicide, but he said nothing.

"Nobody on the show knew Phyl too well," Norman said.

"She kind of kept to herself. Maybe that's why she did it, maybe she was just too damned lonely."

"Yeah," Luis nodded. "Loners kill themselves a lot. When they don't kill other people."

"Boy, I know one thing," Norman said, shaking his head. "When I hear stories like this, I'm sure glad I'm gay."

"Are you kidding? Don't you know the old saying? Show me a happy homo and I'll show you a gay corpse?"

"They got it wrong," Norman said smugly. "It's the straight ones who are lonely. I mean, figure it out. When you're gay, you're like a member of an exclusive club. You can be in any city, and know just where to go to find friends. You've got something to talk about, experiences in common. . . . No, it's the straight people out there who can't connect with each other." He grinned. "I ought to write a book about it."

"Well, I got news for you," Luis said. "Your friend Phyl Wykopf wasn't so straight."

Norman almost dropped his taco chip into the hot sauce. "What are you talking about? Phyl was always mooning after guys. It was the only thing we had in common." He grinned and stuffed the chip into his mouth.

"I'm not saying she was a dyke," Luis said. "She was a trans-sexual."

"You got to be kidding me," Norman said.

"It's the truth. I heard it this morning."

"Where would you hear stuff like that? I thought you worked for the Motor Vehicle Bureau."

"Well . . . that's why I asked you to have lunch with me today. I thought it was about time I told you something."

"Oh, my God, don't say it! You're a trans-sexual, too. You used to be a cocktail waitress named Louise. Only how the hell do they do it the other way?"

Luis didn't laugh. Instead, he said: "I'm a cop, Norm."

Norman's jaw slackened, revealing a tongue red with sauce.

"That's even worse. This is a bust! You're going to arrest me for having sex with a chicken enchilada."

"I'm serious. I'm really a cop."

"Wait a minute. It's something to do with the Sunday Tyler case, right? Well, you got the wrong guy, flatfoot."

"That case is closed, too. I work Narcotics. That's why I was hanging around this place the night we met. There's a lot of action here, you'd be surprised."

"I don't believe this is happening. . . . I thought we were getting along so great, and now you tell me it was all an under-cover operation!"

"Shove that," Luis grunted. "If I wanted to bust somebody big, I'd sure move in with someone besides you. You haven't done more than two sticks since I met you."

"I don't like drugs," Norman said. "They make me sleepy, and when I get sleepy I can't write. And if I can't write, I don't make money. I like money."

"I won't blame you for being sore. I mean, I *was* looking to bust you that first night, but after that, things changed, you know? I just wanted you to understand that."

"Yeah," Norman Levi said, his eyes shining. "I understand perfectly. It's just like a movie! It could even be—a soap opera! What a great idea!"

"A gay soap? Show me one."

"No, I'd have to change the story a little! It'll be a guy chasing this girl he thinks is a big drug dealer. . . . No, wait! Even better! It's a girl cop! She's after this guy! She moves in with him, and then she falls in love! How does that sound?"

"Corny," Luis said. "I've seen it a dozen times."

"That's why it's perfect! Cozy and familiar, that's the kind of story the audience wants! I'll start working on it this after noon. I'll slip a copy to the Badger. . . . He'll go crazy over it. I'll probably get Neffer's job. They're practically ready to dump him now—"

He leaned across the table and gave Luis a loud smacking kiss on the forehead.

"*Madre Dios*," Luis said. "Where do you think you are?"

■ ■ ■

Neffer didn't make his lunch until Harpo's was ready. In truth, the basenji's meal looked more appetizing than his own. There were rich, meaty chunks in his bowl, swimming in gravy. Neffer's meal was processed turkey stuffed between two limp slices of bread. Mothered until twenty-six and wived from that time onwards, he hadn't the faintest idea what to do in a kitchen, or a supermarket for that matter. He thought wistfully about all the restaurants he could patronize, but there was no way he could allow his dog to have lunch all by himself.

Harpo gave the bowl his undivided attention until the door-bell rang. He watched the door open to admit a familiar shape and smell that filled his soul with canine ecstasy. He crammed the last morsel into his mouth and scurried wildly to greet the true love of his life, unconcerned that his master was in a state of shock. He leaped high in the air, all four paws bouncing off Rosalind Neffer's thighs. But of course, Rosalind had the advantage in the rivalry for Harpo's affection that had been part of their contentious marriage: she was at home all day. And now, to Bob Neffer's dismay, she was here, in his secret hideaway.

"All right, goddammit!" Neffer said. "How did you find me? Who told you I was here? It wasn't that cop, was it?"

"Oh, God, you're pathetic," his wife said. "Mark Liebowitz's investigator found you in one day." She patted the animal, indifferent to its passion. "Did you honestly think you could get away with this?"

"You don't really want Harpo!" Neffer said, with a fervor matching the dog's. "You know it was just spite! Let me have him, Roz, please! I know I had nowhere decent to keep him before, in that crummy hotel, but look at this place. It's perfect for a dog. It's got a garden!"

"What are you growing, weeds?" She went to the window that looked out on it, and her lip curled in contempt. "I thought so. You know as much about gardening as you know about cooking. You're such a helpless idiot, Bobby, you know that?"

"I'm a writer," Neffer said weakly. "Writers are like that."

"Don't give me that! Norman Levi cooks, sews, and keeps a cleaner house than I do. And he's a better writer, too, at least of the crap you write."

"You know why I do it! To give you that big house in the suburbs, that big garden of yours! Do you think I *wanted* to stop writing books?"

"We were happier then, weren't we? You didn't work twelve hours every day. We didn't fight all the time. You didn't grind your teeth at night."

"You're right," Neffer said miserably. "We'd probably still be together, wouldn't we, if I'd never taken this job?"

"Yes," Rosalind said. "We probably would."

"Don't you think I've thought of quitting a thousand times? I just never had the nerve. I wake up every morning, waiting for some kind of miracle, some kind of *sign* to tell me what to do."

"You? A sign? Since when did you get religion?"

"I just need *something,* Roz."

For some reason, they both looked at the dog.

Harpo barked.

■ ■ ■

Gene Badger's stomach commented on the *fois gras* he had just digested, but Abel McFee didn't hear it; he was too busy discussing the wine list with the sommelier. Badger cursed the huge breakfast he had stowed away that morning. Of course he had had no way of knowing that the executive producer would invite him for lunch at the most expensive restaurant in the city. He had dined with Abel only once before, when he had been welcomed aboard "Heartbreak Hospital." Was this the other end of the line?

Abel had made his choice: a Mouton Cadet. Badger knew it would guarantee him a soporific afternoon. So did Abel, for that matter, but it didn't worry him. Abel planned to go back to his apartment after lunch and take a nap.

"Well, it's quite a day, isn't it?" he said. "Sunday's killer being arrested. Poor Phyllis committing suicide. . . . And they say soap operas are hard to believe."

"I just wish Phyl had waited a little longer," Badger grumbled. "I know that sounds callous, but the show had enough bad publicity after the murder."

"Well, we've just got to put it all behind us, Gene. Got to forge ahead. Concentrate on those ratings. We looked pretty good right after Sunday's death, but did you see today's Nielsens?"

Badger had forgotten it was Thursday.

"No, I've been too busy this morning. People calling up, asking me about Phyl—"

"We dropped three share points. I'm not ringing the alarm bell. I just want you to be aware of it. You know how those network people are—first sign of weakness, they start to panic."

"Well, Julia Porterfield will be on air in a couple of weeks. Maybe the ratings will pick up when the audience has its darling Andrea back."

"I certainly hope so. The audience doesn't like changes, but sometimes . . . change is inevitable." He toyed with the empty wine glass as Badger wondered what was coming next. What came was the wine. The sommelier uncorked it, and Abel sampled it with approval. With their glasses filled, he gave a toast. "To 'Heartbreak Hospital,'" he said.

To Badger's surprise, Abel drank deeply—not like a connoisseur, but like a man intending to get drunk.

Abel had his reasons, of course. He thought about them now, remembering the sound of chimes in his apartment only two short hours ago. When he had seen Kiki Carney on his doorstep, he had assumed she was delivering the news he had already heard.

"If it's about Phyl Wykopf, honey," he said, "I know all about it. Someone I know called me from the hospital where they took her. Terrible, isn't it?"

"Yes," Kiki said, entering without invitation. "I know you must be very upset, Mr McFee, and I don't want to upset you any further. But I do have to talk to you about something."

"Can you make it fast, honey?"

"My name is Kiki, Mr McFee." She smiled, with the sweetness of a lemon tart.

"Sure, sweetheart, I know what your name is. Now can you make this quick? Phyl picked a rotten time to kill herself. I've got a million things to do today."

"This doesn't have to take long. May I sit down?"

"Sure, we can sit for a couple of minutes." He watched her cross her legs. Very good legs. He hadn't really noticed the associate producer before; Abel liked a bit more maturity in his women. He sat beside her and dropped a hand on a well-turned knee.

"It's about Julia Porterfield," Kiki said, delicately removing his hand without pausing. "About her contract arrangements."

"What about them? Julia knows what we're paying her."

"Mr Badger left the final negotiation to me—he usually does. So naturally I had to get in touch with her agent. The only trouble is, I didn't know *which* agent, and neither did Mr Badger. And as you may know, Miss Porterfield is on the west coast, closing out her apartment."

Abel was starting to feel irritated, particularly after the hand lift. "Why bother me with this? It's just a detail."

"It still has to be settled before Julia actually starts work. When I couldn't reach her in LA, I went through the old files to see if I could find the name of her former agent, when she was on the show a few years ago."

"Listen, cupcake, I've got an idea. Why don't we discuss this over lunch today?"

"I'm busy," she smiled. "But thanks anyway." She opened her purse and removed some folded papers. "I wasn't sure these old invoices were what I needed, since they didn't mention Miss Porterfield specifically. But the name sounded like an agent, so I looked them up in the directory. In more than one directory."

"I'm sure there must be some point to all of this."

"The point is, there doesn't seem to be any agency called Talent Assets, Mr McFee."

Abel was glad his hand was no longer on her knee. It would have turned to ice.

"Naturally, I was curious as to why there were so many invoices from an unlisted talent rep. The company didn't seem to have any office address, either, just a box number, at the post office just two blocks from here."

"Listen, darling, is this some kind of accusation?"

"My name's Kiki, Mr McFee." He had to admire her. Not even Sunday could sustain a mood level like this efficient little blonde. "There's an adorable little man at the collection window," she continued. "When I inquired about Mr McFee's box, he asked if I was going to be picking up the mail from now on, and if I was, I would need signed authorization from you."

"And is that why you're here? To get authorization?"

"No." Kiki laughed. "That's not why I'm here. Actually, I came to talk business. About 'Heartbreak Hospital.'"

Abel poured his third glass of wine and tried to refill Gene Badger's glass at the same time.

"No more for me," Badger said. "That stuff makes me pretty tired, and I've got a busy schedule."

"Well, there's one more thing I have to put on your schedule," Abel said, smiling moistly, a light coating of Mouton Cadet on his lips. "I know poor Phyl's body isn't cold yet, but— we can't afford to be sentimental about this."

"About what?"

"About finding a replacement. I don't think we have far to look. I think we should simply promote Kiki Callahan to the job."

Badger lifted both eyebrows. "Wait a minute," he said. "Kiki doesn't have all that much experience, you know. She was a secretary only ten months ago."

"I don't think that matters much."

"But this is an important job. A tough job."

"Well, she's a tough little gal. I'm sure she can handle it. . . . Oh, I know, you think I don't pay attention to these things, Gene, but I do. I've had my eye on Miss Callahan for some time, and not just on her boobs. That's one smart little girl you have there, and I'm sure she'll do just fine."

"I'm glad you know her so well," Badger said. "And by the way, her name isn't Callahan."

■ ■ ■

The telephone was ringing just as Troy entered his Bleeker Street apartment. He was tempted to let it ring itself out, but the reflex was too strong. When he heard Bagley's growl at the other end, he expected to have his ear chewed off. But the captain surprised him with an almost friendly tone.

"I got news for you, Troy. I think they're going to lift that suspension."

"You mean I can go back to work?"

"The only question is where. I got an inquiry about you this afternoon. Somebody up top wants to know how I'd feel about you transferring out of the unit."

"I haven't asked for any transfer."

"Actions speak louder than words, buddy boy."

"How do you mean?"

"I mean this soap opera case. You made yourself a hero, and now they're talking about moving you to Homicide."

"You're kidding me," Troy said.

"They asked if I could spare you, and I said, hell, the guy's never around anyway. But you think about it, Troy. If you want me to tell them no dice, it's up to you."

When Troy hung up, the word "hero" continued to reverberate pleasantly in his ear. Then he remembered the dangerous felon he had apprehended, little Lottie Orwasher, all ninety-five pounds of her. . . . He shook his head and flopped on the sofa. Homicide, he thought. Some cops thought it was a sinecure, the best job on the force. High rate of arrests and convictions, since most homicides were family affairs, bar fights, gang slayings, mob executions. . . . Real police work, Troy thought, tough, demanding, ugly. . . .

It made him think of Carl Rivera's "serial killer" theory. Detective Rivera must have been disappointed by Lottie's confession. His folder was still on the coffee table. Troy picked it up, and skimmed the contents a second time, looking at it with the eyes of a potential member of the Homicide Squad. . . .

It may have been those eyes which made the difference. He looked at the police photo of Claudine Potter's bloody corpse as if seeing it for the first time. He had taken in no details before, just the broken-doll position of the body, the long hair mercifully concealing her face, the blood spattered on her clothes, the carpet, the scattered debris around her, including what might possibly be a script. . . .

Troy made a hurried search for a magnifying glass. It was in the last drawer he emptied. He put the lens on the object in the photograph and was able to make out the words on the cover, a title of grisly relevance:

LONG DAY'S JOURNEY INTO NIGHT.

16 Painted Dreams

She was actually pleased to see him. He was the man responsible for her loss of liberty, but her eyes, the color of milk under the cold fluorescence, glowed blue again at the sight of him. She folded her hands and leaned her bony elbows on the black formica table, as if waiting for Troy to suggest a game. In a way, he had come to play one.

"I hope you're not mad at me, Lottie," he said. "I was doing what they pay me to do. You understand that, don't you?"

"Oh, yes," Lottie said. "And I don't really mind this place. There's a television set in the community room. I saw Dr Masters at the hospital, so I guess he didn't go away after all."

"It's on tape, Lottie. It was taped some time ago. That's why you saw Dr Masters."

She smiled indulgently, and Troy suspected he was being humored. "Yes, I know. They've explained all that to me, too. But it doesn't matter, as long as I can see my friends. . . . Well! What was it you wanted to talk about?"

"I think you probably know."

"I've talked to *so* many people about it. Some of them were doctors! I asked them if they knew Jonathan, but they didn't."

"I read your statement to the police. There were a few things you didn't seem to remember very well, weren't there?"

She looked down at the table, like a child being chastised. "I was in a terrible state that night. My heart was beating so fast

I thought it was going to explode. It felt just like I was in a dream, walking in my sleep. . . ." She raised her eyes to his, and there was an appeal for sympathy in her unsteady gaze. "I didn't mean to make it so . . . awful. I was just going to do it *once*. When she opened the door. Just once, the way my daddy used to kill the rabbits in our back yard. He always told us, there was a right way to do it and a wrong way. . . . I did it wrong, didn't I?"

"I know one thing you did wrong, Lottie. You didn't tell the whole truth about your talk with Dr Masters. You didn't tell anyone he came to see you in your apartment in Crown Heights."

Lottie made a clucking sound of disapproval, and her eyes moved quickly from left to right.

"Hush! You mustn't tell anyone that! It's supposed to be our secret!"

"Yours and Dr Masters?"

"If people knew he came to visit, they'd be bothering him all the time! You know the way *fans* are." She smiled, excluding herself from the category.

"So Dr Masters made this house call, and asked you not to tell anyone he'd been there."

"Yes," Lottie said. "It was so wonderful. And I wasn't a bit nervous, not after a while. He brought me flowers. I didn't throw them out for a month, not until you brought me the fresh ones he sent. . . ."

"And he sat in that big armchair, didn't he? The one you wouldn't let me sit in."

"I hope you weren't offended. I can't let anyone sit in that chair now. You understand."

"Sure," Troy said. "My father once shook hands with Aldous Huxley and didn't wash his hands for a week. . . . It must have been a very important night for you, Lottie. And for Dr Masters."

"I was so *honored*," the woman said. "The way he talked to me. And it wasn't just because I was in the fan club. I really think he *liked* talking to me. He knew I would understand the way he felt about Andrea, about how that woman was ruining his life. . . ."

"And planning to *end* his life, wasn't she?"

"Yes! He told me that. He said she was planning to kill him, with an ax, right in the hospital parking lot!"

"But he didn't mean it literally, Lottie. Deep down, you must know it's only make-believe. Don't you know that?"

"That's how the doctors talk to me," Lottie said stiffly. "Like I was some kind of retarded child, like I didn't understand the difference between a television show and real life! Of course I understand! I know Andrea wasn't really going to kill him! It was going to be . . . her twin sister!"

Troy sat back, wondering how to handle this.

"That's not exactly what I meant, Lottie."

"Please," she said, her interlocked fingers beginning to tremble against each other. "Don't confuse me the way the doctors do. I thought you came here to be friendly. If you can't be friendly, I'd rather not talk any more!"

"I was just trying to understand—"

"All I know is, if Andrea Harmon had her way, there wasn't going to be any more Jonathan Masters on the show! He'd be dead and gone, and I'd never see him again!"

Her mouth was quivering. Troy, concerned about derailing the conversation, said: "So that was when you decided to help him. All by yourself. That's what you said in your statement. That Dr Masters didn't ask you to kill Andrea, it was all your own idea."

"Yes, it was."

"You're not just trying to protect him?"

"They asked me that, too. The policemen and the doctors. But the answer is no. I've got a mind of my own, you know."

"So you took a knife out of your kitchen drawer, and went to dispose of that destructive woman."

"Yes. That's exactly what I did."

Troy took a deep breath, knowing he was at a dangerous corner.

"Now tell me one more thing. How did you find her?"

Lottie blinked three times in rapid succession.

"How did I *find* her? That was easy."

"Because her address is published in the fan magazines? Or because Dr Masters gave it to you?"

"No! Neither one. It isn't published, and Dr Masters didn't give it to me. I just looked it up, the way anyone would."

Troy reached beside his chair and lifted the attaché case to the table. He removed the Manhattan phone book and placed it in front of her. "Was this how you looked her up, Lottie?"

"Yes," the woman said, actually amused by his simple-minded questions. "Wouldn't you have done the same thing?"

"I guess I would. In fact, I did, just last night. Would you mind doing the same thing for me, right now?"

"What for?"

"Please, Lottie."

She gave a small laugh, and opened the thick directory at midpoint. Then she went slowly through the pages until she found the right one. Her finger slid down a column until it reached its destination.

"There," she said, her voice sweet with triumph. "There it is! A. Harmon. 42 Monroe Street." She saw the corners of his mouth turn down, and said quickly: "Oh, I know, I know! It doesn't say 'Andrea Harmon,' it only says 'A. Harmon.' But I wasn't as dumb as you think. I *called* the number first. And when she answered, I said 'Andrea?' And she said—'Yes.'"

Lottie laughed happily now, not gloating over her success, but sharing it with him.

"When was this, Lottie? When did you call Andrea?"

"You mean the first time? Why, months ago." Her clasped fingers tightened, and she clamped her lips into a thin line. "I called her a couple of times to tell her what I thought of her. She was rude, of course. She always hung up on me. . . ."

"But this time, you went to see her in person."

"Yes, I did."

"You went down to 42 Monroe Street, with the knife under your coat. And you rang the doorbell, and when the woman answered. . . ."

"Oh, don't make me remember it all," Lottie wailed pitifully. "I *told* you it was awful. I thought I could make it happen so fast, but she didn't *die* very fast. And so I had to do it over and over and over again. . . ."

"But you did it all for Dr Masters."

"Yes—that's what I told him. When he came to see me again. I thought he would be so happy! I thought he would —sweep me up in his arms, the way they do on TV. But he didn't. He just looked sick. He had to go into the kitchen to get some water. . . ."

For the first time since the interview began, Lottie unclasped her hands and placed them over her face, forming a mask. Troy waited for the tears to fall, but when none came, he said:

"And it never occurred to you that you might have killed the wrong woman? That Andrea Harmon had moved out of that apartment, that someone else was living there?"

"But—she was in the phone book!"

"The directory changes only once a year, Lottie. People move. Listings stay the same."

"Yes," she said miserably. "I know that now."

"You know that you didn't kill Andrea Harmon? That you killed a woman named Claudine Potter?"

"I know that Andrea is still alive!"

"What?" Troy said.

"I read it in *TV Guide*! She's coming back to 'Heartbreak Hospital'! Because I made a mistake. A terrible mistake!"

■ ■ ■

"You know what I'd call this case?" Dan Lipschutz said. "A tragedy of errors. Eat your heart out, Shakespeare."

"But it wasn't just an error," Troy said. "It was a misunderstanding. A tragic confusion . . ." He let his friend refill his glass. "And it may have been something else. A terrible miscalculation on the part of Milo Derringer."

"So you still think Derringer put her up to it? That he went to Crown Heights deliberately, hoping that Loony Lottie was loony enough to commit murder?"

"I still don't know that answer," Troy admitted. He went to the window and drew aside the curtain, checking on his precious Volvo parked three feet too close to the hydrant.

"He couldn't have known for *sure* that she would do it."

"No," Troy said. "And he certainly didn't know she would try to kill the *character*, not the actress. That there was actually an Andrea Harmon listed in the phone book."

"But why didn't Lottie realize it was the wrong woman?"

"Her vision is pitiful, and Claudine Potter looked just enough like Sunday. . . . She was even holding a script when she opened the door. Lottie struck her down, and kept on striking. . . ."

"That's for sure," Dan said gravely.

"Things might have turned out differently if Andrea Harmon hadn't moved out. She was small and dark—she looked nothing at all like the Andrea Harmon in 'Heartbreak Hospital.'"

Troy returned to his chair, and his drink. He downed half of the vodka before continuing.

"And now comes the question of Sunday Tyler."

"Yes," Dan said. "I'm listening."

"Once you know the first part, the rest isn't so hard. . . . Lottie Orwasher committed her Act of Love. She did what she thought Dr Masters wanted her to do. She got rid of Andrea Harmon. But she had to make sure her beloved Jonathan *knew* it."

"You think she actually *told* Milo Derringer?"

"Lottie definitely told him, and Milo was horrified—not because she killed his wife. Because she *didn't*. He knew that Sunday was still alive, that Lottie had killed the wrong woman, that she had murdered someone she thought was Andrea, and therefore Sunday . . . There was only one logical thing Milo could do."

"My God, Troy," Dan said, in genuine awe.

"There was no weapon found on the scene of Claudine Potter's murder, because Lottie took it home. She put the knife with the feather back in the drawer with all the other knives with feathers. It was there, all shiny clean, when she saw Milo at Crown Heights for the second time. When she told him what she had accomplished. *'Sing, oh! my love, oh! my love, my love, my love . . . This have I done for my true love. . . .'*

"But Milo knew Sunday was alive and well and planning the death of his character and his career. . . . So Milo went into the kitchen and appropriated the knife with the feather on the blade. And Milo rang Sunday's doorbell, and she admitted him without fear. And Sunday died exactly the way Lottie Orwasher thought Andrea had died. . . . And if Milo hadn't sent that bloodstained shirt to the cleaners, we would have found Sunday's blood on it. . . .

"And one other thing," Troy said. "About Fiona."

"Fiona?"

"Abel McFee *did* manage to scare the hell out of Milo at that meeting. He really believed that I was ready to nail him for Sunday's murder. That s why he sent me that lemon pie *à la* weed-killer. . . . He knew I was fond of lemon meringue. Maybe he thought I'd assume it was a gift from the 'Heartbreak' gang. It was worth the chance. Unfortunately, chance decided to let Fiona find it at my front door that day. . . . Now, if you don't mind, I'll leave the messy details to you. I've got to get some sleep," Bill Troy said.

■ ■ ■

Troy walked into Studio 22 and saw Bob Neffer sitting in the waiting area with his dog. Neffer grinned at him, and so, for that matter, did Harpo. "Somebody waiting for you inside," he said.

"Who?"

"Go see for yourself."

Troy let himself onto the set. There had been drastic changes since he had seen it last. The designers had constructed a quaint stone bridge over what appeared to be a moonlit stream. On the bridge, wearing a low-cut gown dazzling with inlaid stones, was a woman with long, cascading hair. There was something familiar about the tilt of her head. It reminded him achingly of someone else. But of course, it couldn't be. . . .

He came closer, and the woman turned. The "moonlight" was artificial, yet its soft glow made her skin radiant. It was an angelic face, but there was deviltry in her eyes.

It was Sunday.

Troy tried to control his wobbly legs. He took a step towards her, and heard her laugh.

"Don't be afraid," she said.

Then she was in his arms, and he was kissing her hungrily, unwilling to release her even to hear her explain the impossible. . . .

"It wasn't *me*," Sunday Tyler said. "That wasn't *me* who was murdered, darling. It was my twin sister! Yes, I do have a twin sister! That's why I've always wanted them to tell a 'twin' story on the show! But now it's too late. My poor sister is dead. My insane husband killed her! She was waiting in my apartment when he showed up with that horrible knife. . . . But at least I'm still alive, and back in your arms, and that's all that matters . . ."

"Yes," Troy said hoarsely. "I don't care about anything else! About Bagley, about Fiona, about the job with Homicide—"

"Homicide?" Sunday said. "What's that supposed to mean?"

He stared at her, feeling a sudden chill.

"But you'd never say that line. Sunday wouldn't say that line in a million years!"

She smiled mischievously. "Then maybe I'm fooling you, too. Maybe I'm not Sunday after all. Maybe I'm her twin, and Sunday is dead. Or maybe I'll just let you find out tomorrow. . . ."

Abruptly, the moonlight was turned off. He was in darkness, and Sunday was gone.

"Sunday!" he cried out, but then realized it was useless. He would have to wait until tomorrow. He was due in court to give testimony, but he'd try to get away in time to watch the show, to find out whether or not Sunday had really returned to him. . . . The recognition that he was trapped inside a soap opera startled him, and he fervently wished himself awake. His eyes opened. He was in his bed, and he had been dreaming, but now the dream was over. No, not over, Troy thought. To Be Continued. He turned his head into the pillow, and waited for the next episode.